GLADIATRIX

THE LAST WITCH OF ROME: BOOK TWO

RHETT GERVAIS

Gladiatrix
The Last Witch of Rome: Book Two

Rhett Gervais
Editor: Paula Grundy
Cover: Jake Caleb, J Caleb Design

Published April 2021
Copyright © 2021 Rhett Gervais

FOLLOW and LIKE:

https://rhettgervais.com/

A SPECIAL OFFER

Building a good relationship with my readers is important to me. I occasionally send newsletters with details about new releases, advanced previews and even the occasional short story. As a bonus if you sign up for the newsletter, you will also receive:

1 - A digital copy of Chosen, the prequel novella to the Last Witch of Rome.

2 - A digital copy of Origin: Children of the Spear: Book One.

3 - A copy of Genesis: Children of the Spear: Book Two.

Just click on the link below and start reading today!

https://rhettgervais.com/new-landing/

P.S I promise, no spam ever!

CONTENTS

PROLOGUE: LOST TIME

Commodus didn't remember throwing the legionnaire to the ground, or wrapping his hands around his throat, but a smile crept onto his face as the weaker man struggled against him, clawing and scraping for every breath, desperate to hold on to the world of the living. The moment was like a waking dream, and he wasn't sure if it was real or not, but he couldn't help but stare with grim fascination as the spark of life faded from the legionary's eyes, and his spent body spasmed one last time before falling limp. With a deep sigh he stood to his full height, dry washing his hands while scanning his personal chambers, unsurprised to find that the room was littered with the dead. Thoughts of wine came to mind, and strangely, he found a pitcher and cup near a fallen chair, condensation still beading on their surfaces.

The world shifted in a cacophony of noise and dazzling light as he drank deeply, and he fell into oblivion once more, with only the taste of wine on his tongue. Later, when reality returned, he found himself with his face pressed against the cool marble floor, staring at the bottom of an empty cup, wine or blood pooling around his cheek, he couldn't be sure. Pushing himself up with a groan, he stuck out his tongue in disgust at the vile taste in his mouth, wondering why he was drinking such a bitter vintage. Wandering from room to room in a daze, he raised an eyebrow when, at one point, he recognized the familiar purple cloaks and fine armor of the dead. They were all Praetorian guardsmen. His men, men whose sole duty in life was to protect him from harm. Commodus blinked, and once again his world shifted and he found himself in front of a full-length, gilded mirror, looking himself up and down, a smile growing on his face when he realized he wore not a stitch of clothing. Turning in place, he flexed his arms and then stomach, marveling at his smooth, unblemished skin and well-defined muscle, a surge of pride running through him at his wide shoulders and narrow waist.

"Truly the son of Jupiter. A god among men," whispered an alien voice in the back of his mind, sending a shiver down his spine.

Commodus beamed with pride at the words, repeating them over and over again under his breath while he continued to flex and pose. The voice understood how important he was, it always did. Satisfied, he decided it was time for a bath and turned to go when he caught sight of a wide scar on his side, glowing white against his bronzed skin.

"Where did you come from?" he whispered to himself, tracing a finger along its length while he struggled to remember where and when he had hurt himself. Suddenly he fell to his knees, his head pounding like someone was driving a spike into his skull. The more he thought about the scar, the more the pain grew, until finally, he pushed the thought of it from his head, and the pain subsided. Reality shifted once more, and he was somehow in the bath, frozen with gooseflesh running up and down his arms, the water far too cold for his liking. Swallowing a cup of wine in hand, he made a sour face, disliking the dry, tangy vintage. He blinked again and was in bed, wrapped up in the blankets, shivering, his skin like ice. "Fire, I need fire!" he bellowed, his deep voice echoing through the empty room. "Where are you? Why are my chambers so cold?"

He wasn't sure how long he waited, but after a time, he threw off the heavy covers and shot out of bed in a rage, cursing at the incompetence of those who served him, the cold forgotten as hot blood raced through his veins. Storming to the entrance of his chambers, he vented his anger with a few vicious kicks to the fallen legionnaires along his path, knocking aside the already battered bodies. Throwing open the birchwood doors of his rooms, he was about to give the men the rough side of his tongue, only to find the corridor leading to his rooms empty, with not a man in sight. Stepping out into the brightly lit hall, undeterred, he raised his chin, boldly heading off in search for someone to punish for this mess. He was halfway down the hall when he came to a halt, his eyes drawn to one of the new images he had commissioned to replace the dreary artwork that Domitian had originally created for these walls. Even as a boy, visiting his father in his rooms, he had hated the original fresco. A series of paintings that were meant to tell the history of the republic, with each part telling the tale of some long, dead fool who had sacrificed or toiled for the glory of Rome.

Commodus would have none of it and had ordered that the entire fresco be destroyed and replaced with something to show his glory. He nodded with pride at one of his favorites, a painting as tall as three men, of Hercules, holding up the sky on his powerful shoulders. The labors of the great hero had inspired him to greatness from the moment he had heard them as a boy, and since those many years ago he had always strived to match the demigod's strength and courage. Commodus had, of course, made sure the hero's features matched his own and he was proud that he could see little difference between Hercules's handsome face and his own. He turned to move on when a chill ran down his spine as he felt like the eyes of the fresco were following him, the pupils of the image strangely flashing a milky white for just a moment. Commodus froze in place, locking his gaze on, to the image, waiting, hoping that it was just his imagination.

"Caesar, are you all right?"

Commodus tore his gaze away from the fresco to find a round-faced servant at the end of the corridor eyeing him, while holding a carafe on top of a bronze tray, his eyes wide. "Come here!" he ordered.

"Yes, Caesar, I was—"

"Just do as you're told," snapped Commodus, pointing at the image of Hercules with the sky on his massive shoulders. "Tell me, what do you see?"

The servant shuffled to his side, the tray in hand shaking as he followed Commodus's gaze. "I don't understand. You mean the fresco? It's, it's beautiful," he stammered, swallowing hard."

"Nothing more?" he asked, pressing his lips together. "Look again, around the eyes."

The man almost caved in on himself, his shoulders hitching higher and higher with each panicked breath. "I don't know about such things, Caesar. I am just a humble servant."

With a snarl, Commodus grabbed the servant by his tunic, wrapping his other hand around his quivering chin and forcing him to look directly at the image. "You don't see its eyes, you don't see them moving, following me!"

The servant squirmed in his grip, hurriedly nodding his head before speaking out of the corner of his mouth, "Yes... yes, I see it now —" he began.

"Then why did you lie to me?" he shouted, shaking him bodily, blood pounding in his temples. "Or are you lying now? Always a foul tongue with you slaves.

Sobs began to wrack the servant's body, and tears threatened in the corners of his eyes. "No, Caesar, I wouldn't lie to you... please," he mumbled with a snort.

Commodus recoiled in disgust as the man's warm snot flowed over the hand holding the man's face. "You slaves are all the same," he growled, wiping his hand on the man's tunic. "I have been too merciful for too long, too kind. I blame Saoterus for that; he always urged me to be kind to the likes of you, but no more."

"Merciful Caesar, please."

Commodus smashed the servant's face against the stone, leaving a bright red stain on the fresco. "Where is my chamberlain?" he bellowed down the empty corridor, letting the sobbing man tumble to the floor, forgotten. "Saoterus! Where in the name of Jupiter are you, man!"

"He is with the gods, Caesar," mumbled a man at his feet, with blood pouring from his mouth.

"What? Who would dare!"

The servant shrunk back against the wall, raising his hands defensively over his head. "This is what you told us, Caesar. No one has seen him in weeks!"

"He had outlived his usefulness," whispered a voice in the back of his mind. "His death has only added to our greatness."

Commodus staggered, using the wall to hold himself up, clutching at his throbbing temples. "Death... added to our... greatness," he muttered, repeating the words over and over.

"May I go, Caesar?" said a small voice that rose above the din.

"Who are you?" asked Commodus to the servant cowering at his feet. "And why am I in the corridor?"

"I don't know. I found you here, like this," said a shaking servant, pushing against the wall to stand, streaks of blood around his mouth and nose.

"Why do you cower so?" asked Commodus, frowning at him. "I am your Caesar. You have nothing to fear from me."

With a shriek, the servant turned and ran, and Commodus almost chased after him before breaking down, laughing from his belly, his shoulders shaking. Given his godlike stature, it was normal for those who served him to be afraid sometimes, and he would let it pass for now. He turned on his heel to return to his rooms when the sound of heavy-soled caligae reached his ear, and a moment later a strange mix of red-cloaked legionnaires and purple-clad Praetorian guards entered the corridor; behind them walked the fat prefect whose name he could never remember, and beside him, the weak-chinned senator, Magnus, whom he knew all too well. "I do not remember summoning you, Prefect, nor you, Senator," said Commodus, strolling down the corridor to meet them. "Or have you come to do your duty and guard my door as you are meant to."

As a group, they came to a halt a few feet away from him, the Praetorian guardsmen at the front unsheathing their weapons. "We have come to do our duty for the empire," slurred the fat prefect, puffing out his chest. "The people have suffered long enough under your incompetence."

"They are nothing but insects to be crushed under our heel," echoed the alien voice in the back of his mind, a tingling heat rising from the base of his spine, spreading up through his chest and down his legs. "Kill them all!"

"The people love me. I am a god to them," said Commodus, flexing his arms, shivering as a surge of adrenaline ran through him. "But if you wish to feel my divine wrath, come then. I will show you."

"You are nothing more than a tyrant," said Senator Magnus, his voice inching higher with every word. "And the senate will do its part to return Rome to its proper rulers, the senate, and people! Kill him!"

At the weak-chinned man's orders, the legionnaires charged like an angry mob, waving naked steel at him as if expecting him to fall easily. Commodus let them come, his breathing steady, his heart calm as if he were out for a pleasant stroll in the palace gardens. The men appeared to be hardly moving, and he easily sidestepped the first wild swings aimed for his heart and head, the whites of his teeth showing as he enjoyed taunting them by pivoting back and forth while knocking their clumsy strikes wide with the flats of his palms. The corridor here was wide enough for ten men, and in short order they surrounded him, glancing at one another with nervous looks when Commodus stopped them with a raised hand. "Are you the fools who are meant to protect my glory?" he began, eyeing each of them in turn, holding them in place with just his gaze. "How are you to slay my enemies if you cannot land a blow on a weaponless, naked man?"

"You are not a man; you're a boy playing at being Caesar," snarled a first centurion with deep-brown eyes and a cleft chin. "And I, for one, am honored with the privilege to kill you." With a roar, the man came at him, striking out with his gladius straight and true, the gleaming blade aimed at his heart.

Commodus didn't bother dodging the blade this time; instead, he caught it in hand, halting the strike just a hairsbreadth from his chest. The centurion's eyes shot open, his entire body trembling when he tried to rip the weapon from Commodus's iron grip. "I am the son of Jupiter, Hercules reborn," he said, tearing the gladius from the centurion's hand, and then faster than the eye could see, he flipped the weapon over and buried it in the other man's heart.

The first centurion's jaw hung open in amazement as he fell in a heap, his blood spreading out like a stain on the cold white marble. Commodus raised the gore-covered gladius and smiled at the men surrounding him, waving them on. They came at him then, in twos and threes, stabbing and slashing like they were an angry mob and not the proud Roman legionaries they represented. Commodus bounded forward to meet them, adrenaline coursing through his blood as he spun the blade in hand, removing the arm of a legionnaire, who had overreached, and then slashing out with a spinning kick at a man trying to sneak in behind him, the blow caving in his chest and sending the poor fool crashing back into Senator Magnus, who was too slow to avoid him. Pivoting to his left, he used the gladius to strike out, viper quick, poking a pair of legionnaires in their chests with enough force to pierce their breastbones, the men falling dead with shocked looks on their faces before they even knew what happened. Seeing how quickly Commodus was dispatching them as a group, the legionnaires halted, closing ranks, and backing away as they eyed their fallen comrades.

"Their weapons are nothing to you, reeds against steel," whispered the voice once more as waves of heat radiated outward from his chest, into his shoulders, and up through his skull. "You are the hero reborn: show them, show them!"

Eyeing the bloody gladius for a second, he let the blade slip from his grasp away, remembering how he had caught the first centurion's flashing blade with his hand and had felt no pain. Even now after battling the guards, there was not a cut or bruise on his bronzed flesh. "The lot of you do not deserve to be called Romans," he shouted at the men cowering away from him. "The legionaries of old would have been ashamed to call you brothers. I am ashamed to even call you men!"

Seeing him defenseless, they gathered their courage, coming at him once more. Instead of defending himself, Commodus locked his arms behind his back, letting the blows rain down on him while smiling like a cat, laughing as their blades glanced off his skin, the steel bending against his bones. He let it go on for a time, relishing at the wide-eyed looks of wonder they gave him, feeling exalted when one Praetorian guardsman threw down his blade and turned to run, his purple cloak streaming behind him. "Cowards!" he shouted, grasping the legionnaire closest to him by the throat, hurling his body at the fleeing Praetorian, bowling the man over as they tumbled together in a heap, knocking the fat prefect off his feet as well. Then, to the surprise of the remaining men who fought him, he caught the blade of a gladius aimed at his head, snapping the steel over his knee in a single, smooth motion. "Those of you who wish to live will stop this nonsense," he began, eyeing each of the remaining men in turn.

"Don't listen to him!" shouted Senator Magnus, struggling to his feet, his face red from the effort. "If we fail here, we are all dead men; he'll see to that."

"You have already failed, and are already dead in my eyes," continued Commodus. "But any of you who wish to live a little longer can help me punish these traitors." He smiled when they lowered their weapons, casting hungry looks at the prefect and the weak-chinned Senator Magnus.

"I am no traitor. I am a patriot!" said the prefect, struggling to unsheathe his gladius, the hilt catching on his round belly. "Don't you remember why we are here? We must be willing to give our lives for Rome. To stop this monster before his madness spreads and it's too late!"

"No coin is worth this," muttered one of the legionaries who then stormed toward the prefect, effortlessly battering aside the man's weapon and forcing him to his knees. "Say the word, Caesar, and I will remove his head."

Commodus threw his head back in laughter as the remaining men followed his lead, some of them roughly grabbing Senator Magnus by his fine tunic and forcing him to his haunches. "What is your name, Legionnaire?" he asked the man who had broken ranks first.

"Cleander, Marcus Aurelius Cleander," said the legionnaire, his blade at the prefect's throat.

"Named for my mortal father," said Commodus, nodding to himself, "and this fool offered you denarii to take my life?"

"We did no such thing," began Senator Magnus, only to be silenced by a look from the prefect.

Cleander cleared his throat, giving Commodus an unflinching stare. "Yes, Caesar, a great deal of denarii. Publius here told us you were weak, a child emperor who spent his days drinking and whoring, but now—"

"But now that you see me, you know he lies."

"Yes, Caesar... although a man could do worse things with his days than drinking and whoring."

"This one has guile, and bravery," whispered the alien voice. "He may prove useful in time."

"You seem like a useful man, and I will be in need of a new Praetorian prefect," said Commodus. "Publius here no longer seems up to the task. Are you?"

Cleander blinked, hesitating for only a moment before giving Commodus a vigorous nod. "For the right coin, I am, Caesar," he said.

"I like you," said Commodus, nodding with approval. "Send this fool to the afterlife, and I will see to it that you have plenty of coin."

"Yes, Caesar," said Cleander. without hesitation, plunging his gladius through the side of the former prefect's neck, Publius gurgling with shock as his heavy bulk fell with a crash.

"Good," he said, turning away, heading back to his chambers. "I will leave it to you to clean up this mess."

"And the senator?"

"You cannot just kill a man of my station," shouted Senator Magnus. "By law, I am entitled to a trial in the senate."

"Trial? Do you think the emperor is a fool?" said Cleander.

Commodus halted, his eyes drawn once again to the fresco of Hercules holding up the sky, meeting the hero's milky-eyed gaze, before talking over his shoulder. "No, it's a fine idea. The senate is an old and outdated part of Roman life, but they still hold a great deal of power, and will explode in protest if we kill a man of his rank without trial, but if they are the ones to expose his treachery, it might be the excuse I finally need to disband one of the last relics of the old republic. Let him go. I will deal with him later... but make sure he is properly disciplined for his insolence."

"We will not stop!" shouted the senator, his voice echoing down the wide hall. "Your rule will be short, I promise you!"

Commodus smiled when the senator's protests were silenced by the sounds of violence, followed by a choking scream. Drawing a deep breath, he felt better than he had in a long time, his head strangely clear. He was himself again, but somehow more. He would have to find a way to show everyone, to make the empire understand, how blessed it was to have him, to let people know that a god walked among them.

ONE

STUMBLING ALONG

Vesper sat perched in the stands above the ludus training grounds with her legs crossed beneath her, relishing in the warmth of the blazing noonday sun caressing her dark skin, trying and failing to find her focus. Furrowing her brow, she tried to block out the spectacle on the sands. A dozen recruits, along with a few more experienced gladiators, were running through the basic forms, grunting and sweating while attacking and defending with heavy wooden weapons, the clatter of sword on shield echoing across the grounds of the Ludus Magnus, driving her to distraction.

Letting out a slow breath, she began, once again, drawing on the Ase in her blood, weaving together threads of power in an attempt to create something from nothing. The concentric patterns on her arms and legs began to glow, and a rush of cold fell over her, sending shivers up and down her spine, while in front of her a long shape, the length of a man's arm, began to take hold. It was transparent at first, shimmering like a distant mirage in the desert heat, vague and undefined. She pulled harder from the well of Ase deep within her; beads of sweat began to roll off her temples as the shimmering ceased, a smile coming to her face when the gleaming steel blade, held in reality, its metal flashing bright in the noonday sun: the smell of its leather-wrapped hilt filled her nostrils. Joy filled her heart as she reached to take the blade with a trembling hand. Her fingers had just brushed the hilt when the weave collapsed, the conjured weapon vanishing in a torrent of light.

"By Olodumare, my block is gone; this should be as simple as breathing now," she muttered to herself. In some ways it was, opening herself to the weave to draw on the Ase that flowed through all things, delving deep into her own being. To draw on the power flowing through her was easy now, but it was the steps beyond, the focus, the creation that eluded her. She felt like a painter with a full pallet, every color available to her, but with no idea how to paint even the simplest works of art. To make matters worse, weeks ago, in the heat of battle, she had conjured a gladius with ease and had deflected waves of dark energy as if it were something she had done a thousand times... but now, without a conflict, when her mind was calm, it felt almost impossible.

"You look like I feel on most days. It is not a look that does you well."

She looked down from her perch to find Linus looking up at her, an easy smile on his weathered face. "Don't be foolish. You look like you could fight a lion, or at least satisfy a dozen highborn women," she said, smoothing her features while pushing her anger away.

"I would make a poor meal for a lion... too old and stringy," said the old gladiator, showing her a sinewy arm that was more bone and tendon than skin and muscle. "And it has been many years since a patrician woman has brightened my door. The ones that would remember me are long dead, I'm sure."

"You're not that old, Linus, and I think you're just trying to make me feel sorry for you so that I'll give you a kiss."

The old man bowed his head, shrugging his shoulders. "You know me too well," he said, glancing around. "Do you wish for me to put out an umbraculum for you? The sun is particularly hot today,"

Vesper cocked her head, giving the old man a questioning look. "Umbraculum?"

"Yes, to shade you from the sun. Most of the patrician women use them when they visit the ludus, or the games at the Colosseum."

Vesper shook her head, waving him off. "The last thing I am is a patrician woman afraid of the heat. The sun is life, Linus, and we should never hide from it."

"Then what vexes you?" he asked, a mischievous twinkle coming to his eyes, "Is it that you miss watching Narcissus with his fat body sweating on the sands, or are you worried that he has run off with some wench?"

"Linus!" she squealed, a hand covering her mouth. "I don't look at him that way! I am a proper Ose girl, not some wild Roman woman. Such thoughts are not—"

"Fear not, fear not," he interrupted with a laugh, raising his hands in protest. "From what I know, he and the new dominus have headed to the auction to procure new slaves. The last batch of recruits looks to be destined for the mines, or at best cleaning out the sewers. Narcissus and the new dominus are off looking for better stock. He will be back by the end of day, I'm sure of it."

The moment she thought of the big man, her face began to itch. Through their strange bond, she could feel all sorts of bizarre sensations no matter how hard she tried not to. With a sigh she looked westward, sensing that he was off somewhere in that direction. "The hairy Celt is the last thing on my mind," she lied, trying to sound dismissive, but her words had no heat, and a smile creased her face when she thought of his broad shoulders and fierce smile. "Besides, with you here, what need to do I have for him?"

Linus barked a laugh, throwing her a wink. "Well then, I will leave you to whatever sorcery you are attempting."

"You are too kind, Linus," she said as the old gladiator hobbled away, barking at the men battling on the sands, his whip cracking over their heads. Drawing in a deep breath she closed her eyes once more, trying to block out the grunts and groans of the day's training. It had been only a few weeks since the battle in the tunnels, and she, Narcissus, and Lady Lucilla had barely escaped with their lives. The Sandawei vodun had been much more experienced than she, and they had survived his attacks by sheer luck, so she had promised herself that she would master her abilities. Narcissus thought so as well, and to that end, had agreed that she take the time to train her skill with Ase, but so far it was slow going, and her frustration grew with each passing day.

The problem stemmed from the fact that she could do only the most basic of things, mostly channeling Ase through her limbs to make herself stronger or faster, or at best infuse a weapon so that it was deadlier. But in the heat of battle she reacted solely on instinct, not really knowing how or what she did. In moments like these, when her mind was calm, nothing came to her, and she was powerless. Worse still, she saw no way of learning what she needed, as there was no one to teach her.

Magda, her aunt, who had begun her training, had fallen to a Sandawei spear long before she could teach her more than the most simple of tasks, and Lillith, the loa spirit that was once her mother, had vanished from her mind after her trip to the past. On occasion Vesper could still sense her presence, but it was more of an echo, a memory of a memory.

Throwing her hands up in frustration a few moments later, she turned her gaze on the men fighting, enjoying the spectacle as they went through the forms with their weapons of choice, or practiced their strikes against the post, a tall rod driven into the ground. Part of her knew that one day soon she would be called once more to fight in the arena, and that she should be down there with them instead of wasting her time on this foolishness. Instead, she just watched, her thoughts drifting to her aunt and her mother, wondering what they would do. Thinking about her people, about her place in the world as a Djambe, her gaze unwillingly shifted, and she found herself seeing the world beyond worlds, and the weave that made up all things. The Ose, her people believed that all were connected, that everything and everyone in the world, from a simple rock or tree, to the bird, to every man, woman, and child made up a tapestry that one could draw energy from, or as they called it—Ase. But here in Rome, something had corrupted the weave, and she recoiled in disgust when she stared at the tattered and worn pattern that surrounded her, forcing her to squeeze her eyes shut in an attempt to push away its vileness.

A high-pitched wail shattered her efforts before she could shift her vision back. Her eyes shot open to find the men standing in a circle, eyeing a fallen thick-waisted gladiator trainee with blood pouring from his ears and nose. She wasn't sure what had happened, but Linus was there suddenly, along with one of the many legionnaires meant to keep them in line, who spent most of their days lounging around the periphery of the training grounds. The old gladiator pushed the men back, threatening them with the whip and then going to his knee. Wanting to get a better view, Vesper stood, and to her surprise for the first time since she had been in Rome, she could just see the threads of life that connected the men to the weave. Back home in her village where the weave was full and complete, the connections between people were clear as day, but here, mired in the corruption of Rome, there was not a hint of them. Now, for some reason, she could make out the flickering filaments of green and amber, despite the darkness, and she could sense that the tapestry was clearer, stronger. Looking down at herself, she could see her own silver thread, along with the golden one that flowed off to the west, her connection to Narcissus.

Her curiosity growing, she leapt from her place in the stands, landing gingerly on the balls of her feet, and then striding toward the bleeding trainee while her heart raced with excitement. As she got closer, Nabil, the wiry gladiator who had felled the trainee, sneered at her, snapping at her in an unfamiliar tongue and waving her off.

Although she couldn't understand the words, his meaning was clear, and she had been at the ludus long enough to know him. Nabil had been a champion in Carthage, and had made his way to Rome to make a name for himself. He had a habit of looking down his nose at everyone, and as such had no interest in speaking the common tongue to people he felt were beneath him. Instead, she looked to his round-faced companion who served as his translator. "Tahir, what in the name of Olodumare is he going on about?"

Nabil continued to spout harsh words at her until Tahir silenced him with a raised hand, finally giving her a pained smile that never touched his dark eyes. "Forgiveness, Nabil here seems to think you are overstepping your bounds."

Vesper's brow shot up, and she frowned at the pair of them. "Bounds? Exactly what bounds is he talking about?"

"I dare not repeat his true words in polite company," said Tahir with a tight-lipped smile, "but his meaning is clear. He... we... would prefer if you were away from sight. He says that you are not in charge here and should stop behaving like you are."

"In charge?" she asked, looking at the men surrounding them.

Tahir looked away, pressing his lips together before continuing, "Sitting up in the stands like some sort of queen while the rest of us sweat in the dirt."

"Have you been hit in the head one too many times?" said Vesper, scoffing in disbelief. "I am doing no such thing. Narcissus and Dominus gave me permission to spend part of my day off the sands."

Tahir leaned forward, sneering at her. "Permission to practice your vile arts; we have heard of such things. Among our people, those who show such tendencies are cast out, or better still, have their tongues removed."

"But we aren't among your people, are we?" said Linus, stepping in between them all. "This is Rome, and if Vesper wishes to walk naked through the streets, no one will say a word!"

Vesper held back a smile, placing a hand on the old gladiator's sinewy arm. "I am a gladiator, just like you," she began, eyeing Nabil up and down, "not some monster that needs to be hidden away. And if the sight of me offends you, you can look away."

The wiry gladiator spat a curse of some kind at her, his voice inching up with every word. Beside him Tahir cocked his head, nodding along in agreement. "Nabil says the ludus is no place for your kind. Your evil is an affront to Almighty God."

"Well, you can tell him that among my people—"

"A moment, please," said Tahir, furiously shaking his head as the two men argued, the round-faced man swallowing hard before speaking again. "Nabil also says that just because you lay with the sheep lover does not mean you should be permitted to be among us."

Vesper's eyes shot open, her hands balling into fists at her sides as a collective gasp erupted from the circle of gladiators and trainees. Without thinking she met Linus's eyes. "Get me a weapon," she said simply.

Linus pulled her back from the circle of men, his face creased with worry when he spoke, "This is a bad idea. It isn't about you. He's just trying to goad you."

"Well, it worked!" she said, throwing the wiry gladiator a hard-eyed look.

"No... you don't understand. The day he arrived at the ludus, Narcissus made an example of him, shamed him. He's been looking for a way to strike back ever since."

Vesper narrowed her eyes, her gaze shifting back and forth between Linus and Nabil as her mind worked furiously. "Does everyone in the ludus think Narcissus and I are... you know..."

"Don't you?" asked the legionnaire who stood with them, the guard she knew as Rainar.

Linus gave her a shrug, looking down at his feet. "Of course, even the legionary who guards the ludus thinks so," he said, pointing to Rainar. "We see the way he looks at you... and you at him."

"But there is nothing between us," said Vesper in a hurried tone, her nostrils flaring. "I have never even kissed a man, much less lain with the hairy Celt."

"Truly?" choked Linus, looking like he'd swallowed his tongue. "Apologies, but as they say, rumor is believed faster than truth. This is the way of the world, give it time, the men will forget this before long and find something else to gossip about."

Looking around at the men and the guards around the training grounds, Vesper could see in the way they looked at her, that they all believed it. Even Linus looked like he thought that she was with Narcissus, that they had lain together as man and woman, despite her doing nothing to encourage such a story. "As I said, bring me a weapon so that I can silence this fool," she said, drawing on the Ase that coursed through her blood, singing a few words under her breath, while combining it with the few wisps of power she could draw on from the corrupted weave that surrounded them.

"Vesper, the man is a former champion! He—"

"And I have my honor to defend," she snapped, cool tingles running up her spine and spreading outward to her arms and legs, making her skin as strong as steel and giving a bounce to her step as she returned to the circle. Locking her gaze on to the former champion of Carthage, she directed her words to Tahir, "Tell him that he if we wishes to apologize, I will let this matter pass without shaming him."

The round-faced man broke into laughter, shaking his head while translating her words. When he was done, he folded his arms across his chest, nodding to Nabil.

The wiry gladiator didn't bother to wait for Tahir to translate, dragging a finger along his throat. "I kill you... and your sheep lover," he said in a broken tone.

Vesper saw red as Linus thrust a heavy wooden gladius into her hands along with a round shield, all sense of calm vanishing as she charged at Nabil, her titanic blows and furious strikes thundering off his shield. Powered by the flood of Ase in her muscles, she was much faster than the wiry gladiator, and he quickly fell back on his heels, raising his shield high in a vain attempt to ward off her wild swings, his eyes going wide with each bone-shattering blow. Trying to regain the upper hand, Nabil ducked a wild swing and spun on his right foot to slip past her defenses, but Vesper was faster, catching him with her shield with a bone-crunching hit as he turned, knocking him off-balance.

Growing more desperate, he pushed her away, reversing the grip on his gladius so Vesper's sword strikes were deflected instead of blocked, her wooden blade slipping over the length of his, allowing him to get in close enough that she could smell his rancid breath just before he kneed her in the belly, and then slammed his forehead into the bridge of her nose. Clutching at her head, she shook off the stars appearing in the corners of her vision and resumed her original stance, more cautious now.

"Is that the best you can do?" Vesper seethed, gritting her teeth through the needles of pain shooting through her throbbing skull. In response, she slammed the hilt of her sword under his chin, driving him back and opening the distance between the two of them once more.

The former champion on Carthage spat blood, waving her on with a hungry look. Vesper wasted no time, striking out with her gladius in a series of powerful jabs that left deep punctures in his shield, the tip of her blade splintering from the force. Nabil's eyes flicked to the gashes in his shield, and he gave her a wide-eyed look. Dancing away, he reversed his grip once more, trying to match her fury with his own, lashing out with wide strikes aimed for her head, only for Vesper to take the heavy blow, locking the wooden blade between her shield and flank, ignoring the pain. Roaring like a beast, she slammed the pommel of her blade into his forehead with enough force that Nabil's eyes rolled back, showing the whites as his body went limp. In the heat of the moment she forgot herself, hitting him again and again, mercy forgotten. Then without warning, Linus was there, holding her back with what seemed like half of the ludus, including Rainar, all straining against her while she snarled like an animal.

With a shudder she came back to herself, the fire of her rage fading away like the setting sun as she slumped against the old gladiator in exhaustion. "Remind me to never anger you," said Linus, slipping under her arm to hold her up. "And before you do the same to me as you did to that poor fool, accept my deepest apologies."

Vesper looked at his weather-worn face and shook her head, gratefully accepting his aid as they walked back to the stands while the other men saw to Nabil. "I know that you mean no harm, old man," she said, a hand going to her side where she had taken Nabil's wild strike, "but Ose women are meant to stay pure until they are betrothed, to have everyone think I am with a man not my husband... it shames me."

"Well, I don't think anyone will be talking of anything but your fury on the sands. I was sure you would crack Nabil's skull if I let you go on," said Linus, helping her up the steps.

She opened her mouth to answer when she suddenly bent in half, her stomach rolling like someone had just kicked her in the belly. "By Olodumare, what's happening?" she said, choking back vomit as a vile odor filled her nostrils.

Linus helped her sit, his head moving like it was on a swivel as he searched for what had made her ill so quickly. "Are you injured from the battle with Nabil?" he asked, frowning out at the wiry man who was only now getting to his feet. "I didn't see him get in any—"

"No!" she said, knowing the smell, having experienced this pain one time before at a villa that had been wiped out, the entire country-side turned to ash. Sucking in deep breaths, Vesper struggled to her feet, shifting her gaze to the world beyond, in the same moment, a small gasp escaping her lips.

"What is it?" asked Linus, following her gaze, in confusion.

"It's clearer," she said, a slow smile creeping across her face as she watched hints of color return to the weave surrounding them, the darkness receding like a morning fog.

"Now I'm sure you got hit in the head a little too hard," said Linus, his brow coming together. "I think it would be best if we took you to see Jacob. Some time with the medicus would probably do you well."

Pushing the old man away, she gasped in wonder as she saw flashes of cobalt and crimson, the threads of the weave pulsing strong and true. Vesper was about to jump with joy when the blast hit her, a wave of force that knocked her off her feet and onto her face. Shaking off the blow, she sat up just as the receding darkness began to coalesce, forming a thick shaft of pitch black in the distance that blocked out the sun, the strange pillar stretching from the earth to the heavens and beyond. Then, without warning, a tremor of fear pulsed through her connection with Narcissus. And to her horror she realized that the towering pillar of filth, the darkness, was right above the slave market, and Narcissus was at the heart of it.

TWO

STRANGE VISITS

Lucilla kept her face still while the weak-chinned senator droned on, her heart pounding faster with each word that tumbled from his bruised and battered mouth. Wetting her throat with a bit of wine to calm herself, she tried to keep her voice steady when she was at least able to get in a word. "If what you say is true, why would he let you, of all people, live?"

Senator Magnus raised a cup to his lips, his shaking hand spilling some of the dark vintage on the wooden tabletop. "I am aware of how Commodus feels about me, and by all rights I should be dead along with Publius, but it is my understanding that the only reason I live is that he means for me to stand trial for high treason. He wants to send a message to the senate, to all the patricians. That is why he had his men beat me so, so you could see that he has no respect for the highborn, and what we have done for Rome."

Her husband, Tiberius, who sat across from the senator rose to his feet, passing a hand through his graying hair. "And then you, in your foolishness, darken our door, wasting my time with your whining," he said with a sigh. "Do you not think that just by coming to our home, that you are putting us in danger? Implicating us in a foolish plot we want nothing to do with!"

Lucilla hugged herself, a chill running through her despite the heat of the morning sun. She and Tiberius had been in the villa's garden, enjoying their morning meal of bread, dates, honey, and some watered wine when a slave had barged in, nervously announcing the senator at their door. Her husband had initially told the servant to send the man away, but Lucilla had been hungry for news, and had convinced her husband to let the man in to say his piece, much to her dismay. "And you say your weapons did not cut his skin, that he—"

"Enough!" snapped Tiberius, not looking at her. "Ignore this fool and his lies. He is just trying to frighten us with tall tales to garner sympathy for himself and his cause. Commodus is just a man! The son of Marcus Aurelius, not Jupiter. I knew him as a child. I was there when the wet nurse put him to her breast. Let us not get caught up in delusions."

Lucilla nodded in agreement with her husband, and after hearing the senator's story, her thoughts fled back to the fateful day a few weeks past, in the tunnels under the city. She had spearheaded her own failed attempt on her brother's life. Commodus had shown an unnatural strength and had taken blows that would have killed an ordinary man. Now that she thought about it, his strangeness had started months before, exactly when she couldn't be sure, but something about him was different, and now the senator's story confirmed it. Pushing herself away from the table, she stood, giving Magnus a hard look. "Senator, I think it would be best if you left our home. Your very presence here marks us as traitors to the empire."

Senator Magnus blanched, sputtering as his eyes darted back and forth between her and her husband. "But... but... we have to stand together! The only way for us to survive is to defy that monster, and return power to the senate."

"I will not risk my station, or my life, for a foolish cause," she said, meeting her husband's approving gaze. "Finish your wine and get out. I will not ask so nicely again."

"Tiberius," said the senator, giving her husband a pleading look, "Lucilla may be too soft to want to harm her brother, but surely you—"

"Watch your tongue," said Tiberius with a growl. "As far as I'm concerned you are a dead man walking. I know Commodus, and the only reason he let you live was so that you would lead him to the rest of your conspirators. Now, do as my wife says, and get out of my house before I throw you out!"

"I will see him out, Husband," said Lucilla.

The senator put down his wine, paling like a man who had just been told when he was going to die. "You will regret this, Tiberius, you and everyone else who stands aside when Rome needs you most."

Her husband shook his head, dismissing Magnus with a wave of his hand. "I very much doubt that. Rome will endure, just as it always has. Now get out of my sight."

"Come, Senator, I will at least grant you the courtesy of escorting you to your carpentum," she said, motioning for him to follow as they left the garden, making her way through the wide corridors of the villa with the hapless senator in tow. They were nearly to the entrance, out of earshot of her husband, when she glanced at him over her shoulder. "You are certain Publius is dead?"

Magnus bobbed his head, sucking in a deep breath. "Yes! I saw the gladius plunge into the drunken fool's neck, watched as his blood pooled on the floor beneath him."

Lucilla paused, waving away the pair of their personal legionnaires who stood guard at the door. "How many men did you have?"

"We sent in a group of cohorts to do the deed; we assumed ten men should have been more than enough. But when we heard nothing after a time, Publius and I were sure he was dead, or something had happened, so we went to see with another set of cohorts, men who were well paid for their—"

"Come, we can't stay here," she said, raising a hand to quiet him, glaring at a slave girl who just happened to be cleaning the floors nearby. They walked into the courtyard of the villa, Lucilla wincing when the full light of day beat down on her fair skin.

"Your husband is having you watched?" he asked, lowering his voice.

"I can't be sure, but he has plans to leave our villa here on Palatine Hill and go to our country estates, but so far I have convinced him to stay," she said. "Not that it matters now. What are you and your people going to do now?"

"Ready my defense, rally allies to my cause," he said with a shrug. "I only hope things go better than they did here."

"It seems you've brought your entire household with you," she said, eyeing the line of hard-looking men surrounding the senator's waiting carriage. Along with a young boy who served as a footman, and a kindly looking old slave with bronzed skin, who served as a driver.

Magnus wrung his hands in front of him, casting a worried look at his meager forces. "I cannot be too careful. Commodus killed every man we brought with us, or frightened them enough to switch sides. I'm afraid if we can't convince men like your husband to join our cause, that we are doomed, and the emperor will simply have us killed one by one."

"You and the men of the senate control much of the empire's wealth," she scoffed. "I find it hard to believe— By the gods!" shouted Lucilla, her gaze torn to the sky above the city. "It can't be real."

Senator Magnus followed her eyes, stumbling back like a drunkard when he saw what had drawn her attention. "What is that?"

Lucilla said nothing, ignoring the sputtering man as she walked around the senator's carpentum to get a better view. Above the city, the sky was black as if the sun had turned its back on Rome. Stranger still, the darkness was centered over only a portion of it, in what looked like the western market. She was about to send the senator on his way when it hit her, a vile wind that smelled of rotting meat that made her gag, a smell she knew all too well. "This can't be happening!"

"I don't understand; what has you in such a panic?" asked the senator, his brows coming together.

"You don't smell that?"

"Smell what?" he asked, frowning at her.

She gave him a sidelong glance, her mind racing. The incidents had grown worse over the last few weeks, and she had done her best to investigate them. With her husband watching her like a hawk, it had been difficult, but now, with the darkness falling over the city, and the smell of death reaching her even here, it appeared that matters had made a turn for the worse, and she had to act before it was too late. Steeling herself, she turned to the driver: "Sicilian, you will take me to the city, to the western market."

"You cannot just take my man and my carriage," said the weak-chinned senator in protest, moving to block her way.

"Senator Magnus, I will need your men too. There is more at stake than you can imagine," she began, pushing him aside and nodding for the driver to continue. "And right now, I need to be in the market, so you can come with me, or stay here—I don't really care. I'm taking this carriage whether you like it or not."

Magnus glanced up at the sky once more before bobbing his head yes and leaping into the seat beside her. The driver snapped the reins and they were off, with Lucilla praying to the gods that they could get there in time to stop what was about to happen, or at the very least, find the cause for these events and at last find some way to stop them.

THREE

GIFTS

Narcissus pushed his way through the densely crowded market, his massive frame cutting a path through high and lowborn alike, all the while his eyes were ever moving, hunting for threats. A shout up ahead, followed by men cursing made him tense, ready to do violence, but as he drew closer, it was clear it had been a simple accident with a few rickety carts spilling their produce, knocking over an older slave who wasn't paying attention. Snorting in frustration he turned to the lanky man, with a boyish face, who followed close behind him. He was dressed in a fine white tunic embroidered with gold thread, a purple striped toga wrapped around him. "I don't know why you insist on coming to the market, Cassius, most of the slavers who supply us would be more than happy to bring their wares directly to the ludus for inspection."

The lanky, boyish-faced man raised his chin, fumbling to rewrap part of his toga that had been dragging in the dirt. "And let those idiots from the ludus dacicus have the first pick of the new stock? I don't think so," he said. "I am now the chief lanista of the greatest ludus in the empire now. It's best if I inspect the new recruits myself, lest the riffraff think they can take advantage of me. Yourself included."

"Of course... Dominus," said Narcissus, looking away and rolling his eyes. Cassius had been one of three lanista's who administered the ludus magnus. He had been mostly responsible for supplying gladiators for private events, as the Roman patricians were always hungry to be seen alongside the heroes of the arena. The death of Epstein a few weeks ago had changed all that, and he had been given more responsibility and was now accountable for acquiring new talent as well.

"You find something amusing," said Cassius, frowning up at the big Celt.

Narcissus pushed aside a toothless beggar who had gotten too close, putting the fear of the gods in him with a feral snarl before continuing. "I do. I was not aware you had such lofty ambitions, but you take well to power, and luckily for you, purple suits you well."

Casting a wary eye at the milling crowd, the lanista shook his head. "I did not want this. I was just a simple man trying to make a living before you and the emperor's sister had Epstein killed. For no good reason, I might add."

"Epstein was a nuisance, even at the best of times. Sending him to the underworld was a gift to the ludus, and once told, you agreed with her decision... did you not?" said Narcissus. "And I find it strange that despite your claims not to want it, you take every opportunity to mention you are the new head lanista of the ludus."

"True, in both regards," he said with a half grin, pushing past Narcissus toward a rough-looking group of men in chains, standing atop a wooden platform. "But I can't help myself, and it would be best if we forgot all of that. Come, let us see what the market has to offer."

"I can't protect you if you rush off like that," growled Narcissus, elbowing his way through the crowd after him.

"Apologies," said Cassius, dry-washing his hands when they arrived in front of the platform, giving polite nods to some of the other buyers that he knew. "But if I don't have a place at the front, I won't be able to see the quality of the flesh, and this will all have been a waste of time."

"I know how it works, Cassius. I just hate this place," he said, wrinkling his nose at the bizarre mixture of unwashed bodies and sweet perfumes. The entire market was like that wherever he looked. Unwashed men and women in chains to be sold as cheap labor stood next to perfumed and pretty courtesans that would go to the city's brothels or, in many cases, directly to private citizens looking for pleasures of the flesh. Children, the younger the better, were often the cheapest, as they took time to mold into their roles, but were often the most loyal once trained, depending on who bought them, of course. Those in highest demand were the men whose strength or skill was obvious, men who could become gladiators with the right training.

"Why?" asked Cassius with a smile. "The slave market is the most interesting place in all of Rome."

"It is a place of pain and suffering, of sadness."

The lanista spread his arms wide, a grin coming to his boyish face as he began, "Sadness?? Never. It is a place of opportunity, of joy," he said, just as an older man in a stained tunic appeared on the platform, poking and prodding the men in chains with a heavy wooden rod, shouting at them to stand up straight. Smiling at the sight, Cassius continued, "You see, the senate, even the emperor himself, would tell you the empire has been built by their wisdom, by the strength of our legionnaires, but the truth is Rome has been built on the backs of men like you see before you. Slavery is the true legacy of Rome."

"The men standing on that platform do not look full of joy."

"That is true," said Cassius, his voice full of excitement, "but that is because they don't know the truth yet."

"And what is that?" asked Narcissus.

"That their lives will be better from this day forth. They will live under the Pax Romana. They will not know war, or hunger. Living in safety with a roof over their heads and food in their bellies. It will be a far better life than the one they knew before."

"How could you know what their lives were like before they came here?" asked Narcissus, his brows knitting together.

"You have lived in Rome for too long, my friend, and I fear you have forgotten," said the lanista. "This is the heart of the civilized world, my friend. Life beyond our borders is savage. Filthy people living in little more than mud huts, trying to scrape enough together to eat, constantly warring with their neighbors over tiny parcels of land that could hardly feed a few people."

"Yes, but they are free."

"Free to what?" he scoffed. "To live short, brutal lives wallowing in their own filth! No, being a slave in Rome is far better than living free in some hovel with a toothless, smelly wife and a pack of mewling, hungry children."

Narcissus looked up at the browbeaten, filthy men, a pang of sympathy in his heart. "Do you truly believe that the Roman way is better, that a life in Rome is better, even as a slave?"

"Of course. Look at all we have created. We are superior to these savages in every way. They need us to take care of them, to decide for them. It's just better this way."

Narcissus looked around the slave market, eyeing the Roman patricians with their trappings of wealth. Fine clothes, full bellies, and the coin to buy whatever they wanted. "Yes, but at the end of it all, strip away their titles and clothes, and how do you tell which man is patrician and which is slave?"

"Our greatness would be obvious," laughed Cassius, shaking his head.

"As you say," said Narcissus, looking away to hide his anger. Men like Cassius would never understand slavery. How could he? He had been born a freeman, and had lived a privileged life, thus could analyze slavery from the outside. Narcissus didn't have such luxury. Once, long ago, it had been him up on that platform, little more than a frightened young boy, taller and wider than some of the grown men who stood beside him. He had been sold like livestock and had spent every day since answering to one dominus or another: his life, his choices, never his own. "Would you have bought me?"

Cassius hesitated, a slow smile coming to his lips. "Of course. Look at you. Look at all that you have achieved! You were a hero of the arena, and are now a great doctore. Your life has been made better in every way!"

Narcissus began to object when the auctioneer shouted over the chattering masses, and Cassius shushed him to silence, his attention focused on the men on the platform. Keeping one eye on the crowd and another on Cassius, Narcissus mulled over the lanista's words, his blood growing hotter each time a man in chains was sold. Part of him wanted to snap his neck, just as he had done weeks ago with Epstein, but he held back, knowing that the law was such, that every slave in the ludus would pay the price with their lives if he was found out. Instead, he did what he always had, controlling his anger and focusing on discipline and duty, which today was keeping Cassius safe.

The purchase of new stock did not take long, and once Cassius had arranged delivery of the men to the ludus, he gave Narcissus a leering grin while patting his coin purse. "We have a few extra denarii; why don't we take advantage of all the market has to offer."

Narcissus kept his face still, his breathing steady, knowing what the lanista was hinting at. "It would be better if we returned to the ludus; it is difficult to keep you safe in those places."

Cassius barked a laugh, patting the big man on the shoulder. "Come now, my friend, you don't have to watch. I will see to it that you get to enjoy yourself as well."

"The last thing I want is some whore used by every man in the city."

The lanista cocked his head, tapping the side of his nose. "Oh, don't worry, I won't tell your little Ose whore a thing; your perversions will remain between us."

"What did you say?" he snapped, bristling with rage at the lanista.

Cassius flinched, swallowing hard. "Apologies," he said, shrinking away with a simpering smile. "I didn't mean to offend. It was just—"

Narcissus balled his meaty fists, ready to silence the lanista by ripping out his vile tongue, but he knew better, and somehow managed to calm himself by letting out a slow breath, sure that anything he did to Cassius would only encourage talk at the ludus. "Never mind, let's just get on with it," he growled, cursing his own stupidity for even reacting.

The lanista sighed in relief, his boyish grin returning. "Excellent! I know a brothel not far from here with the most luxurious baths. It will be a fine afternoon filled with delights."

Narcissus grumbled noncommittally under his breath, falling in beside Cassius as they sped down narrow, graffiti-covered streets, his thoughts lingering on Vesper all the while. He could not understand how the rumors of them had reached so far. Neither one of them had done anything to encourage them, and Narcissus, for one, treated her no differently than the other men. Thoughts of her amplified the sensations flowing through their bond, and despite him being in the shade of the market, he felt the heat of the sun on his skin. And he felt that for some reason she was irritated and annoyed. Their connection was the strangest thing he had ever felt, and to make things more difficult, there were times he could barely feel her, and he forgot that the bond even existed. But if he lingered too long on thoughts of Vesper, her dark eyes or the soft curves of her hips, the sensation from her surged to the front of his mind, and it could be hours before the feeling died down again.

"It won't be long now," said Cassius. "Just around the next corner."

Looking around the unfamiliar street, Narcissus frowned into his beard. "Where in Hades are we?" he asked, realizing he had let his mind wander and had no clue where they were.

Cassius perked up, pointing across the square to a run-down insulae painted in garish colors, its flaking paint showing its age. "Hunter's Square, in the old market. It was part of the original city, where men gathered to sell meat when they returned from their hunts."

"A dismal place," said Narcissus, eyeing the grime-covered walls and garbage-filled alleyways, frowning when they passed a group of filthy children in rags begging for denarii. "Do the cohorts ever patrol this corner of the city?"

"No, they police the better parts, where the bribes are more lucrative," said Cassius with a laugh.

Narcissus wrinkled his nose, hints of nausea bubbling in his belly from the smell of the place. Staring at the hungry children, he fished a few coins from his belt, tossing them in the dirt in front of them. "Where are their parents? They can't all be orphans."

"The children? Who cares? They're nothing but filthy urchins," said Cassius, frowning at the coins Narcissus had thrown to the group. "Their mothers probably work in the brothels lining the square. As to their fathers... who knows? I doubt any man with good sense would claim to have sired such filth. And you should not have shown them your coin. I'm sure they would cut your throat for less."

Putting a hand on the lanista's shoulder, Narcissus stopped him. "I know you have your perversions, Cassius, but this is not a good place; everything about it makes me uneasy. Why don't we head—"

"Is the great Narcissus afraid," he said, raising his voice, "of some street urchins? Come now, this can't be!"

The big Celt shook his head, eyeing the small groups dotting the square, feeling like they were being watched. "I have survived for so long because I trust my instincts, and right now, my instincts are telling me that we need to be gone from this place."

"Oh, come now, you're not the type to believe in superstitious nonsense... and I doubt these fools would try anything. Not with you around, so let's just go have some fun."

"As you wish," said Narcissus, bile rising in the back of his throat from the sickly odor wafting through the air. "Hopefully the brothel will smell better than out here."

"I don't smell anything," said Cassius with a shrug, strolling across the ancient square with a spring in his step while whistling a tune Narcissus couldn't quite place.

They had just arrived at the garishly painted door of the brothel, when a commotion behind them caught his attention. Narcissus turned, his hackles rising when he saw a pair of tall, dark-skinned men with cracked white paint smeared over their faces, leading a half-dozen naked men and women bound in iron shackles, their faces covered by dark hoods. Something about the whole scene shook Narcissus to the core, and the bitter taste of fear filled his mouth when he recognized the crowns of bone they wore, and the threat they represented.

"What in the name of gods are they doing?" asked Cassius, behind him.

"I don't know, but we have to stop them," said Narcissus, just as one of the men raised a hand in the air, and wisps of shadow began to circle his palm, a dagger, black as midnight appearing in his hand after a moment.

"Stop them? Have you lost your mind? No, we need to get inside, away from this mess."

Narcissus shook his head, his eyes never leaving the dagger in the man's hand. "These are very dangerous people; you have to get inside, Cassius, and don't come out until I get you. Understood?"

The lanista hesitated, his voice full of irritation. "But... No, I am dominus here. We will both go inside and mind our business; that is the reason people come to this part of the city, to not be bothered."

Snarling in rage, he turned to face him. "Get in the damn broth-el... or there won't be anything of you to return to the ludus." Before Cassius could say more, Narcissus picked him up bodily and shoved him through the door, slamming it shut behind him. A bloodcurdling scream filled his ears, snapping his attention back to the square, and he turned just in time to see the shadowy dagger ripped from the chest of one of the slaves, their blood, a woman's blood, staining the weapon a bright red as she fell in a heap.

"Scum of Rome," shouted the man who had stabbed her, raising the bloody dagger above his head for all to see. "We are the Sandawei, the first people created by the almighty Olodumare in his own image, and we have come to bring justice to your corrupt empire."

The Sandawei with the dagger grabbed another slave behind him, showing Narcissus his back. Seeing his chance, he broke into a sprint, adrenaline filling his veins as he raced to save a life. He had managed only a few feet when he was blasted back on his heels by a choking wind that brought tears to his eyes. Struggling to see, he squinted in horror as the dagger pierced the chest of another slave, his screams echoing across the entire square as a wave of shadow rolled over everything he could see, turning day to night.

Raising a meaty hand to protect his eyes, he pressed forward, ignoring the burning and itching in his eyes. With a roar, he bowled into the Sandawei's back, sending both of them tumbling over in a mangled heap, elbows and fists flying in all directions. Narcissus battled to get the upper hand, but just as he managed to roll on top of him, a jet-black dagger appeared inches from his face. Acting on instinct, he grabbed the dark-skinned man's wrist, bending it back at an unnatural angle until her heard bone snap, a guttural scream filling his ears. Not wasting any time, the big Celt bounded to his feet, dragging the screaming man with him. "Enough," he shouted, shoving the Sandawei out in front of him and locking his arm behind his back, using him like a shield. "Stop, or I'll break his neck."

The Sandawei holding the chains stared at Narcissus with a milky-eyed gaze, while a chilling smile spread across his painted face. "This be none of your concern, big man," he said, overpronouncing his words with a halting cadence. "Go about your day and be gone."

The man in his choke hold began to chant under his breath, and Narcissus tightened his grip, cutting off his air to silence him. "I know who you are," he said, recognizing the milky gaze and guttural dialect from their fight with the emperor's chamberlain, the man who had almost killed them only a few weeks ago: Saoterus. "I know what you are, what you represent. So do as I say. Let the slaves go and leave this place."

"Come come, you are not some Roman. You be a slave, made to bow and scrape for your dominus. You should be helping us punish these wretches, not defending them," he said, tugging at the chain, pulling the remaining slaves in front of him.

Narcissus flinched like he'd been struck, knowing there was truth in his words. He had been a slave since he was a teenager and owed the Romans nothing, but the whimpers and sobs coming from the hooded slaves told him these Sandawei were no better. "No! Those aren't Romans you're killing; they're simple men and women who hunger for life, no more than me, so why would I let you murder them in cold blood? Why would I let you finish whatever sick ritual you're performing?"

A smile crept on the Sandawei's face as he ducked behind the slaves, unsheathing a bone dagger that he held up for Narcissus to see. "The Ẹbọ have already begun; no stopping it now, big man," he said as the darkness around them grew deeper.

"If I break this one's neck, I'm sure it will stop," said Narcissus, shaking the man he was holding before continuing, "There's nothing like death to silence a fool's tongue."

"The Sandawei and death be old friends," he said, lightly dragging the bone dagger along a trembling slave's throat. "Gonna be your friend too, unless you run along."

He crooked a finger at Narcissus, speaking, whispering hate-filled words that echoed across the square, and the burning in Narcissus's eyes intensified, while sharp needles of agony spread over his skin, reddening his pale flesh as if he had plunged his arm in boiling water. "Have it your way, then," he growled through the pain, twisting the body in his hands with all his might. A sharp snap filled the air, followed by a choking rattle as he crushed the windpipe of the man he was holding, blindly charging forward with the spasming body.

He was almost on top of the Sandawei when the bone dagger flashed in front of him, and by reflex he threw the broken body to the left while he went right, the razor-sharp weapon clipping his arm, drawing a thin line of crimson along his bicep. Ignoring the cut, he dodged behind a woman chained at the neck, and then pivoting to his side, kicking out with a heavy boot, catching his attacker in the groin, the brutal strike folding him in half.

To his surprise, the woman grabbed a length of the heavy chain binding her to the others, and with a wild screech lunged for the injured Sandawei, tying the iron chain around his neck while pulling back with all her weight. Narcissus was about to help her when she shouted, "Kill him, quickly, before he calls more."

"I doubt he can do anything with that chain—" Narcissus paled when the flailing warrior uttered a single word that rumbled like distant thunder, and a wave of cold spread over him, a chill running up his spine. Sandawei warriors began emerging from the shadows a heartbeat later, appearing as if by magic from filthy alleys all along the edge of the square, many of them half crouched like animals, loping toward them. "By the gods."

"Not the gods, only Sandawei tricks," said the hooded woman in a strained voice, pulling at the chain as the painted warrior gasped for air, "but I think we are too late."

Balling his fist, he pummeled the choking man in the head, his eyes rolling back as he fell to the ground. "That will be enough of that," he said, reaching to help the woman remove the hood. The burlap material was attached to the collar around her neck and was near impossible to easily remove, so Narcissus helped her tear holes so that she could see and breathe properly.

They had just managed it when the woman's eyes went wide. "Look out!"

Narcissus turned just in time to see a bone-tipped spear flying toward his chest, a pair of half-bent warriors almost on top of him. Not bothering to move, he snapped the hissing weapon out of the air, spinning it around in a single smooth motion and lashing out, using its razor-sharp tip to pierce the heart of the lead warrior. Not slowing, he used the back end of the crude spear to deflect a clumsy thrust from the second Sandawei warrior, then, without mercy, grasped him by the throat and spun in place, hurling the hapless man back toward his allies, where he landed in a heap.

"If that's your only trick, I think we're going to be in trouble," said the woman, appearing at his side, the chain off her neck while she struggled to remove the remainder of the hood.

"We are full of tricks," he said as pulse of warmth passed through him, and Narcissus felt a knowing tug, a smile coming to his face as he fell into a ready stance. "When she comes, we will attack."

"What?? Who? Have you gone mad?"

A bright flash of light cut through the cloying darkness, and Narcissus looked down to see a golden cord pulsing at his midsection, stretching out to the woman who had just appeared, glowing as bright as the sun. "It took you long enough," he grumbled.

Vesper smiled her brilliant smile at him, and a surge of heat pulsed in his blood. "I was busy," she said, glancing around the square. "But it looks like you've made some new friends. How did so many get into the city?"

Narcissus shook his head, frowning at the closing circle of Sandawei warriors. "I don't know, but they don't seem to like me; they've already tried to kill me twice today."

"Let's teach them a lesson, then," she said, singing under her breath. An instant later a fine gladius appeared in her hands, and a set of metal bracers grew like vines, suddenly covering his forearms.

"It looks like you've learned a few tricks," he said, eyeing the ornate metal covering his forearms. "Let's put them to good use."

"Together." Vesper smiled, charging ahead, her glowing form banishing the darkness with every step.

"She's like a Celtic woman," he muttered, watching in awe as she leapt into battle, her gladius moving like the wind. "In the best way." Roaring, he followed after, never feeling so alive, or so happy.

FOUR

THE BURDEN

The horses drawing the carpentum were in full lather by the time Lucilla descended into the city proper, with thick streaks of frothing white sweat pouring down their sleek-muscled flanks. Bouncing around in the cabin, her patience was wearing thin, and she wanted to get out and whip the horses herself, but doing so would not have been proper for a woman of her station, and would have started unwanted rumors for the senator's guard, who followed them closely behind. Instead, she ground her teeth while shouting out the window, "How much longer, man?" she said, her eyes drawn to the dark column twisting above the western part of the city.

"We are almost there," shouted the driver, his whip in constant motion, cracking over the frothing horses. "By the luck of the gods, we seem to be the only fools charging headlong into this mess."

Lucilla couldn't help but agree as she watched the steady stream of plebeians and slaves flowing in the opposite direction, wide eyed with fear. "What do you expect to find?" asked Senator Magnus, pulling her attention away from the window and the streaming mass of humanity. "I mean it's just a cloud of darkness, is it not?"

Lucilla blinked, almost having forgotten that senator Magnus was with her. He was too quiet for his own good, and she wondered how spineless men like him clung to power. Just looking at him made her wish that her brother *had* killed him. In fact, with his slight frame and small hands, she was sure that it would be easy enough to do it herself, more enjoyable too. Instead, she smiled politely without showing her teeth, drawing in slow breaths through her nostrils, and out through her mouth to calm her nerves. "The darkness, the smell are signs of incidents that have been happening for months now. At first they were small in nature, strange attacks, people vanishing, but with time they grew. It was not long before we found entire insulae filled with nothing but blood, or entire villas with the people all gone, the land surrounding it as black as night."

The senator sputtered, rolling his eyes. "Of course, I have heard of such things, even seen some of them for myself. But these are affairs for the legionary, or at the very least the city guard. Why would a woman of your station take on such a burden?"

Cocking her head, she leaned forward, her eyes never leaving his. "No one was willing to do anything; no one cared, so I took it upon myself."

"Surely your husband, or—"

"No one!" she said, her voice cold. "So I took it upon myself."

The senator shifted in his seat, looking away. "Well... I'm sure I could have. Or at least—"

"Would you have taken action if I had come to you with some wild story about an empty insulae... or worse, dead slaves?"

"I would have gone to someone who could do something."

"You have spent too long letting others take the reins, Senator. All of us in positions of power have. But I have learned that sometimes you must get your hands dirty, especially when something so precious as Rome herself is threatened."

"Well, you are braver than I," he said with a frown. "Charging headlong into danger without so much as a dagger. I pray that Jupiter will protect us."

Looking out the window once more, Lucilla kept her face still, realizing he was right, and that she had nothing to defend them with. "I doubt the gods have time to play with mortals, but pray all you want. I will find a way to stop this." They rode on in silence for the rest of the journey, with only the shouts of the driver and the crack of his whip breaking the monotony. She wished it was somehow possible to send a message to Vesper, but in her haste she left without her guard, or even a slave to send word.

Gooseflesh ran up and down her pale skin as the carpentum passed through some invisible threshold, and day turned to night. Across from her, Senator Magnus cringed, a squeak escaping his lips while his entire body started to shake. "No, no, turn us around! I will not stand for this madness of running headlong to our deaths," he said, looking out the window and then quickly shrinking back into his seat.

Watching the senator panic, Lucilla drew herself up, her resolve growing the more he cowered. "Was it not our first Caesar who claimed that cowards die many times before their deaths, and that fortune favors the bold?"

"How dare you!" he said, his face reddening. "I am a senator, a man of honor. My family—"

"I was not speaking of you, Senator," began Lucilla, a tiny smile playing across her lips. "I was only saying that if we fall, you shall be remembered for your bravery, perhaps even deified by the senate itself and remembered as a god."

The senator, his fear forgotten, opened his mouth to speak, only to snap it shut when the carpentum ground to a halt, the driver shouting back from his seat, "My lady... I... I am not sure where you intend for us to go, but there is an entire group of cohorts from the city guard blocking the road—"

"I understand," she shouted, quickly stepping out of the carpentum, hunting for the centurion in charge, comforted by the sight of a full centura, almost a hundred men, standing at the ready. "What are you called, Centurion?" she said at last, her eyes falling on a legionary carrying a vine staff, with a mushroom-shaped head that had been polished to a high shine, marking him as the leader of this group.

The centurion, a wide man with a pronounced limp and dark, thoughtful eyes gave her a nod, looking her up and down as he adjusted a fine gladius on his hip. "Albus Flavius, my lady."

"And do you know who I am, Albus?"

"I do. I was part of the legions that invaded Parthia with your former husband, Lucius Verus."

"A great victory, one that should have seen you elevated beyond such a low station," said Lucilla, raising a fine brow at the man. "How is it you find yourself with the unenviable position of leading legionnaires in the city guard?"

The first centurion pressed his lips together, tapping his knee with his staff. "I took a spear through the knee, and it never healed well. My captain rewarded me with an easy posting close to home, although I'm not so sure how easy that will be today," he said, looking up at the darkened sky.

Putting a hand on the man's shoulder, she leaned in close, speaking low so that only he could hear, "Rome has need of your bravery once more, Albus. I have need of you. I have been investigating these troubles on behalf of my brother. I—"

Albus pressed his lips together, meeting her eyes. "I'm sorry, I have orders. No one may pass until we receive word from the city prefect."

"It will be too late by then," she said. "I have seen what happens after these incidents. Bodies burned to ash, families murdered, legionnaires vanished. I cannot stand by and wait for it to happen again: we must act."

"I am three years from my twenty-five," he said with a sigh. "You ask me to defy orders, throw away my future?"

"I would never do such a thing," she said, raising her chin, "but Roman lives are at risk, so I ask you, instead of waiting here, come with us. You may end up finding glory in doing some good once more."

Albus licked his lips, glancing over his shoulder at his men who shifted in place, their eyes flickering to the sky constantly. "Perhaps, the gods know these men could use some glory... and we heard screams earlier. It would be in poor judgment to stand idly by while the people of Rome need us."

"You are a wise man," she said with a laugh, patting him on the shoulder. "Follow closely, and I will see to it that you get a better posting." Returning to the carriage, she settled in across from the senator, who gave her a half grin but said nothing as they resumed their breakneck pace, Albus and his hundred cohorts falling in behind the senator's guard.

It did not take them long to reach the heart of the darkness, the old city, built when Rome was no more than a series of outgrown villages and towns that banded together for safety and commerce. As such, the buildings were made mostly of baked, ugly brown clay and aged wood. To make matters worse, this part of the city did not have proper plumbing and smelled of a latrine mixed with the vile smell of rot that grew stronger with each incident, making it impossible to find the source of the strange odor.

"How do you expect to find anything in this darkness?" said Magnus. "This, it is a fool's errand, let us return to your home, to your husband."

She silenced him with a raised hand, waiting, watching until she saw what she was looking for, another brilliant flash of light, cutting through the darkness once more. "There she is," she said, showing the whites of her teeth. "It seems somehow she is here too, a light guiding the way."

"What?" said the driver, blowing out his cheeks in confusion.

"The light! The flashes! Follow them, quickly," she shouted to the driver, who wasted no time heading off, the near spent horses whinnying in protest as they raced toward the light, to Vesper, and hopefully to the answers she had been seeking for so long.

FIVE
ẸBỌ

"By Olodumare! There are too many of them," rasped Vesper, breathing hard while battling back a wave of Sandawei warriors, gasping when a bone-tipped spear slipped through her defenses, scraping across her back, leaving a deep groove in the leather vest she wore.

"I don't know where they keep coming from, but it looks like a full-scale invasion," said Narcissus at her side, catching a charging Sandawei warrior mid stride, turning his momentum against him and slamming the hapless fool against the mud-brick wall, dust filling the air as the paint-covered man crumpled to the ground.

"Yes, this is starting to feel like one of those situations where I should have looked before I leapt," said Vesper with a frown. When they realized how many Sandawei were pouring into the square, she and Narcissus had cut a path to a narrow alley, battling through a horde of relentless warriors in the vain hope that they could control the tempo of the battle in a smaller space, while fighting back to back. The alley was a good position to limit how many Sandawei could come at them at once, but they now found themselves pinned on both sides, growing more exhausted with each wave of new enemies.

"Above us!" shouted Narcissus, using his bracer to deflect a spear meant for his heart, and then smashing his attacker's nose flat with a pair of quick jabs.

Vesper looked up just in time to see a pair of warriors on the roof of the mud-brick building, drawing back to hurl their spears. Without thinking, she drew on the few ragged threads of power she could siphon from the weave, blasting them off the roof with a powerful gust of wind. The falling men tumbled on top of the warriors at the front of the alley, throwing the entire formation into disarray for a heartbeat as the Sandawei fought to reform their line, cursing and screaming in their halting tongue all the while. Taking advantage of the momentary chaos, she struck, stabbing and slashing with her gladius, felling Sandawei warriors faster than they could defend. "We can't keep this up," she said, glancing over her shoulder when she heard the big Celt scream, her heart pounding harder when she saw a spear lodged in his shoulder, while another glanced off his thigh, leaving an ugly red gash on his hairy leg.

"Can you get us up on the roof?" he shouted, sucking in ragged breaths as he snapped off the end of the spear, leaving the tip buried in his shoulder. "Like how you jump from place to place."

"I don't think so," she said, raising her shield to block a wicked blow that left her arm numb, "but I can try something else." Vesper had felt it when they fought their way into the alley, sensing the long dormant seeds in the mud brick and fallen timber that made up the ancient insulae, a small spark of life in such a dismal place. Vesper began to sing under her breath, and the concentric patterns on her arms and legs began to glow, pushing back strange darkness that covered the square as she drew on her own deep well of strength, combining it with the faintest threads of power from the weave, until finally channeling it all through the seeds in the wall. Her voice grew from a whisper to a high crescendo as the mud brick began to vibrate, filling the alleyway with choking dust as the ancient brick came apart, blinding some of the attacking Sandawei, but oddly not touching her or Narcissus.

"What in the name of the gods is this?" said Narcissus, staggering back into her as her glow brightened, pushing back the dark.

"A way up!" she said, smiling as vines and thick branches full of emerald-green leaves burst from the walls on both sides of the alley, while razor-sharp thorns reached out like clawing fingers toward the oncoming rush of Sandawei, curling around their dark-painted limbs, choking, restraining any who came too close. Vesper raised her arms higher, and the newly minted vines snaked their way up the walls, replacing the faded, old mud brick with the vibrant colors of life. "Climb!".

Wasting no time, Narcissus grabbed ahold of a sturdy-looking vine, heaving himself up arm over arm like he'd done it a thousand times before, quickly reaching the top and vanishing over the edge. Taking his lead, she did the same. Having spent much of her youth playing in the great tree at the heart of her village, Vesper easily scrambled up the vine-covered wall like it was second nature, climbing as she did in her youth. She was almost at the top when something pierced her calf, and she slipped, fighting the pain while she dangled from one hand. She looked down to find a spear buried deep in her calf, while blood rained down on the alley below. On the ground, the Sandawei, blocked from the alley changed tactics, hurling spears at her despite the vine barrier deflecting most of their throws she had created, the one in her calf being the sole exception.

Thinking quickly, she sang again, focusing her power through one of the tattoos on her shoulder, and a heartbeat later, the vines grew thicker, obscuring her from sight. Above her Narcissus appeared, sticking his head over the edge. "Take my hand!" he shouted, reaching out for her over the side of the building.

Gritting her teeth through the pain in her leg, she swung her body upward, catching the Celt's outstretched arm while at the same time climbing with her good leg. The thick muscles in his arms flexed, and he swung her up as if she weighed nothing, the pair of them falling over in a heap, with Narcissus on his back while Vesper fell on top of him. They lay there together, eyes locked, covered in blood and dirt while they both struggled to catch their breath. From fighting, or something else, Vesper wasn't sure, but part of her enjoyed his warmth, drinking in his scent, that for some reason didn't seem so bad anymore. "Apologies," she sputtered after a moment, her voice catching in her throat when she realized she was on top of him.

Narcissus reddened, his eyes looking everywhere except at her. "I don't know my own strength sometimes, and you're lighter than I imagined."

"Of course, it was nothing," said Vesper, rolling off him with a wince, clutching at her calf when she tried to stand.

The big Celt opened his mouth to speak, but fell to silence and his eyes went wide. With a grunt he pushed her aside, his knee catching a Sandawei warrior in the chest, knocking him over the edge as he tried to clamber onto the roof. "They're climbing, even though the thorns," he said, leaning back to avoid a hurled spear that hissed by.

Limping over to the edge, Vesper leaned over to see the white-painted warriors stained red as they climbed, ignoring the thorned vines and leaving horrid gashes up and down their flesh. "That's inhumane," she said, recoiling in disgust.

"We will be far more exposed up here," said Narcissus, looking around. "We won't last long."

"We are not dying here today," she said through gritted teeth. "My aunt once told me that the Sandawei gave up being truly human a long time ago. I think it's time I stopped treating them as such, that I stop trying to show them mercy." Ignoring Narcissus's questioning look, she shifted her vision to the world beyond, collecting the thin threads of power she had weaved into the climbing vine and thorn wall, drawing out every last drop until the plants that were once a vibrant green, turned to a sickly yellow and brown, leaving the whole plant dry and fragile. Then, without missing a beat, she focused the power, concentrating it into the palm of her hands.

"What are you going to do?"

Vesper eyed the heat radiating off her glowing hands while

kneeling at the edge of the insulae. "Burning them, burning them all." The dry wood lit up the minute she touched it, killing flames licking up and down its length and breadth. Ducking back from the edge, she squeezed her eyes shut, trying to block out the screams of the men and women in the alley who burned, reminding herself that they killed her aunt. That given the chance, they would have killed her and Narcissus without a second thought.

"It shows great strength to weep for your enemies," said Narcissus, reaching out to lay a hand on her shoulder but then pulling away.

"They are monsters, and I don't want to be like them," said Vesper, gingerly touching the wound on her leg, and then seeing that it wasn't too bad, grabbing his hand just as he pulled away, using it to stand but still not letting go once she was up. "But I will do what I must."

"There are more of them," he said, squeezing her hand, pointing to the other side of the roof with his chin.

Vesper's shoulders slumped as beads of sweat rolled down her temples, exhaustion threatening to defeat her even when the Sandawei could not. Returning the squeeze, she ran to the other side of the roof, crouching down to remain hidden, when she found the square in chaos, filling with Sandawei. Eyeing the tall warriors painted in white, flaking paint, her stomach roiled, and she had a terrible sense of déjà vu when the Sandawei started going from insulae to insulae, pulling men, women, and children from the buildings, and then lining them up in the square, killing any of the poor stragglers who moved too slowly for their liking, or tried to run. "They did this in my village the night they killed my aunt," she began, looking up at the darkened sky, her jaw falling open when she saw, for the first time, some of the Sandawei were connected to each other by threads of black filaments that vanished a few feet away from them, connecting them to something, although she couldn't say what or where they led. Swallowing hard, she continued, "But it was nothing like this; there were never so many."

"I don't know how they managed to sneak their numbers into the city, but they must be foolish if they think that a small group of tribal savages could challenge the might of Rome."

"I'm not so sure," muttered Vesper, her eyes locked on to the writhing filaments, "Some of them are like Saoterus, drawing on a power I don't understand. And if they are anything like one of the vodun I have met, they must have arrived here by traveling along the path in the world beyond."

At the mention of the dark place with its cobblestone path and wailing spirits, Narcissus paled, his voice trembling when at last he was able to speak. "That place," he grunted, "I pray to never see it again."

"We won't, I promise," said Vesper, nodding in agreement, remembering that it was the only time she had ever seen the big man afraid. He had almost died there, trying to protect her. She had sworn that day, that even if she knew how to get back there, she never would, not by choice anyway.

"She is still alive," said Narcissus suddenly, crouching down beside her.

"Who?"

"There," he said, pointing. "With the hood on her head. She was one of the slaves they brought with them. They killed the others with a dagger made of shadow."

Vesper's brows drew together when she caught sight of the hooded woman, and for the thousandth time she wished her aunt was still with her or even her mother. It was clear the Sandawei had performed some kind of ritual, but the why and the how were a mystery to her, and she felt like a child given a puzzle that she couldn't figure out. "My aunt once told me that the Sandawei were the first to be gifted the access of the weave, but they were heartless monsters, who used the great gods' gifts for conquest, for evil. Olodumare, in his infinite wisdom, removed his blessing, leaving them powerless, but now it seems they have found a new source of strength to continue with their conquering ways."

"But you can stop them, just as we did with the emperor's chamberlain."

"I am grateful for your confidence," she said with a smirk, "but Saoterus almost killed us, and he was just one man..."

"Yes, but he surprised us. Lucilla had told us that Commodus was a drunken fop, and that his chamberlain was little more than a sycophant, bowing and scraping for scraps of power and influence."

"I know there is truth in your words," she said, shaking her head, "but I have no idea how I do the things I do. I can draw on power from the weave, from myself, but to shape it, I don't have a clue. It feels more like luck than skill, and I fear one day that luck will run out."

A boyish grin broke out on his face, and he patted her shoulder. "We Celts know that the world is a mad place, and you are better off to be lucky than good!"

"But—"

"Your luck has saved us more often than not, so why change anything now?"

Vesper shook her head, not believing what she was hearing. "So you think we should just jump in and hope for the best? That's madness."

"Well, it's worked so far, has it not?" he said with a shrug. "And if that doesn't work, can't you breathe fire on them, or hurl lightning from your eyes? I mean, I've seen you angry."

"I know you are trying to be funny, but you just end up looking more frightening when you smile like that," she said with a wink before continuing, "but it does not work that way. Even if I knew what I was doing, reality fights back when we do the impossible."

"But the vines?"

"Vines growing out of the walls are possible: fire coming out of my mouth, not so much."

"Bah, then what's the point of your fancy sorcery if you can't crush your enemies with it!" he said, frowning in a way that made him look terrifying. "And I can see in your eyes, you like my jokes."

Ducking back, Vesper tried not to smile at him, instead focusing her attention on the cut on her calf, and the snapped-off spear in his shoulder. When looking at the wounds in the world beyond, she could see how it would be possible to stitch them back together, and she had done so before, in the heat of combat with her life on the line, but in the moment, it was all beyond her. "Well, we're both hurt, and there are a few hundred of them down in the square. Those don't look like good odds, no matter how brave we are... and your jokes are terrible. I only smile because I was raised as a proper Ose girl, and taught to be polite to my elders."

"Elders!" he sputtered. "I'll have you know I'm—"

Before he could finish, a horrible clatter filled the air, and they turned to find a carriage, led by a full team of eight horses crashing through the square from a side street, the frothing horses trampling over the Sandawei warriors in a mad frenzy. Followed behind the carpentum was a mishmash of cavalry, legionnaires and a group of hard-looking men who looked to be ordinary citizens armed with whatever they could find. "By Olodumare," she said, eyeing the reactions of the few vodun in the square, watching as the black filaments surrounding them writhed and pulsed, growing thicker with each passing moment. "If they are to stand a chance, we have to stop the vodun."

"The who?" asked Narcissus, cocking his head.

"Vodun! The men like Saoterus, given the chance they'll kill everyone, no matter how many men attack."

Narcissus gave her a feral grin, flexing his arms. "Then we have no choice; we must attack! Now, while their attention is diverted."

Vesper was taken aback, her brow coming together. "Are you mad!? You want us to just jump into that chaos without even a hint of a plan?"

"Our plan is to crush the head of the snake before they know we're here," he said, standing to his full height, his eyes roaming the square. "Let's pray that your luck holds!"

Letting out a slow breath to calm her racing heart, she started looking for a way down when Narcissus stepped to the edge of the insulae. "What in the name Olodumare are you doing?"

"Jumping! That one over there looks soft," he said, pointing.

"You'll die!" said Vesper, grasping for his hand.

"Don't worry, the fat man over there will break my fall."

"No wait... please, I have an idea," she said, shifting her gaze to the world beyond, her fingers brushing the amber cord that connected them. "I'm not sure it will work, but we'll have a better chance of surviving all of this if it does."

The big man stopped, crouching once more with her. "That always feels so strange, like you're touching the inside of my skin."

"I know," she said, having felt the same way often enough, "but I think we can use this connection we have for more than just annoying each other. I am going to try and transfer my Ase to you, to share my strength so that you are stronger, faster. Perhaps fast enough that you won't die on me today."

A feral grin split his face as he settled in beside her, "Do you know how I have survived all these years, despite most gladiators having a very short life?"

"Because your smell kept your enemies off-balanced?" she joked, concentrating on doing the one thing she knew well, enhancing her strength, her speed. But instead, transferring that strength to him.

"Bah, you would prefer a perfumed weakling. A man like that wouldn't do you much good right now, would he?" said Narcissus.

"I'm sorry, I am glad to have you with me, always," she said quickly, pouring Ase through their bond, unfortunately to little effect. "I have come to appreciate the way you smell... even miss it when you're not around. Sorry I interrupted you... what were you trying to tell me?"

He smoothed his short beard, his eyes never leaving hers. "I don't remember much of my people. I was captured and enslaved not long after the first hairs appeared on my chin," he began, "but the one lesson I took from them was that your life was forfeited the moment you entered battle, and only in victory would you find life again."

"That sounds scary," she said, her eyes starting to blur from the strain. "But brave, and freeing, in an odd way."

"Yes, it is, and this has served me time and time again, especially in the arena. Because I never expected to live to see the next day, so I fought with every ounce of strength I possessed, holding nothing back. After all, the dead have nothing to lose."

Vesper cocked her head, a disturbing thought coming to mind. "But what about your family, your friends. The people that love you?"

Narcissus blinked, his brow shooting up. "I don't—"

"Wait! I have it!" she said, her heart catching in her throat when she felt a tiny flow of Ase pass between them. "I think we can do it." Vesper drew on the power in her blood, combining it with the remaining energy she had pulled from the vines, and did the only thing she knew for sure would work. Then, using their bond, she poured the strength, stamina, and durability she normally poured into herself into the big Celt, sharing her power with him.

"By the gods," he laughed, sucking in a deep breath. "I feel like I could uproot a tree!"

Vesper gasped at the sense of wonder flowing through their bond, her heart racing with joy. "I have no doubt. I sometimes forget how strong you are, more so now."

"By Jupiter! I will put this gift to good use," he said, rising to his feet. Vesper's heart caught in her throat when, without another word he leapt, laughing like a madman as he fell. She almost tumbled off the roof herself when she looked to see if he was all right. A smile lit up her face when Narcissus landed on a heavyset Sandawei warrior he had pointed out, crushing the man beneath his big body. The pair of them fell in a heap, and for a heartbeat she worried that he had broken something, or worse, was unconscious or even dead, only to gasp with relief, when the big Celt bound to his feet, looking up at her with a boyish grin plastered on his face.

"It's official, he's a madman," she muttered to herself, "and worse still, I'm following him!" Watching him wade into a group of

Sandawei warriors who were unfortunate to have their backs to him, she decided to follow his lead, and was about to leap off the building, when a surge of adrenaline from Narcissus surged through their bond, making her heart race and blood boil. Gripping the edge of the roof, she almost fell, all sense of reason fleeing her mind, and all she wanted to do was break bones and rend flesh with her bare hands. Falling back from the edge, she clutched her chest, trying to slow her racing heart. Fighting to remain calm, her mind fled back to quieter times, memories of her childhood, climbing the great baobab tree in her village, sleeping away the afternoon in its branches, and spending her evenings gazing up at the stars while her aunt braided her hair. Vesper let out a breath as the rush of anxiety faded, still there, but somehow she had managed to push it back.

"I am dead, and only victory will grant me life once more," she said, leaping off the roof without fear and for once without regret. Ready to die but with the hope of living on.

SIX
STREET TO STREET

The carpentum came to a grinding with halt with a harsh jolt, and Lucilla had to hold on for dear life or risk being thrown from her seat. In front of her, Senator Magnus had taken on a hint of green in his pale complexion, and she frowned in disgust, remembering the man's weak constitution. "Take deep breaths, Magnus. I don't want your breakfast all over me."

"Apologies, I have a weak belly. It has been this way since I was a child."

Knowing him well enough, she began to agree, when a piercing scream filled the air, followed by a hollow thud as their driver fell from his seat. "Stay here," said Lucilla in a rush, circling behind the carpentum for cover, cursing when she saw the rough shaft of a spear sticking out of their driver's chest.

"Get back inside, it's not safe out here," shouted Albus, cringing when he bent his knee to duck down beside her. "I don't think we can make it to that pillar of shadow, and I was about to order the driver to turn around. That doesn't look like it will be happening now, so the safest place for you is inside."

Ignoring his concern, Lucilla peeked out, seeing that the senator's men were engaged in a chaotic melee with a group of dark-skinned warriors, with flaking, white paint drawn over their bodies in strange patterns. "What is the meaning of this? Who would dare attack us here, in the heart of the—"

"I don't know, but they were lying in wait for us," he said, his voice calm despite the chaos around them. "The senator's men, I told them to wait, fall back, but they've charged ahead, and now are being cut to pieces."

"And the men of the watch you brought with you?" she asked.

"I ordered them to fall back to cover the minute we were attacked."

"A wise man indeed," said Lucilla, squeezing the first centurion's shoulder. "We can't let these invaders get a foothold in the city. We must get to the source of all this, root them out before it's too late. Can we have the men press ahead with a phalanx?"

"You know a thing or two about tactics?" he said, his thick brows shooting up in surprise.

"I traveled a great deal with my first husband," she said, catching a glimpse of a man hurling spears, with deadly accuracy from the roof of the insulae. "We couldn't bear to be apart when we were first married. I spent more hours than I could count in the corner of a tent, listening to his advisors discuss war and tactics."

"Very well," he said, falling back to organize the legionaries. "I will have the men form up."

"Albus, one last thing," she said, eyeing the men on the roof.

"Yes?"

"Take your best javelin throwers, the men with the strongest arms. Make sure they are well supplied from the rest of the men. Have them throwing from the rear to cover the phalanx from the attackers on the roof."

"You have a good eye. Goddess Diana would be proud to call upon you for the great hunt," he said, giving her a salute. "I will see it done."

While Albus headed off to organize the men, Lucilla darted back into the carpentum, wrinkling her nose in disgust when the sour odor of vomit filled her nostrils. "How in the name of the gods did you manage this? We were stopped!"

"Forgive me," said Magnus, holding his stomach. "Given the events of this morning with your brother, and now this attack on our great city—"

"It doesn't matter!" she snapped. "I need you to keep your wits about you! The city is under attack, and we are in deadly peril if we stay here. I am going to take the driver's place and try to get us out of here alive."

"This again! Let my men—"

"Your men are being cut to pieces," she said. "Albus and his men are proper legionaries, and are our best chance to fight our way out of this."

Magnus shrank back into his seat, clutching at his chest. "I cannot endure this. Jupiter, save me."

"Coward," Lucilla muttered under her breath. Albus and his men sped past the carpentum, their heavy-soled caligae clattering in unison on the cobblestone, while above her, the whistle of javelins filled the air, followed by the heavy crash of bodies falling from great heights.

Climbing in the driver's seat, she took hold of the reins and the driver's whip, cracking it above the horses to set them in motion. Ahead of her the legionnaires had formed a phalanx, a deadly configuration where each man's shield interlocked with the man next to him, making the line near invincible. Advancing with the hardened discipline that had crushed all the challengers to the empire, they were able to deflect or ignore the disorganized attacks from the invaders despite their greater numbers. At the first centurion's command, the men heaved in unison to push the chaotic mob away, opening their defenses for only a heartbeat, a wall of spears stabbing out with deadly precision, then reforming the impenetrable wall just as quickly.

Rolling past the fallen invaders, a shudder ran through her when she saw some of them had died with their eyes wide open. and their pupils were covered with a milky-white film. Noticing that those with the strange eyes were covered from head to toe with bizarre tattoos made her stomach twist into knots if she stared too long. Tearing her eyes away, she snapped the whip once more, urging the horses to go faster, her sense of unease and desperation growing with each passing moment, determined to protect the city she loved.

SEVEN
BERSERKER

He landed on the Sandawei with a horrible crash, the other man's body absorbing the brunt of his fall, while he felt invincible as the hapless warrior crumpled under his weight. Not wasting a moment, he rolled to his feet with a wild howl, using his bracer to smash in his skull for good measure. He had barely taken a breath when another Sandawei warrior, wide as he was tall, appeared in front of him, his painted face snarling with rage as he attacked without mercy. The Sandawei's spear thrust came at him viper quick, its bone tip aiming for his heart, but Narcissus was faster, catching the weapon in a meaty hand and easily snapping the shaft in half.

Undeterred, the Sandawei never slowed, plowing his shoulder into Narcissus's gut, trying to use his lower center of gravity to knock the big Celt from his feet. Narcissus cursed as his sandals slid on the cobblestone, his big body hunching over the other man. Battling to stay on his feet, he pounded his elbows into the warrior's back, knocking him to the ground just as they slammed into the side of a building, their titanic impact leaving deep cracks in the mud brick, blasting the air from his lungs.

The Sandawei warrior rolled to his feet, a dagger appearing in hand as he glanced over his shoulder "Come. Come brothers and sisters," he shouted over his shoulder. "We have a Roman pig to gut!" Behind him a dozen warriors answered his call, breaking off from the looting and killing, charging toward them with wild hoots and shouts.

Narcissus growled while he pushed away from the wall, kicking out and catching his attacker in the gut. "I am no Roman," he said, his nostrils flaring with anger from the insult. "And if I am to die today, I'm taking all of you with me!"

Counting the overwhelming odds facing him, he drew on his anger, delving into memories long buried. Remembering the day the Romans had taken him during his first battle, the humiliation of standing on the slave block and then sold like livestock, naked and exposed to the world. Every sting of the whip on his young skin came back to him, the gut-wrenching fear of the first day at the ludus, locked in a dark cell with strange men he didn't know. The hurt, the pain of his first wounds in the arena. He drove it all into a deep well of profound rage, and at his core, something snapped, and he forgot who he was or what he was doing, the entire world around him turning to a dark shade of red.

He charged the Sandawei coming at him, then, seeing but not seeing, a passenger in his own body. Crashing into them in a mad frenzy, he felt no pain, their wicked spears little more than stinging gnats on his hardened skin, their vicious blows rolling off him like summer rain. Narcissus lashed out with his long limbs, every part of his body a living weapon that broke limbs and shattered bone, his fury relentless as the Sandawei begged for mercy, their screams echoing across the square. More came at him then, their chalky-white faces enraged at first by his defiance, quickly turning to wide-eyed fear when spears shattered on his skin, and shields broke under his fists. Battling on, he lost all sense of time, knowing only his rage. Then, suddenly, he could sense Vesper beside him, her fury matching his own as their attacks synchronized, a dance of violence that felled every enemy in their path.

He had just cleared a circle around him, when in the distance he saw a man floating above the ground with thin filaments of black void swirling around him. Thinking he must be one of the vodun that Vesper had mentioned, Narcissus charged, intending to crush him under his heel, when a wave of darkness passed over him. The square, the warriors, everything vanished, and he found himself in a dull, gray place, unseen voices sobbing while screams came from every direction.

"Little Celt, thinks he is so brave. Nothing more than a coward at heart," whispered a voice, speaking with the cadence of a Roman highborn."

"What... where... what is this trickery?" said Narcissus, his breath frosting as he sucked in deep breaths of stale air. A hollow feeling forming in the pit of his stomach when he realized where he might be.

"No, Bràthair," said the voice. "No trick. I wish to speak to you before I send you to the other side."

"Bràthair... brother, I'm not your brother. Show yourself, so I can rip out your tongue for speaking the language of my people."

"Here... I am here."

Narcissus flinched when a man with a slight build emerged from the darkness. He was dressed in the fine white toga of a Roman patrician while wearing a crown made of bone tied to the side of his head, his face hidden behind a mask made from a ghastly skull, colored with flaking, red paint, its teeth yellow and grotesque. Without missing a beat, Narcissus lunged for him, only to find himself held in place by some unseen force. "What have you done to me? Where are we?"

"You are here by my will," said the man, fully emerging into the light, giving Narcissus a slight bow from the waist.

"You are Roman," spat Narcissus, his mouth going dry when he at last recognized the place, with its cobblestone path and howling shades in the distance. The place Vesper called the world between worlds, a place where he almost died. The cords in his neck bulged as he struggled to reach for the man, who stood just beyond his outstretched hands.

A hoarse laugh echoed in all directions as the man threw his head back, his entire body shaking with laughter. "I am no Roman. I am like you, an insect trapped in the empire's web."

"I don't care what you are; let me go from this place, and I promise to kill you quickly," he said, his heart pounding as he fought against the fear growing in his belly.

"In this place, you couldn't kill a fly without my say-so."

"Then what the hell do you want?" snarled the big Celt.

"For you to join me, to join us. The Romans are nothing but parasites, sucking the life out of everyone for their selfish needs. Leaving only death and destruction in their wake."

Narcissus rubbed his skull, his ears straining. "And you are better, are you? A symbol or virtue and hope for all mankind."

"We Sandawei offer a better life, freedom for all, and not just a privileged few!"

"Your people are killing children in the square, innocent men and women. I don't think so," he said, hearing the one voice he wanted to, even over the cacophony that surrounded them. Rubbing a hand on his belly, a smile came to his lips when he felt the connection once more, the connection that had become such a part of him, that he did not want to live without it ever again.

"Roman whores and faithless men, we are killing those who must be cleansed."

"Freedom for all," said Narcissus, reaching out, feeling her energy, her Ase as she called it, "except those you judge unworthy."

"Yes," said the masked man, leaning forward, a hunger in his voice.

"Why would the world trade one set of tyrants for another?" said Narcissus, "There is another way, and together, I think we can find it."

"We?"

"Vesper!" he shouted, ignoring the strange man as he reached out through their connection, a feeling of warmth pulsing through him, banishing the cold of this place.

A burst of amber light blossomed from his midsection, pushing back the darkness, and he raised an eyebrow when the Roman flinched, and he could see him fully. He was slight of build with pale skin that made him look sickly in the light. Behind his mask, his blue eyes were darting in all directions, hunting for the source of the light. "It looks like you're the coward here," said Narcissus, smiling when the masked man shrunk back.

She appeared then, a welcome sunrise banishing the curtain of night with a blinding light. "I'm here," she said, touching his arm. Narcissus squeezed his eyes shut, and when he could see once more, the other place, the masked man was gone, and he found himself in the square where it had all started, dead Sandawei everywhere he looked, the brilliant light of the noonday sun shining down on him. Standing around him were a group of legionaries staring at him with their mouths agape and whispering in awe.

"What happened?" he asked when no one spoke, the silence broken only by his heavy breathing as he tried to calm the wild rush of adrenaline coursing through his blood.

Vesper looked away, motioning to the carnage in the square. "I don't know how to explain: somehow you were drawn into the world between worlds. For a time I thought I had lost you."

Narcissus frowned at her, narrowing his eyes. "It was the masked man. He drew me to that horrid place."

"The who?" she asked.

"You must have seen him. He was floating above the battle, and then in the other place. He said he drew— But you didn't see him... did you?"

Vesper pressed her lips together, shaking her head. "No I'm sorry, I know I promised you—"

Lucilla appeared suddenly, striding with her head held high as if she owned the square, a limping first centurion in tow. "The pair of you have done the impossible," she said, raising her voice so that those in earshot could hear. "You and these men are heroes, having defended Rome herself from a terrible invasion."

"Lady Lucilla," said Narcissus, smiling when a pulse of amusement flowed from his bond with Vesper. "Not that we are ungrateful, but how is it that you are here? With the city watch, no less."

"The column of darkness could be seen from miles around... and I could... The smell of rot filled the air, and I feared it was another incident, like the others. So I rushed to investigate."

Vesper hugged herself despite the heat, nodding along as Lucilla spoke, "I think you're right. There were vodun here, like Saoterus. They were performing some sort of ritual, bringing in more of their numbers... and something else, something not human, but I don't know for sure. Narcissus was here first, and he stopped—"

"The woman!"

Lucilla raised her chin, frowning at him. "What woman?" she asked.

"There was a woman, one of the sacrifices. She and the others were hooded, wearing chains," he said, scanning the square, and then setting off to where he had last seen her.

"What would it matter? She was just a slave," said Lucilla, stepping gingerly around the bodies, Vesper not far behind.

"You don't understand," he said, stopping in front of the building where he had last seen her. "The Sandawei, they brought the slaves with them. She might know their plans or, at the very least, how they got into the city."

Vesper put a hand on his shoulder, a pang of sympathy flowing through their bond. "I remember her," she said, "but she was struggling to remove the hood, and even a skilled warrior would have been hard pressed to survive during an attack like that. She most likely is among the dead or, at best, managed to run and hide."

"I am not most people, Daughter!" said a woman emerging from a shadow-filled alley next to the brothel, the hood gone, but the collar remaining around her long neck.

Narcissus cocked his head, thinking that he had seen the woman somewhere before. Though he was sure he would remember her if he had. She was stunning, with a high forehead and cheekbones, flaw-less brown skin, and dark eyes that seemed to look through him. She wore little more than rags, and he couldn't help but stare at her round hips and full breasts. He was about to speak when a sense of shock pulsed through his bond with Vesper, and he turned to find her staring at the woman, her mouth agape while the woman stared back.

"How is this possible?" asked Vesper at last, grabbing on to Narcissus to steady herself.

"I don't know," said the woman, giving them all a full-lipped smile that never touched her eyes. "But I am here, fully this time."

"I don't understand," said Narcissus. "Who is she?"

Clearing her throat, she spoke with a voice full of dread, uttering a single word over and over, "Mother."

EIGHT

LILLITH

Vesper squeezed her eyes shut, wanting to laugh and cry at the same time. Part of her wanted it all to be real, that her mother was alive, in the flesh this time, and not some vile loa clinging to the world by a hairsbreadth. At the same time, praying that the woman in front of her was a figment of her tired mind, and she wouldn't have to deal with the consequences of what it all meant. Lillith was dangerous, her ambitions without limits.

"I am very real," said Lillith, reading her thoughts.

"You are dead," said Vesper bluntly, her eyes snapping open to see that her mother was still there, back straight with her chin raised high, looking like a queen despite wearing only rags that hardly covered her lush figure. "Or at least lost in time, somewhere along the weave."

Her mother looked down at her herself, flexing her fingers and then running a hand along the complex braid that started at her forehead and ran down to her shoulders, "I... I think I was," she began, drawing in a deep breath, giving them all a brilliant smile before continuing, "but something pulled me back, to this place, this time."

"What did you do? What vile ritual did you perform to cheat death?" asked Vesper, giving Lillith a hard look.

Before her mother could answer, Lucilla stepped between them, cocking her head. "I remember you," she said, brushing a hand across her own cheek. "You were a friend of my father's; you would cup my face and call me—"

"Little Empress," whispered Lillith, her brilliant smile growing wider as she took Lucilla's hand. "By Olodumare, how you've grown."

"You know her?" asked Narcissus, crossing his arms. "You both do?"

"Yes," said Lucilla, fawning over Lillith, hugging her and then holding her at arm's length, her brow furrowing. "She was my father's... What did he call it? Djambe! Yes, it was her duty to protect him."

"I was many things to your father," said Lillith in a strained voice, "but that was long ago. I promise we will take the time to catch up, but for now, I am exhausted, and I wish to speak with my daughter."

Lillith tried to push past her, but Lucilla stood her ground, blocking her way. "But It was so long ago. I couldn't have been more than five or six, yet you look the same; how is that possible?"

Vesper enjoyed watching her mother squirm, and waited for the explosion of anger, but instead Lillith gently put a hand on Lucilla's shoulder, speaking to her in a soft voice, "There are more pressing questions than my beauty regimen... like how the Sandawei got into the city, and what were they doing?"

"Apologies," said Lucilla, backing away to stand between Vesper and Narcissus. "Of course, of course. I forget myself sometimes. Protecting the city from these travesties is far more important than my foolish questions."

"Mother, please," said Vesper, crossing her arms across her bosom. "Times are desperate. You need to tell us what you know. Why did the Sandawei bring you here?"

Facing off against all of them, Lillith spread her arms wide and shrugged. "I don't know any more than you do. The last thing I remember was that night of drinking with Quintis," she said, looking away and brushing a hand over her eyes. "I have memories of those few fleeting moments with you and Magda on that horrible day in the market, lost in time. Then I woke up here earlier today with a Sandawei vodun standing above me, his face hidden by a painted mask that resembled a skull."

Beside her she felt Narcissus stiffen, worry passing through their bond, making her own stomach turn with fright. "A red mask worn by a pale man, slight of build," blurted the big Celt, his hands twitching as if he wanted to throttle someone.

Lillith cocked her head, frowning at him. "Yes, how would you know that?"

"Because I saw him. Today!"

"Here in the square?" asked Lillith.

Narcissus looked at Vesper, his face flushing a deep shade of red, almost matching his beard. "No... yes, one minute I was in the middle of the battle, the next, it all vanished, and I found myself in the other place, the place between worlds."

Her mother's lips pressed together into a thin line, her nostrils flaring. "You know of the other place? You risked much going there. It is a door that is not easily closed once open."

"It was not by choice: it never is," she said, giving her mother a sidelong glance.

"I don't know who this vodun was," said Lillith, "but if you suddenly found yourself in the other place, that means that they traveled through the place in between, and opened doorways for their people to enter the city. You must have stumbled through one by accident."

"That makes sense," said Narcissus. "One moment it was just a pair of Sandawei with a few slaves in chains, the next we were facing hundreds who appeared from thin air."

"Not that I don't believe you, but it should have been impossible for the Sandawei to invade as they did," said her mother, crossing her arms over her ample bosom. "When I was Djambe here, I protected the city by channeling a portion of the Ase of all who lived here into a great web over the city, thousands of threads of power that would entangle any attempting to pass through a portal, trapping them forever in the weave, never again able to touch our world."

"The weave over Rome is in tatters, corrupt and deadly," said Vesper, narrowing her eyes. "Surely, you must see it... even feel it."

Before her mother could answer, Lucilla spoke up in excited tones, "Is this the meaning of all of these incidents, then, all this death? To bring their people into the city?"

Lillith nodded, ignoring Vesper's question. "Part of it, but it does seem more complicated than that. A ritual of this magnitude would require a great sacrifice, a powerful soul. And would be a great risk to the one opening the portal. Sometimes, other things come through," she said, her entire body shivering. "Tell me about the other incidents. The only one I was aware of was the one at the villa in the countryside, with the shadow creature."

"There have been many," said Lucilla, "more than I can count, but they have always been the same. Bizarre events where normal people are taken by madness, slaughtering friends and family, or fellow soldiers. We have found entire insulae filled with nothing but blood, no bodies... and always the smell. It grows worse with each incident."

Vesper nodded along, adding her thoughts, "I think the ritual we stopped today was meant to be something similar, a sacrifice that would be the catalyst for some Sandawei evil."

"That is how it began," said Narcissus, nodding along.

Before he could go on, they were interrupted by a limping centurion carrying a staff decorated with flowing vines carved along its length. "Lady Lucilla, you need to see this."

"What is it, Albus?" asked Lucilla, irritation marring her fine features.

The centurion hesitated, his eyes darting between them before he cleared his throat. "Forgive me, but the bodies of these savages—the bodies are turning to dust, like they've been dead for years... and the smell. I cannot explain it."

"Show me, please," said Vesper before anyone could speak, her belly churning with worry.

Lucilla gave Albus a nod, and they headed off through the mayhem of broken bodies and fallen weapons, stepping around pools of blood, the all-too-familiar smell of rotten meat that had been left out too long in the summer heat, filling Vesper's nostrils. Falling back to walk beside her mother, she put a restraining hand on Lillith's shoulder. "I know that we began to mend things before... before you were lost to me," she began, choosing her words carefully, "but I know you well enough to know you are not telling us everything: you are too cunning for that."

Lillith matched her pace, a small smile dancing on her full lips. "I see your caution has grown, Daughter; this is wise. The world is full of dangerous people with wicked intentions."

"That is not an answer to my question," said Vesper, matching her amused smile with one of her own. "Tell me, what's really going on here? My knowledge of Ase is nothing compared to yours, but from what Magda told me, Olodumare cut the Sandawei off from the weave ages ago. They do not have the power or the will to do what they did today."

"You are right, Daughter," said Lillith. "Something has emboldened them. What—I cannot say, but this was far more than a simple attack; this was a tiny nation declaring war on the Roman Empire."

They walked in silence for a time, Vesper bowing her head. "And what about you, Mother?" she asked. "Now that you have returned, should I fear for my life, my soul?"

Lillith let out a throaty laugh, putting an arm over her shoulder. "No, you are now and forever my evening star, my beautiful girl, and the thing I love most in this world."

Vesper locked eyes with her, searching for the lie, searching for the con. "You speak in riddles," she said, looking down. "Speak plainly."

"The only thing I want is to be your mother, no more. I have my soul... my body is young and strong once more. What else could I possibly desire... except your big Celt perhaps. Olodumare knows I would put those big hands and wide shoulders to good use."

"Mother!"

Lillith let out a throaty laugh, and Vesper felt the tension drain from her shoulders. "I mean you no harm, Daughter. I am simply grateful for a second chance, a chance to do things right this time."

"What would that be?" asked Vesper, narrowing her eyes.

"Vesper! Come see this," shouted Narcissus up ahead, waves of nausea flowing through their bond.

"We will finish this later," said Vesper.

"I look forward to it... Daughter."

Ignoring her mother's look of amusement, she raced ahead to find the legionaries, along with a few merchants who had businesses in the square, piling the dead in preparation to burn them. "What is it?" she asked, covering her nose in a useless attempt to block out the smell of rotting meat, along with the more foul odor she now recognized as corruption caused by the Sandawei rituals.

Lucilla stood silent and pale over a set of Sandawei bodies that were laid out in front of her, some of them withered and emaciated, looking years dead, while others hardly bled. "Come and tell me what you see, Vesper."

Frowning, she stood beside the taller woman, while a legionary bent over and opened one of the dead Sandawei's eyes. "What is it that you want me to— By Olodumare! Are they all like that?" she gasped, wrapping her arms around herself as she stared at a milky-white pupil.

"Not all of them, but those marked," said Lucilla, pointing to a series of twisted markings covering the body with the milky-white eyes. "And their flesh does not rot like the others. If I didn't know better, I would say they were asleep, not dead."

Vesper sucked in a deep breath, feeling lost. "He looks just like the vodun Papa Jufari."

"It's more than that," said Lucilla, finally facing her. "During our battle with Saoterus, just as he fell, my brother... his eyes glazed over like this... for just a moment."

"Are you sure?" asked Vesper.

"I've had nightmares about it every day since our battle in the tunnels."

Staring into the corpses' milky eyes, she steeled herself. "What do you intend to do?" she asked, already knowing the answer to the question.

Lucilla looked up at the sky, shaking her head slightly before continuing, "I have put it off for too long, despite all the risk. I must go to him, find out what in the name of the gods has happened to him."

"You don't have to go alone. We will come with you," said Vesper.

Beside her, Narcissus grunted in agreement. "With us at your side, you have nothing to fear."

To Vesper's surprise, Lillith stepped forward. "The imperial palace was always one of my favorite places. I would be glad to see it again," she said, her eyes twinkling with amusement, "and I might serve as a distraction. From what I remember, your brother spent a great deal of time staring at my bosom."

Lucilla's shoulders fell, and she let out a breath. "Thank you, my brother is a monster at the best of times. I can only imagine that he has grown worse. We will take the senator's carpentum."

"You have my word, Little Empress. We will keep you safe and, if necessary, bring Olodumare's justice to the boy," said Lillith, linking arms with Lucilla.

"I am grateful. Perhaps if he is distracted by your breasts, he will listen for once."

While Lucilla and Lillith walked arm in arm to the wooden carriage, laughing like old friends, Narcissus held Vesper back. "Apologies, but given the stories you've told me of your mother, this does not feel right."

Vesper cursed herself for telling him about Lillith, but it would have been impossible to tell him stories about her Aunt Magda without including her mother, and her fall from grace. Leaning in close, she wrinkled her nose at his musky odor, lowering her voice, "I'm not a fool. The last thing I intend to do is trust her. I'm not sure that I ever could, not after everything that has passed between us. But right now I need her. Even after weeks of trying, I am no further along in my skills with Ase. At least she can teach me."

"A wolf can only teach you to be a wolf, nothing more, no matter how much you wish it otherwise. She can only teach you her way."

Vesper sighed, trying to find fault in his words, but finding none. "My mother was once a great hero to the Ose, wise and powerful with a profound sense of justice. That is what we need now."

"Yes, but then she lost her way. Did she not try to steal your body, your soul. Her time has passed, and you stand at the ready—"

"But I'm not ready," said Vesper, shaking her head.

"From what I've seen, you are," he said. "You protected me in the other place, when I had fallen and was on the edge of death. You protected all of us during the battle with Saoterus in the tunnels under the city."

"That was instinct, and a bit of luck. It had nothing to do with skill or understanding of what I was doing," she said, her nostrils flaring. "What happens when my luck runs out, and you or Lucilla get hurt, or worse, some innocent that was in the wrong place at the wrong time?"

"You won't. Send your mother away, and we can figure this out ourselves," he said in a stranded whisper, a fierce determination flowing through their bond.

Vesper looked at her mother as she squeezed in beside Lucilla on the driver's seat. "Maybe I want her here," she began. "At least I won't have to bear this burden alone anymore. My mother could be Rome's shield against the dark, while I take the time to learn all that I need to know to fulfil my duty, a duty that will only fall on me far in the future, as it was meant to."

"Once you have outgrown the safety of your mother's womb, you cannot go back," said Narcissus, shaking his head. "And you are not alone. I am with you."

"I know," she said, relishing in the warmth flowing through their bond, "but—"

"Look around you," he said, taking her by the shoulders. "We had a great victory today, you and I together. Don't ignore what we have done, what we are capable of."

With a sigh, she did as he told her, blinking in wonder when she realized how many Sandawei there had been, and somehow they had not only managed to survive, but to be victorious. Without thinking, she reached up and put her hands on his shoulders, pulling his face closer to her own, a shudder running through her as she kissed his soft lips. "Thank you."

"What was that for?"

"For opening my eyes, for helping me bear this burden, for being you," she said, reluctantly letting him go.

"Now is not the time for that!" shouted Lucilla, a mischievous smile coming to her fine features.

"We will finish this later, I promise," said Vesper under her breath, squeezing Narcissus's hand.

Entering the cool dark of the carriage, Vesper shrieked, almost jumping out of her skin when she realized that a thin man with a balding pate and a weak chin was already in the carpentum. "Who is the name of Olodumare are you!?" she asked.

"Decimus... Senator Decimus Annius Magnus. You're in my carriage." He squeezed his hands, nervously shredding the gold embroidery from his fine white tunic, his eyes growing even wider when Narcissus squeezed in behind her. "May I ask why?"

Before Vesper could think of an answer, the slat between the passenger compartment and the driver's seat slid open, revealing Lucilla's wide smile. "Magnus, you came to my home this morning looking for allies. Well, you've found them, myself included. Now let's go get cleaned up, and find a way we can make my brother's rule over the empire as short as possible!"

NINE
A HERO'S MURAL

Gliding down the wide marble corridors of the palace, Lucilla's heart beat out of her chest, feeling far less confident than the last time she had come here. This time her mouth was dry, and she shook with fear, terrified of what her brother might do. "All of you be prepared," she said over her shoulder. "Commodus is erratic, often drunk, and prone to bursts of anger, so say nothing unless I speak to you directly. Don't even look at him if you can."

"I'm just amazed that we could simply walk into the imperial palace without anyone stopping us," said Vesper, looking around with childlike wonder on her face. "I have never seen such exotic things, so much wealth... and it's all just left out in the open. It's beyond imagining."

"I think you will find, Daughter, that if you walk with confidence, and greet those that cross your path with a kind smile or nod, most will assume you belong.

"All of this has been plundered and stolen, no doubt," said Narcissus.

"It does help that you walk with the wife and daughter of the past two emperors, not to mention the sister or the current one," said

Lucilla, knowing that the fine tapestries that decorated the walls and gold inlaid doors made of rare and exotic woods, brought in from every corner of the empire, were often taken without care of whom they belonged to. "The wealth of the empire has been built up over centuries of expansion, war, and conquest. But none of it matters; they are just things, and serve no purpose beyond impressing the simple minded."

"I could not have said it better myself," said Lillith. "The riches you see here are only symbols of the one true currency in the world. Power. This is what you see on display here, not the gold and silver, but the power to take what you wish, when you wish, with not a soul being able to stop you."

"Well, I don't think I would mind taking back some of that gold and silver," began Narcissus, with a grunt. "I think it would—" As a group they fell silent when Lucilla turned to lead them down a wide fresco-lined corridor.

"What is all this?" asked Vesper, slowing her pace to stare at the towering murals decorating the hall.

"The delusions of a crazed mind," said Lucilla in a quiet voice, stopping to gaze.

"I'm not sure I understand," said Vesper, her eyes narrowing. "They look like Commodus but—"

"They are meant to represent The Twelve Labors of Hercules," said Lucilla. "The son of Jupiter who, when driven mad by the goddess Juno, kills his wife and sons. When his sanity returned, he begged the oracle at Delphi, a high priestess of Apollo, for a path to redemption."

"A foolish tale," snapped Lillith, her tone full of spite. "The boy has destroyed Domitian's priceless history of Rome, all to put his face on these immature drawings. I suppose he still thinks of himself as Hercules, then?"

"Yes," said Lucilla, her face reddening with shame.

"I had told your father to give him the rod and beat some sense into him," she said, "but he had a soft heart, indulging the boy in hopes that he would outgrow the fantasy. I see now that your brother has only grown worse with time."

"The guard," said Narcissus suddenly, pointing with his bearded chin to a half-dozen purple-clad legionaries standing in front of a set of gold inlaid doors.

Lucilla's attention fell onto the Praetorian guardsmen, her lips pressing together in a thin line. "I don't know any of these men."

"Should you?" asked Lillith.

"Yes... at least some of them," she said, a hollow feeling forming in the pit of her stomach, fearing what it meant that the faces she knew were absent. "Come, let us find out what my brother has done, and pray that it does not bring us to ruin."

They were halfway down the corridor when Lucilla stopped short as the doors to the emperor's private chambers swung open, revealing her brother dressed in his full regalia. She had not seen him since that fateful day in the tunnels under the arena, and to her amazement he looked lucid, his eyes clear and his gaze sharp. His tall frame was covered by a fine white tunic, while a rich purple toga was expertly wrapped around his broad chest and waist to highlight his muscular physique, and finally, a gold-leafed laurel crown sat adorning his head, glittering like the sun. The moment he saw her, a smile creased his handsome face, and he pushed past his guards to greet her with wide-open arms. "Sister! It has been too long," he began, striding toward her with purpose. "I feared that I would be forced to send an entire legion to find you, just so that I could be graced by your beauty."

Lucilla tensed, every muscle like steel. Despite the fear churning in her belly, she hugged him, praying he could not hear the pounding of her heart. "Brother, I come with news from the attack on the western market."

To her surprise, he nodded, casting a curious glance at those behind her before continuing, "We have been informed. This along with the attempt on my life is cause for great concern. We were just on our way to the Curia Julia to address those fools in the senate."

"An attempt on your life! Has the whole world gone mad!? Where in the name of Jupiter was your guard?" she asked, feigning surprise.

"Here, in this very hallway where we stand," said Commodus, shaking his head.

Lucilla looked to the floor and gasped, noticing for the first time that blood had seeped into the porous rock, and couldn't be completely washed away, leaving a faint crimson sheen on the white marble. "Did you find the conspirators?"

"Publius," he spat, saying the name like a curse, "the fat drunkard, and some of my own guard," he shouted, his handsome face twisting with rage. "It is only because of my divine constitution that I was untouched."

"Thank the gods you survived," she lied, looking back at the others to cover the fact that she already knew. Senator Magnus had told her of the attempt when he visited her and her husband this morning, but hearing it from Commodus himself made it real, made it deadly, especially considering that she tried to send her brother to the afterlife not so long ago. "But what does this have to do with the senate?" she asked, wanting to change the subject.

"Publius was not working alone. Magnus, that pathetic excuse for a senator, was mixed up in this. The pair of them paid my own men a godly sum to have my head."

"Then why did you not have him apprehended? Surely even the senate could not defend a man trying to kill the emperor."

"Bait on the hook, Sister," he said with a self-satisfied smirk. "The man is a worm, and I have used him like one to fish out his conspirators."

"That explains much. Magnus was at our villa this morning begging for an audience with my husband. I don't know the details, but Tiberius promptly had him thrown out."

"Good, at least I can be sure that you and Tiberius are with me. With luck, Magnus will lead us to those who would betray the empire, to those who have no loyalty to me." Before Lucilla could ask more, a swarthy, unshaven legionary dressed in the purple-and-black-leather armor of a Praetorian exited from her brother's chambers, strapping on familiar ornate scabbard and gladius to his hip and adjusting his tunic.

"Who's this?" she asked as he strode toward them while glaring at her with piercing green eyes that seemed to weigh and measure her in a single glance.

"Ah, this is Cleander," said Commodus, a smile creeping onto his face. "He stood with me when the other Praetorian guards made their foolish attempt on my life."

Lucilla drew herself up, returning Cleander's stare with one of her own. "I see that with Publius gone he has been rewarded, elevated to the rank of prefect."

"Yes, and more," said Commodus, resting a hand on Cleander's shoulder. "Since Saoterus ran off some time ago, I have been without a chamberlain, but good that Cleander here has agreed to take up the task."

Lucilla's eyes widened, and she coughed into her hand to cover her shock. "Are you sure? That is an enormous amount of responsibility," she began, using every ounce of her willpower to keep her the heat out of her voice, "to let a man you hardly know—"

"He is my choice, Sister. He and my other prefect, Perennis, shall take the burden of the day-to-day running of the empire," he said, cocking his head as if listening for something before nodding and continuing, "I don't have the time, not to mention that the wailing of the plebeians and patricians alike set my nerves on edge. My place is to make the grand decisions that elevate us as a people, not get lost in the boring details like roads and sanitation."

"Those things are important, Brother. Perhaps it would be wise to take advantage of the more experienced administrators at your disposal, such as my husband, or at least a senator who knows—"

"I've had enough of the senate," exploded Commodus, his face reddening with anger. "Do you think I'd want anyone of those rats in my presence? They resent my divinity, and there have been whispers that they wish to return to the ways of the republic, where true power rested in their hands."

"You can't imagine the entire senate was involved in the plot to kill you?" she asked.

"Why wouldn't they!" sneered Cleander. "When you see one rat, often there are more... many more."

"Some where you least expect them," she snapped back, giving the new prefect a hard look.

"There are traitors everywhere," said Commodus, suddenly calm once more, "and it was my hope that Magnus would lead me to the rest of his conspirators in short order, but this attack on the city has thrown my plans into chaos."

"What plans?" asked Lucilla.

"The senate has grown too bold since my ascension, sticking their noses in places they don't belong, questioning my authority, but no more," he said, shaking his fist. "Those old men have forgotten their place, and I intend to make an example, with blood if necessary."

"Commodus, these are powerful men, from ancient families whose roots run deep throughout the empire. You cannot simply cull them without consequences," said Lucilla.

"I will not let the attempt on my life stand." He seethed. "If I allow these men to defy me, without punishment, they will only grow bolder."

"He is right," whispered Lillith, leaning in close so that only she could hear. "Even under your father, the men in the senate were conniving, doing everything they could to undermine the power of the emperor."

Lucilla swallowed hard, smiling at him once more. "I am in agreement, Brother, but what are we to do about the attack? We cannot let that stand either. It is all related to the incidents I have been speaking about for months."

"Cleander here will take care of it," said Commodus, waving a hand dismissively, "for now I must make my presence felt in the senate. You are welcome to join me if you wish; however, your friends are not permitted."

"They are called Sandawei, Caesar," said Vesper, stepping forward, her dark eyes narrowing. "They are dangerous, very dangerous."

Before Lucilla could silence her, Commodus gave her a hawkish stare. "I remember you," he said. "You are Lucilla's little gladiatrix, the girl who survived her execution. Come forward, let us see what my sister has made of you."

"Yes, Caesar," said Vesper automatically, looking like a child as Lucilla's brother towered over Vesper, eyeing her up and down with a half-smile. She looked like she was about to speak, but he silenced her with a harsh look and a raised finger.

"You've certainly cleaned up well," he said, circling her like a predator. "If I recall, Saoterus had some interest in you."

At the mention of the dark-skinned chamberlain, Lucilla felt her blood run cold, gooseflesh running up and down her arms. "Vesper and her companions only came to the palace with me because the streets were dangerous. Now that I have your protection, I am more than happy to accompany you to the senate. We should let her and her companions return to the ludus."

Her brother ignored her, cupping Vesper's chin and forcing her to look up at him. "You are from Africa Proconsularis, are you not?"

"Yes, Caesar," said Vesper, shooting a desperate glance to Lucilla from the corner of her eye. "The Sandawei—"

"Will be dealt with. Won't they, Cleander?" he began, a hand falling on Vesper's breast before he continued. "I remember that day I first saw you battling on the sands; you were impressive. I wonder if you are the same with the pleasures of the flesh. I have rarely enjoyed the pleasures of your people, but I've been told that they are vigorous lovers, far more aggressive than the soft Roman women we are accustomed to."

"You leave her be," growled Narcissus, behind her.

"It would please me greatly to see you fight on the sands, to get my blood hot, and then after... sometime in the baths perhaps."

"Commodus, please," she said, as Vesper went rigid from his touch, her eyes wide with fear. "This woman belongs to me; her womanhood is untouched, and I intend to keep her that way until a time of my choosing."

"I am accustomed to your eccentric behavior, Sister, so I won't kill you, or your man for his insolence, "said Commodus, his hands circling Vesper's waist, making Lucilla worry that he would drag Vesper into his chambers."

"Brother!?"

"So pretty," he said, showing his teeth. "Perhaps another day, when I have more time. For now the senate awaits. In fact, why don't you come along with my sister? You might enjoy this. In fact, I insist." Without another word, he brushed past her with Cleander in tow, their small group forgotten as if they didn't exist.

Lucilla let out a breath she didn't know she was holding, brushing a hand across her eyes. "Vesper and I will go with him," she said, her limbs weak, as though she had been holding up a great weight for too long. "The rest of you return to the ludus; it will be safer... for all of us."

"I am going to drown that man in his own blood," growled Narcissus, glaring at Commodus through hooded eyes as he vanished around the corner.

Lucilla was about to ask the same when Vesper crumpled to her knees, hugging herself, rocking back and forth. "Are you all right, Daughter?" asked Lillith, kneeling at her side.

Vesper shook her head, her breathing quick. "How could you just stand there like that?"

Lucilla pressed her lips together, cursing her brother for his perversions. "I'm sorry, my brother is used to having women throw themselves at him; the whores he deals with refuse him nothing. In the—"

"It was not that," said Vesper, shaking her head and eyeing them all at once. "Could you not feel it? Surely, you must have, Mother?"

"Feel what, Daughter?"

"I'm not sure, but my limbs were frozen, and it felt like I was drowning in filth, choking on sewage."

"He behaved more like himself than he had in a long time," said Lucilla with a shrug. "I didn't feel or see anything beyond his normal behavior. If anything, he seemed calm and collected."

Narcissus picked her up off her knees, and her breathing steadied as she continued, "There was something coming from him, a stink. Like the corruption we witnessed at the villa in the countryside... only more. The smell, the feel, was the same. I think he may be the source, the cause of these events."

Lucilla replayed every conversation she had with Commodus in the last few months, feeling like her greatest fears had come to pass. "He has not been himself for months, but I always thought he was drinking too much, not getting enough sleep... and I suspected something after the battle in the tunnels, but now, if what you say is true, we must act, or all of Rome may suffer."

"We tried that," said Vesper. "We did not fare well."

"True, but things are different now," said Lillith.

"How so?" said Lucilla.

The dark-skinned woman gave Lucilla a smile that gave her hope and at the same time sent shivers down her spine. "This time... you have me!"

TEN

NEW CONNECTIONS

"So what are your intentions with my daughter?"

Narcissus bit his tongue, blushing a deep shade of red. "W-what?" he stammered, stumbling as they walked down the wide avenue that led away from the palace. "I'm... we are... nothing—" he said finally, keeping his eyes forward, not daring to look at her.

Lillith threw back her head, her melodic laughter filling the streets of Palatine Hill as she clutched at his forearm to stop herself from falling over. "By Olodumare, this will be fun; you're as bad as she is."

"As who? You mean Vesper," he groaned, covering his face with a meaty paw. "I am her doctore, nothing more... she is a fine woman, but she has made it clear that proper Ose women do not entertain such thoughts."

"Proper Ose women!?" said Lillith, rolling her eyes. "Oh, how I wish I had been the one to raise her and not my sister. I would have kept all those ridiculous provincial attitudes from her. Not that it matters. This little dance the two of you are having will be over soon."

"Over? Why?" asked Narcissus, his brows drawing together.

"Calm yourself, big man," she said, squeezing his arm. "What I mean is that, given the way you two look at one another, I am sure you will be arguing over the name of your first child before the summer solstice. We Ose women are very fertile," she said, once more breaking into laughter.

Narcissus looked away, rubbing a thick finger under his nose. "You're a madwoman."

"But not wrong, I'm never wrong about such things."

"We should move along," he said, looking around to see if anyone was watching them. "This is no place for a slave." Narcissus had spent very little time in the part of Rome that housed the emperor's palace, not to mention the sprawling villas of many of the city's wealthy. Wherever he looked, he was dazzled by some grand home with towering columns in the style of the Greeks, or some gaudy fountain with nymphs dancing like drunken fools. The streets were wide and clean, dominated by monuments capped with gold status all dedicated to the glory of Rome. Even the road was different here, looking as if some servant had taken the time to wash every brick to cleanliness: the air filled with sweet-smelling roses, cypress, rosemary, instead of the normal odor of refuse that dominated much of the city.

Lillith sighed, her gaze following his. "Don't worry, the wealthy who live on Palatine Hill have no interest in the lowborn unless they own them, and if anyone asks, we are simple-minded servants on a task for our dominus."

"Let us return to the ludus quickly, then," he said. "I have been away long enough, and I'm sure that Cassius, the lanista that accompanied me to the market this morning, has already returned."

"You know," began Lillith, smiling at him with a crooked smile, "it's not every day a woman comes back from the dead. I want to celebrate, a bit of wine and a song, maybe a game of dice would do me well. Do you have any denarii you can loan me? I promise you a king's fortune in return."

Narcissus stopped once more, cocking his head. "Vesper told me you were once the witch woman to Emperor Marcus Aurelius, someone of wealth and power; why would you drink and gamble like a common plebeian... or slave? And why would you wish for coins when you can just conjure them up from thin air?"

Lillith's eyes narrowed, and Narcissus tensed, fearing that violence was about to be done. "I am no witch!" she said bluntly, raising her chin. "A witch is an evil creature in league with the underworld. My daughter and I are Djambe, wise women. Seers tasked by Olodumare to guide the world to a better future."

"Apologies, I did not mean to insult," he said, blinking in surprise, when just as quickly as it appeared, her anger vanished, replaced once more by a lopsided grin that promised mischief.

"You must understand something, boy. I have spent many years among the rich and powerful of Rome, and I can tell you, I have learned that the plebeians and slaves of this great city have far more fun than its patricians. The rich live hidden away in gilded gardens and cages, turning up their noses at those they think beneath them. They pass their days drinking too much wine while the world passes them by," said Lillith, smoothing down her braid. "And as for winning coin, seeing the look of pain in your opponents' eyes when they lose, is far more fun than pulling them from the weave."

"You are not what I expected," he said, Vesper's stories about Lillith coming to the front of his mind. "But it is early in the day, and such things are better done under the cover of night."

"I don't know what my daughter sees in you: you're far too serious."

"There is nothing going on between Vesper and—"

Lillith took his hand, flashing him a brilliant smile and changing the subject. "You're right, it's early in the day, but I know just the place where we can look respectable, a dark corner in the light of day where they practice all the lecherous things I enjoy!"

He pulled his hand away, drawing up to his full height to tower over her. "I have tried to be kind, but Vesper has told me all about you," he began, crossing his arms across his thick chest.

"Truly, and what did my lovely daughter have to say about me?" she said, not backing away.

"She said that you were once a great hero, a guardian of Rome, but in your desire for power, you fell to darkness, and died betraying everything and everyone you were sworn to protect."

Lillith's beautiful face twisted into a mask of rage, her eyes flashing dangerously. "You have no idea of who and what I am, boy." She seethed, showing him her teeth. "You have been told half-truths and third-hand tales, and you think you know me: that is foolish... and dangerous. If you have any sense in the thick—

"And while Vesper is willing to forgive you," growled Narcissus, speaking over her, "I don't trust you."

"Ah, there it is," said Lillith, her smile returning suddenly despite his harsh words.

"W-what?" he stammered, taken aback.

"The reason my daughter likes you," she said, backing away while nodding. "You are a man of conviction, with a strong spine. You will make a good husband."

"What in the name of the gods is that supposed to mean?" he growled, his head spinning in confusion.

"Powerful women require powerful men to tame them."

Narcissus shook his head, sweat starting to roll down his temples. "I don't wish to tame her; she is not a beast to be broken!"

"Bah, don't be a fool," said Lillith, putting her hands on her lush hips. "Don't you think she will tame you as well? This is the way of men and women. Those that are destined to have a love that lasts will break each other over and over again, like tempering steel; each break will make the final love stronger... better, until the entire world shall tremble in fear at your combined power."

"You are a madwoman. I'm sure of it now," he said, barking a short laugh. "Not that it changes anything. I don't trust you, and I will not let you hurt her. I would die before I let anyone hurt her," he finished in a whisper, bowing his head.

"Good!" she shouted, slapping her palms against his thick shoulders. "You shouldn't trust me. Trust no one with your heart I know from personal experience that path leads to ruin."

Narcissus was about to say more, when Lillith turned away, wiping a hand across her eyes. "Are you all right?" he asked, pressing his lips together. "We Celts can be too harsh with our words, even when we mean not to."

"Oh, how I know, boy," she said, clutching her chest, a pained look crossing her face, "but if you learn one thing from me, it's that you should fight for love; don't wait for tomorrow. Seize it today while you still can because tomorrow it will be gone, and you will be left with only ashes and regret."

He bowed his head, shame coming to his heart. "I'm not sure if you're speaking of days gone by or of Vesper and I," he said, drawing in a deep breath. "I suspect both.. It does not solve the problem of what to do with you."

Lillith's shoulders raised and fell, and after a deep sigh, she turned and walked toward him. "Let me tell you something, and take it to heart. I am a monster. I am every horrible thing you and Vesper think of me. I have murdered men in cold blood, slaughtered entire villages, not just the men, but the women and children too."

Seeing the coldness in her eyes, Narcissus backed away, prickles of gooseflesh running up and down his arms. "I did not mean—"

"I have set entire cities ablaze without an ounce of regret," she said, grasping him by the front of his tunic to hold him in place. "You and Vesper may have just started battling the Sandawei and their darkness, but I've been fighting them before either of you drew breath in this world, and because of that, I've saved more lives than I can count. Your entire home province of Gaul would have fallen to madness and chaos if not for me, if not for my sacrifice."

"Apologies," he croaked, wanting to back away but finding himself paralyzed as she drew closer, her fingers digging into his flesh, while the other hovered over his chest like a claw.

He tensed, wanting to scream when suddenly thin, black filaments snaked out from the tips of her fingers and plunged into his chest. "I would have preferred to make this easy on you and do it in some dark corner after many cups of wine," said Lillith, smiling as the alien threads dug deeper into his chest and tears rolled down from his unblinking eyes, "but sometimes you must take the roll of the dice given to you."

Narcissus wanted to scream as the filaments crawled under his skin, boring deep into his muscle and then down his spine, spreading from there to every inch of his body, all the while driving him to madness like an itch that he couldn't scratch. "Why?" he whispered with his last breath, choking as his throat closed.

Lillith shrugged, sweat rolling down her temples as she showed him her brilliant smile. "Because of your unique connection to my daughter, because you will not remember any of this," she said, lowering her voice to a whisper. "Because I am a monster, who will do anything to keep this world safe."

ELEVEN

THE SENATE

"Senators of the republic, stand at attention," boomed Cleander, slamming open the ornate doors, and leading the way onto the main floor of Curia Julia, the principal meeting place of Rome's senate. A dozen fully armed Praetorian guards followed in his wake, their purple cloaks flowing behind them like flags in battle, while their polished leather armor glowed in the bright shafts of golden sunlight that shone through the high windows, dominating the room.

"What is the meaning of this?" began a white-haired senator as Cleander walked past him. "You have no right—"

Cleander's ornate gladius was in his hand and at the senator's throat before he could say another word, the new prefect's swarthy face breaking into a smile when the tip of his blade drew blood. "Another word... and it will be your last," he said, turning his gaze on the rest of the chamber. "That goes for all of you. Today is not the day to stand in defiance, but to kneel in supplication."

"Apologies," said the senator in a trembling voice, falling into his seat and clutching at his chest as Cleander sheathed his blade and moved on.

Turning to face the entryway, Cleander raised his voice. "Today you are blessed. Imperator Caesar Marcus Aurelius Commodus Augustus shall address this corrupt body in his divine right as imperator and pontifex maximus."

Commodus entered after his full title was announced, ignoring open looks of revulsion from the senators as he strode down the main aisle of the chamber. Reaching the front of the chamber, he climbed the low dais built into the back wall that held a single chair, a chair made of wood and brass, polished to a high shine. Above it, attached to the wall, was a golden eagle, its wings spread as wide as a man was tall, the letters S.P.Q.R engraved on a plaque held in its talons. Settling in the chair, he took the time to arrange his toga while his guard, led by Cleander, took up positions in front of him. The entire chamber was deathly silent while the senators waited for him to address them.

Vesper watched the entire spectacle from the vestibule, and she and Lucilla were the last to enter, completely ignored by the waiting senate, as all eyes were on Commodus. "It's beautiful," said Vesper in a low voice as they snuck into the main chamber, a smile creeping across her face as she lost herself in the dazzling stone mosaics decorating the walls and floor, delighted by the sheer array of vibrant colors that shimmered in the afternoon sun. "It is like they tried to imitate the tapestry of life that we Ose see, but only smaller."

"We should not be seen here," whispered Lucilla, pulling her behind a column that was part of the colonnade holding up the high-vaulted ceiling. "Women are not permitted, regardless of rank or station."

"Why?" asked Vesper, studying the old men who, as Lucilla told her, were the most powerful people in the empire aside from the emperor himself.

Lucilla frowned while hints of anger smoldered in her eyes. "A foolish tradition that should have been abandoned long ago—shh, it appears that Senator Adventus has run out of patience."

Vesper's gaze returned to the front of the curia, where the senator who had spoken before, stood up and cast a defiant look at Commodus. "You break hundreds of years of tradition! When the senate is in session, none are to enter," he began, his deep baritone voice reverberating off the high roof and walls.

Commodus made a tiny gesture with his hand, and the senator was silenced by a pair of guardsmen that were suddenly at his side, wrestling Adventus to the floor, the scrape of steel on leather filling the air as one of them pointed a gladius to the helpless man's throat. "He has gone mad, truly mad," whispered Lucilla, beside her, her unblinking eyes riveted on the spectacle on the senate floor.

"This gives me the right," shouted Commodus, bounding to his feet and pointing to the ornate golden eagle behind him. "Senātus Populusque Rōmānus."

"What does that mean?" whispered Vesper, eyeing the Roman letters on the plaque held in the eagle's claws.

"The senate and people of Rome," whispered Lucilla. "A reminder that we are a republic, where the people have the last word, and not a king."

"But Commodus is more than a king, he is—"

"I am Rome!" shouted Commodus, pulling her attention back to him. "As first council and imperator, I represent the senate, the people. All of you serve at my pleasure."

"You are nothing more than a boy tyrant, pretending to be a man," screamed Senator Adventus from the floor, struggling against the men holding him, his face red from the struggle. "Not worthy of the people of Rome!"

"The people of Rome love me," snapped Commodus, "just as much as they hate all of you."

"It's happening again," said Vesper, putting a hand on her belly.

"What do you mean?" asked Lucilla, not looking at her while she held on to the column with a white-knuckled grip.

"Can you not smell it, the rot?" she said, wrinkling her nose as she fought the urge to empty her stomach, all while the senate floor erupted in a flurry of defiant shouts and outright anger.

Lucilla drew in a breath, a sour look coming to her face. "A little, but does that mean—"

"It does. I'm sure of it. Commodus is drawing on some form of Ase that I can't see," she said, "but I feel it in my bones; something terrible is about to happen."

"These men are the only people in the empire with the power and influence to stop my brother!" she said, her eyes wide with panic. "With them out of the way, there will be no limit to what he can do."

"Would he not listen to you; can you talk to him?" said Vesper.

"I can try, but I doubt he will listen. You saw how he was at the palace. One moment he is calm and seems to be the brother I remember, growing up, loving but naïve. Then in the span of a single breath, he is something else, a monster who thinks of himself as Hercules, a god made of flesh."

"Then we have to stop him, here and now, before he has no one to limit his madness or his power," said Vesper, squaring her shoulders, wondering how she managed to get herself into a situation like this once more.

"The last time we faced him, we almost lost our lives," said Lucilla, swallowing hard, "and that was with Narcissus and Quintis at our sides."

"I know," she said, drawing on the well of Ase in her body, in her blood, shuddering as her limbs grew stronger, her skin harder, but still feeling weak, tired, "and after the battles in the market today, my strength is mostly spent, but we must try."

"I will go to his side, make him see reason."

"No, look, his shadow falls over the senate, and they don't even realize it," said Vesper, pointing to the chamber floor, where the area around Commodus had grown darker despite the bright shafts of sunlight streaming through the large windows, as if the sun had hidden behind the clouds. "Something about your brother is very wrong, and I'm afraid of what will happen to you if you go down there."

Lucilla swallowed, her eyes going wide. "Then I will serve as a distraction, from here."

"Wait for my signal; you will know it when you see it," said Vesper, moving toward a narrow platform that ran behind the senator's seats while Commodus continued to rage.

"I was content to leave you be and ignore your crimes against the people of Rome, but then you sent your gang of thugs to the palace this morning, not even having the courage to do it yourself."

Another senator, a dark-skinned Sicilian with a cleft chin and silver at his temples stepped forward, his reddish-purple-striped toga draped over one arm. "We have done nothing but the people's business, Caesar," he said with a pleading look on his face. "What would make you think so ill of us?"

Sneaking to a point halfway between the main door and the dais, Vesper ducked down behind a chair, fighting the urge to vomit, the sickly smell of dead flesh growing the closer she was to Commodus. From this distance she could clearly see the red-faced rage and wild-eyed madness that had taken hold of the emperor. "Senator Sabinus, I expected better of you," he said, addressing the man who had spoken. "That rat, Magnus, claimed that the senate wanted me dead. I will be merciful and let him have a trial by his peers, but I want justice. I want him executed, along with any other conspirators in this gang of traitors."

The senators looked at one another, a murmur of confusion running through the group until Senator Sabinus cleared his throat, raising his hand for silence. "Apologies, Caesar," he began in a respectful tone, "but Senator Magnus must have been lying to shift blame for his ambitions, whatever he did. He did it alone; we had no part in it."

"Lies!" shouted Commodus, shaking his fist at the silver-haired senator.

Fearing that Commodus was about to carry out his threat, Vesper shifted her vision to see the weave, wanting to draw on what little power she could from its tattered corruption. The instant her sight slipped beyond the mundane, she gasped, finding herself immersed in an inky darkness, blind, with only a vague sense of shape of the chamber. Vesper could still feel the chair in front of her and the cool marble beneath against her skin, even hear Commodus and his ranting, but nothing more, as if she had fallen into a void of some kind. Cursing under her breath, she squeezed her eyes shut to return her vision to normal. Her breath caught in her throat as a wave of pain shot through her, flowing like molten fire from her connection with Narcissus. Falling to her knees, she tore at a burrowing sensation that started at her breast, and then drilled deeper under her skin, as if something was crawling in her veins.

Commodus and the senators became a distant echo while she fought for breath, their words a cacophony of noise but nothing more. The meager amount of Ase she had managed to pour into her limbs faded, slipping through her grasp like flowing water. With a start her vision shifted back to normal, and she realized the floor rushing toward her. Thinking quickly, she threw her hands out in front of her, catching herself before her head bounced off the unyielding marble.

"Are you all right?" asked Lucilla, appearing at her side, her whisper piercing the chaos and yelling on the chamber floor.

"I don't know," she said, sitting up with Lucilla's help. "Something happened to Narcissus. There was pain, then panic, and now nothing."

"Do you need to go to him?" she asked, raising a fine eyebrow.

Vesper touched her chest where she had felt the pain, wanting nothing more than to find him, to make sure he was safe, unhurt, but a scream pulled her attention back to the senate floor. One of the senators was on his knees in front of the dais, a growing pool of blood under him. "Narcissus is alive," she said, pushing her feelings away, "and we'll find him, but this will be a slaughter if we don't act now."

"I agree, but you don't look like you're in any condition to fight," said Lucilla.

"True, what little strength I had has slipped away," she said, just as the Praetorian guard dragged more senators from their seats, forcing them to kneel in front of Commodus. "But sometimes duty doesn't give us a choice."

Lucilla nodded in agreement as Commodus paced on the dais, his voice full of spite as he addressed them, "You are all guilty by association, whether you knew of Senator Magnus's plans or not. I want every Roman to know of his crimes. I want him to pay for his attempt. If you cannot do that, then you will stand in his place, and die in the arena. One of you every day until he is found, or the senate is no more. Given how much they hate you, I'm sure the citizens and slaves of Rome would enjoy seeing the lot of you brought low."

"Can he do that?" asked Vesper, cocking her head. "Among the Ose, our lawgivers and leaders are revered, respected for the sacrifices they make to guide and protect our people. If these men are the same, he cannot just kill them. There must be rules. Why else would the senate exist?"

"Maybe," said Lucilla, licking her lips. "I'm not sure, and to be honest it might be for the best. When Rome was a true republic, the senate were the true rulers of Rome, with the people's best interests at heart. Today it's a shadow of its former self, full of corrupt men that hoard all of the empire's wealth for themselves. The only reason the institution still exists is because the senators use their wealth and influence to make sure they can hang on to the power it symbolizes."

Vesper looked at the fat bellies and soft hands of the senators, and understood what Lucilla meant. They had the look of men who had never toiled for their food or drink, who slept on soft beds without a care in the world for the labors of others, but it was also clear by the confused looks on their faces and outright denials, that most of the men on their knees played no part in the attempt to kill Commodus. "There is more going on here than we can see," said Vesper. "These men are likely to be guilty of many sins, but we cannot let whatever evil that has taken hold of your brother to spread further. I fear if he kills these men, it will only grow worse."

"You will be the first, Senator Adventus," said Commodus, "just as you were the first to speak out against me! Tomorrow, in the Colosseum, you will die, Ad gladium."

"Can you make me a weapon, like last time?" asked Lucilla.

"We cannot win this battle with weapons," said Vesper, eyeing the Praetorian guard, the fleeting hope of an idea forming in her mind. "Where is Senator Magnus?"

Lucilla's fine brows drew together as she frowned. "I sent him with Albus, the first centurion from the market. He is on his way to my villa on Palatine Hill."

"Good," she said, rising to her feet. Vesper walked down the narrow aisle, threading her way through the throng of startled senators. "We know where he is, Caesar," she shouted, the nausea growing in her belly the closer she came to the emperor. "The senator you seek."

Commodus raised a hand for silence, and Vesper did her best not to flinch when every eye in the curia fell on her. On the dais, Commodus frowned, his face contorting and flushing to a deep shade of red. "Why did you not inform me of this sooner?" he said, adjusting his lavish toga.

"We tried, when we came to see you," she lied, walking slowly down the main aisles toward him, on shaking legs, the smell growing worse with each step. "But did not have the chance."

"It's true, Brother," said Lucilla from somewhere behind her, playing along with the lie. "I will have him sent to the senate for his trial."

Vesper fought the urge to turn and run when Commodus lit up, his red-faced anger forgotten, instantly replaced by a wicked grin that sent a chill down her spine. "Trial? No, a trial would be a waste of time, and in my role as pontifex maximus, I find him guilty!" he said, descending from the dais toward Vesper. "He will face death in the arena, with all of Rome standing witness."

"Whatever you wish, Caesar," said Lucilla.

"We will have a whole day of games, a tournament for the privileged," shouted Commodus as Cleander and the remainder of his guard fell in behind him. "And you, you will be my champion."

Vesper held her ground as he stopped in front of her, eyeing her up and down with a proud smile on his face. "I don't understand; what does it mean to be champion?"

"I remember fondly your first day on the sands of the arena, you ignited the crowd, and impressed me with your victory, despite the odds. I wish to see you fight once more, and as thanks for bringing Senator Magnus, you will have the chance, as my champion."

"Brother, that's not fair," said Lucilla, appearing at Vesper's side. "To punish her—"

"It is not punishment. It is an honor!" he scoffed.

Lucilla opened her mouth to speak, but Commodus silenced her with a raised finger. "To be my champion means that you will be part of a grand battle in the Colosseum, a contest to see who will be granted the privilege to execute Senator Magnus, along with any other traitors we root out in the coming days. The only way to win will be to kill every man or beast placed before you."

"That does not sound like a privilege," said Vesper.

"It is not," said Lucilla, shaking her head.

"I have decided," said Commodus, smiling like a boy who had been given a sweet. "A grand battle on the sands, and then an execution of the guilty."

Commodus went to move past her but Vesper blocked his path. "I will not do this," she began, raising her chin in defiance despite the bile rising in her throat. "I am not some plaything for your amusement. I was, until a few months ago, a free Roman citizen living a life in peace until I was taken against my will and dragged to this city. All because of a lie against my father, a lie that has been proven false many times over."

"And now you are a slave, with the privilege of serving me. You should consider it a blessing. Few have the honor of fighting in my name."

"My people, my mother and father were loyal servants to the

empire, and now you are telling me I should be proud to fight like an animal, to kill a man who has done me no wrong."

Commodus looked around the senate chamber, grinding his teeth together before he returned his attention to her with a tight-lipped smile. "Do not mistake my desire to see you battle on the sands as a sign that you can defy me. You will fight! You will be a true gladiatrix. A hero to the people of Rome, loved by all. Don't you want to hear the crowd cheering your name, to be a legend whose victories are echoed throughout time?!"

"No," she said, lowering her voice. "I was raised to protect life, not take it. I am not a murderer."

Commodus's smile widened as he leaned in close enough that she choked on the overwhelming smell of rot. "But you are so good at it," he said, matching her tone. "So, in the end, you will fight, and win. I am sure of it."

"To kill a man in the heat of battle, when there is no choice is one thing, but to kill for sport, to execute a man in cold blood—this is not the way of the Ose. It's not my way."

"Make it your way!" growled Commodus. "Or I will have Cleander here remove your head. Would that be better?"

"Brother—"

"Shut up, Lucilla!" He seethed, showing the whites of his teeth. "I have been nothing but kind and merciful, but I've had enough of those trying to defy me for today. Say one more word... one more word."

In that moment, Vesper saw a flicker of madness in his eyes, heard the hysteria in his voice, and felt the uncontrolled rage smoldering just under the surface. "I will do it," she said, worrying what Commodus would do to Lucilla, and the senators, if he was pushed too far.

"Good!" he said, throwing his hands up. "It's settled, then." Without another word, Commodus and his men pushed past her, with Cleander, the emperor's new chamberlain, sneering at her as he walked by.

They were almost to the ornate doors when she called out to him, "I want one more thing," said Vesper, surprised to hear the words coming out of her mouth.

"What are you doing?" asked Lucilla in a strained whisper.

Commodus turned to face the assembly, raising an eyebrow, in that moment looking very much like his sister. "You are a bold one! Very well, if you are to fight, what do you want from me?"

Vesper swallowed hard, her heart beating out of her chest. "If I win, if I do this thing that goes against who I am. I want my life returned, my freedom."

"What?"

"And that of my doctore as well, Narcissus," she said, fighting the urge to cover her mouth, feeling like she was losing her mind.

"Doctore... you mean the beast of a Celt with all the hair?" said Commodus, throwing back his head in laughter.

Vesper ground her teeth, and she surged forward, balling her fist. "He is a good man who has earned his freedom many times over—"

Commodus cocked his head, and for a heartbeat she swore his eyes flashed a milky white. "If you survive the day, and do as you're told, I will give you and your Celt your freedom."

A smile crept onto Vesper's face against her will as a surge of excitement ran through her. "Thank you—"

"But if you want it for the both of you, then you and your hairy Celt will stand alone," he said.

"What?" she said, feeling like she had been slapped.

"You wish to refuse my kindness, my blessing? This is the price!" said Commodus, raising a finger, looking pleased with himself. "It will be a story for the ages, barbarian savages from opposite corners of the empire, facing off against the heroic gladiators of Rome."

"That would be a death sentence, Brother."

Commodus looked around to the assembled senators, frowning at Vesper. "Such is the price of greed," he said, pointing at her. "I offered her the role of my champion, to be a hero to the Roman people, and she spurned it! So, instead, she and her doctore will face off against men of my choosing."

Lucilla opened her mouth to argue, but Vesper put a hand on her shoulder, speaking first, "I accept your challenge," she said simply, holding his gaze.

"Good. In three days' time, we shall have this contest," he said, crossing his arms, tapping a finger on his lips, "and if by some miracle of the gods you survive, we shall have that time in the baths," he said, turning on his heel and leaving without another word, his men following in his wake.

Vesper sank to her knees the moment the curia doors boomed to a close, her entire body trembling like she had spent the day hammering rocks, "How... how—I'm such a fool."

"You're not a fool," said Lucilla, falling in beside her. "You stopped him from killing everyone here. You saved lives," said Lucilla, her eyes lingering on the doorway.

"All I did was give us a few more days, nothing more," said Vesper, clutching at her chest while drawing in a shuddering breath. "Now, we must find Narcissus."

Lucilla nodded, and they moved to leave when Senator Adventus and some of his colleagues approached them, the white of their togas stained and bloodied. "That is the bravest thing I have ever seen," he began, bowing slightly at the waist. "I was sure that I was going to die today. On behalf of the senate, we offer our gratitude."

Vesper blinked in surprise, sharing a look with Lucilla. After her description of them, she had not expected anything from these men, and certainly not thanks or kindness. "The world is a strange place, Senator," she said, choosing her words carefully before continuing, "and we must protect one another, or else people like Commodus will destroy everything."

The senator looked back at the others behind him, a look passing between them before returning his attention to her. "We cannot help you with your battle on the sands," he said, "but if you survive, and have need of anything, you may call on us."

Beside her, Lucilla gasped, and for a moment, Vesper couldn't find her voice. "Thank you, Senator," she said at last, not sure what to say.

The remaining senators moved away, but Adventus stayed, giving her an expectant look. "Something else?" asked Vesper.

The senator looked down at the blood on his robes, shaking his head. "Win," he said, showing her a feral grin. "Win and shame that tyrant. Do it for the people of Rome."

Vesper smiled, sighing deeply. "I will, Senator. I will."

TWELVE

THE HOUSE OF BACCHUS

"I don't understand how you can know where he is," said Lucilla, dragging her feet in the late afternoon heat, exhausted in mind and body from the events of the day, "and how can you feel what he feels?"

At Vesper's urging, she and Lucilla had left the Curia Julia not long after Commodus, returning for the second time today to Palatine Hill. Wandering the wide, tree-lined avenues where Rome's rich and powerful made their homes, desperately searching for any trace of Narcissus—so far, with little to show for it. Looking past a sprawling villa with a magnificent garden and brilliant arches, Lucilla sighed, knowing she was close to home and could, with a short trek, spend the rest of her day cooling in her private baths, washing away the dirt and grime of the day while enjoying a few cups of sweetened wine, but the haunting look in Vesper's eyes pushed her on.

It was late in the afternoon and the heat of the day was fading when they stopped to rest at one of the many elaborate fountains that dotted the avenue. Vesper half sat, half fell on the concrete lip, her shoulders slumping as an exhausted sigh escaped her cracked lips. "Narcissus and I... we are connected," she said, answering Lucilla's question while motioning for her to sit, "but since that moment in the senate, he feels... distant, weak. And he was right here, on this spot, when it changed."

Lucilla gratefully plopped down beside her with a sigh, taking off her sandals and rubbing her feet. "It must be a great comfort to know the ones you love are safe," she said, her mind wandering as she stared at the jets of water that flowed from the bronzed animal heads decorating the fountain. "My first husband and I were very close, and I feared for him terribly when he was away on the field of war. To have been able to know he was well, it would have been wonderful."

"What happened? Was he killed in battle?" asked Vesper.

"No, he was returning to Rome when he fell ill. The medicus said it was something he ate, but it never sat right with me, and after my father passed in the same manner, I suspect that he was murdered," said Lucilla, squeezing her eyes shut, pushing back tears. "Apologies, it still hurts, even after all this time."

"Commodus?"

"I've always suspected, not that it matters anymore, but yes. He was the one with the most to gain," said Lucilla, "but the worst part is not knowing. Lucius was dead for weeks before I was told of it. If I had known such connections existed. I would have asked it of your father. But he never spoke of such a thing."

"You knew my father? How?"

"Yes, a little. After your mother vanished, he took her place as Djambe. One night my father asked him to cast out the demons possessing me!" said Lucilla jokingly.

"What!?" laughed Vesper, scrunching up her face in disbelief.

"We Romans are very progressive in most things, but the body of a woman is not one of them. The first time I bled, my father feared I was possessed," she said, thinking back. "Your father, he tried to explain that my moon flow was normal, natural, but the great Marcus Aurelius would not hear of it, and insisted that your father use his magic to fix me. It became a monthly ritual for us. When it was my time, he would spend a few hours with me 'to cast out' the evil in me.

To pass the time, we would discuss all sorts of things: life in Rome, or about his home among your people, the Ose, and their history, it was fascinating."

"I did not realize you were so close to him," said Vesper. "You more than likely spent more time with him than I did. After my mother died, he was forced to spend more time in Rome, as was his duty. As I grew older, he came home less and less, leaving my Aunt Magda to raise me."

"I was young, and he was exotic to me, so different from my father's other advisors. I became obsessed with the idea of magic and witchcraft, and I think he showed me much more of it than he should have," said Lucilla, narrowing her eyes. "In the end, I think he was just grateful to have someone to talk to. He always seemed sad, like something was missing."

Vesper put her hands under a bronze lion's head to catch the stream of fresh water, cupping a handful, drinking deeply and then washing her face. "Ase is not magic or Roman superstition. Chosen, those who can channel Ase, like me and my parents, we are not witches: we are seers and wise people, meant to guide and protect our communities. If you truly listened, you would know such things."

Lucilla noticed a small group of women frowning at the pair as they walked by, and she glared back at them until they looked away. "Apologies," she said, "but he did speak of you often. He was so proud of you, and it was clear he loved your mother very much."

"I wish I had known either one of them as well as you did," said Vesper in a hoarse voice.

Lucilla cursed under her breath when Vesper looked away, and she caught a glimpse of unshed tears brightening her eyes. "Men, they are all the same," she said, speaking quickly. "My father and husband were the same, always off on some distant frontier. Expanding the borders of the empire, fearing the barbarians at the gates."

"It is not only men," said Vesper. "My mother was just as guilty. She spent most of her life in the saddle, at the side of Marcus Aurelius, your father, using her skill in Ase to win wars... all in the name of keeping us safe."

"A strange woman, your mother. Stranger still that she has somehow managed to do the impossible and return from the land of the dead."

"Again, you probably knew her better than I did. She had died not long after I was born and I never knew her," said Vesper.

"I have only a few vague memories of her," said Lucilla, narrowing her eyes at a pair of women who sat not far away, whispering to one another and giving them sidelong glances. "From what I remember, she was... intense, driven, but always quick with a jest or a smile, and she and you your father looked to be the best of friends. She was one of the few people who spoke to him without holding back, or bowing and scraping. I knew your father better, I suppose, because I was older when he came to advise my father."

"Why do they look at us that way?" asked Vesper, pointing with her chin at the women who had been staring before."

Following Vesper's gaze, Lucilla glared at them, sending them scurrying up the road, not daring to look back. "Because of the way we look."

Vesper frowned, her brows drawing together as she looked down at the simple tunics they both wore. "Is it because I am from the provinces... or because I am a slave?"

"Neither" said Lucilla, shaking her head. "Romans don't care for such things. In fact, there are many slaves who live in Palatine Hill who are far more respected and claim higher status than many freemen. No, it's because we're filthy, looking far too common, too poor for this section of the city."

"I will never understand you Romans," said Vesper, gesturing to the fine homes surrounding them. "You put so much effort into beauty, into the physical, yet you leave nothing for the spirit."

"What is that supposed to mean?" asked Lucilla, leaning back.

"Look around you. This fountain flows with more water in a day than most villages drink in a week. And the wealth of one of these homes could feed the thousands of poor that you have living, from day to day, in the slums of this city."

Lucilla stood, her cheeks getting hot. "The poor of this city live better than the wealthy in many places," she said, clenching and unclenching her jaw. "Commodus may be many things, but he makes certain that those in need have their daily bread, wine, and a roof over their heads. In fact, just by the very existence of Rome, civilization, art, music, all these things have flowed to the barbarian tribes in and out of our borders. The world is a better place because of us." As the last words left her mouth, Lucilla came back to herself with a start, realizing that she had been screaming, and now a small crowd had gathered, watching them.

"Apologies," said Vesper, pursing her lips while squeezing Lucilla's shoulder. "I didn't mean to offend. The Ose live far different lives than the people of Rome. I must adapt."

"No, I'm the one who is sorry," said Lucilla, squeezing Vesper's hand. "Today has been exhausting, and I think I need some wine."

"You can go home. I can find Narcissus on my own."

"I can't let you do;, he may be hurt or—" Lucilla fell silent when Vesper stood, her eyes going wide.

"He's back!" she said, sucking in a deep breath before darting off. "This way, quickly!"

Despite her legs shaking like a newborn calf, Lucilla ran after her, a surge of adrenaline giving her the strength to keep up. At the pace Vesper set, they rapidly descended into the city proper, the larger villas of Palatine Hill giving way to the more common-style domus, the modest homes of Rome's ne'er-do-wells that were often made of cheaper materials, poured concrete and wood instead of marble and fired bricks. The streets were narrower too, made of a dull, hardened clay that was drab when compared to the bright white streets of Palatine Hill. Vesper ducked around a corner, and for a heartbeat, Lucilla was sure she had lost her.

"Over here," shouted Vesper, and Lucilla backtracked to an alley she had passed, to find Vesper standing in front of a door. "He is in here, still faint, but here."

Walking to her side, Lucilla's brow shot up, and her entire body stiffened when she saw the painted image on the door, that of a man holding a wine-cup in one hand and a bunch of grapes in the other. "This is no place for us," she said with a tight-lipped smile, pulling Vesper aside as the door swung open and a pair of men staggered out, singing loudly and reeking of wine. "If he is here, it's best that we leave him be."

"They are just drunk," she said with a laugh, "and I have been in Rome long enough that I have been to a pompina; they are a little rough, but a bit of drink and food never did any harm. I might even indulge. I'm starving, and the wine was quite good last time, though the pain in my head the next—"

"That's not a good idea," she said more firmly this time, her pale cheeks flushing pink. "While you might find some wine here, this is more of a place to explore the... uhh... pleasures of the flesh."

Vesper's bright smile vanished, and her expression turned to stone. "What!? Why in the name of Olodumare would he come to a place like this?" asked Vesper, her harsh tone making Lucilla flinch involuntarily.

"Who can truly understand the desires of men," said Lucilla, "but places like this exist to... to allow them to pursue their base instincts of flesh and debauchery. It can be a good thing, leaving us to be left in peace to live virtuous lives." The words had just left Lucilla's mouth when the door opened once more, and a tall woman with dark hair and deep-brown eyes emerged, one of the straps of her embroidered stola falling off her shoulder, while the bottom half of the garment was stained with wine.

"You were saying something about women being virtuous." Said Vesper, glaring at the woman.

Lucilla's cheeks grew hotter, and she cleared her throat. "Well, some women can be just as bad—" Another woman emerged, squinting up at the late afternoon sun, almost falling over the first one. Catching a glimpse of the woman's face, Lucilla's breath caught in her throat and she spun on her heel, doing her best not to be seen.

For a moment she thought she had succeeded, only to cringe when the woman called out to her, "Lucilla, darling. Is that you?" said the second woman, slurring her words. "I thought when you married Tiberius, you had given up the bacchanalia and all its joy!"

Lucilla's shoulders fell, and she turned to face the woman. "Octavia," she said, putting on her most pleasant smile. "You look... well."

"You're the best of liars, Lucilla. I look like I've spent my day enjoying the gifts of Bacchus... and not just the wine." She giggled, falling over the other woman while the pair of them shrieked with laughter.

"Bacchanalia?" asked Vesper through clenched teeth.

"By the gods, Lucilla," said Octavia, catching her breath, "is this one yours? She's stunning. Look at those eyes, so fierce, almost dangerous, like she would murder you in your sleep for speaking ill of her! Now I understand why you've abandoned your friends. I would do the same if I had such a slave."

"Lucilla. What are these fool women talking about?"

Octavia fell back, touching her chest. "And defiant too, that must make it exciting, to be so out of control."

"Nothing, come quickly," said Lucilla, wrapping an arm around Vesper's waist and pushing past Octavia and her friend. "Just the ramblings of women who have had far too much wine."

"But—"

"It was good seeing you, Octavia," said Lucilla over her shoulder, ignoring the drunken women and their questions, pushing Vesper through the door and into a sumptuous, yet gaudy vestibule. They continued down a dim hallway that was decorated with a mural that ran its length, depicting an androgynous figure floating above a group of naked men and women harvesting grapes, dancing, and drinking in an endless celebration.

The mosaics of the hall continued into a large, colorful room, made bright by a wide skylight that sent light dancing off a small reflecting pool that shimmered in the late afternoon sun.

"What is this place?" asked Vesper, eyeing the small clusters of men and women sitting on padded wooden benches in twos and threes, or laying on thick, patterned carpets and leaning on comfortable-looking cushions, most of them wearing clothing that left little to the imagination.

"I will find a priestess, and she will find Narcissus for us; it would be best if we wait here."

Vesper glanced around the room with a pained look, scrubbing a hand across her eyes. "You mean if *I* wait here."

Lucilla licked her lips, trying to think of words that would soften the blow, but one look at Vesper made it clear she was no fool and could see what was happening all around her. "Yes," she said, clearing her throat. "I don't think this is the kind of place you would enjoy. While this kind of behavior is common in Rome, I know you well enough to know you wouldn't approve. And to be honest, it would not do you well to find Narcissus doing whatever it is he is doing."

Vesper bowed her head sheepishly, staring at the half-naked patrons from the corner of her eyes. "Why would he do this?" she whispered after a moment, her voice so full of pain that Lucilla felt like her own heart was breaking.

"I don't know," she said, taking Vesper by her shoulders, "but we will get to the bottom of this. Sit, have some wine, and I will find him," said Lucilla, guiding her to one of the empty benches.

"And what then?"

Lucilla pressed her lips together, looking everywhere but at Vesper. "I don't know, but trust that you are not alone in this. I am here for you."

Vesper laughed, while tears flowed freely. "I can't—I don't know what to do," she said, holding her chest.

"Are you well?" asked Lucilla, taken aback, worried that Vesper had lost her mind. She had seen it happen, more than once, ladies who lost their wits over a man, herself included.

"I think so," she said, catching her breath. "It's just that he told me the same thing only a few hours ago, that he was here for me."

"Well, unless someone removes my head from my shoulders, I *will* be here for you. I promise."

"Thank you," said Vesper, wiping her face.

"I will be back shortly." Lucilla gave Vesper one last squeeze on the shoulder and then left to find a priestess or at least a slave to help them, doing her best to ignore the inviting smiles and gentle caresses as she passed through the room. The primary rites of the cult had to do with wine and fertility, and most Romans worshipped him through drink and sex, often to excess. Places like these were rare, often moving from week to week, as the worship of Bacchus had to be done in secret. The cult was outlawed centuries ago during the republic for fear that it would corrupt the people beyond redemption. She knew all too well the allure of such places and had happily lost herself for weeks and months after Lucius had died, enjoying every moment of it... until her father had forced her to remarry. To her frustration, Tiberius had little appetite for the pleasures of the flesh and insisted she stay away from such places. Pushing aside her urges, she followed a pair of men down another dimly lit hall and through a heavy curtain, finding herself in a crowded room filled with people of all ages milling about, drinking and speaking in low tones. Pushing through the throng, she found a bar running the length of the room, attended by a slim, young man with fiery red hair and wearing a near transparent tunic, pouring out cups of wine.

"Thaddeus," she said with a coy smile. "It's been too long."

The slim man's eyes narrowed, flashing with anger. "Not long enough."

Lucilla's shoulders slumped, exhaustion taking her. "What was I supposed to do? My father—"

"You said you would leave it all behind," he said, leaning in closer. "We were to leave all of this together."

She reached across the bar, taking his hands in hers, a shudder running through her when the memory of them running up her own body passed through her mind. "Apologies, I wanted to, dreamed of it day after day, but family obligation is not such an easy thing to cast aside. My father had a new husband for me by the time he returned to Rome. What could I do?"

Thaddeus looked away, pursing his lips. "I know," he said at last, pushing away her hands.

"I sent denarii," said Lucilla, speaking quickly, her fingers twitching to reach out for him once again. "Enough that you could have started a new life anywhere in the empire."

"Without you!?" He frowned, shaking his head. "What would be the point? No, better to stay here... drinking the days away."

Lucilla wanted to take him somewhere quiet, to better explain, but Vesper needed her, needed to find Narcissus. "We will talk more on this. I will return, I promise," she said, locking eyes with him, "but, for now, I need a favor, to find someone for a friend."

"Who?" he said, a spark of hope crossing his face.

"A big man, red hair, with a great beard."

"He is here," said Thaddeus. "A hard one to miss. If I didn't know you better, I would say he was for you, but given your tastes..."

"You are my tastes," she said fondly.

"Then I will find him for you... but only if you promise to come back to me one day."

"I should have come back, at the very least to explain," she said, and leaned forward once more, gripping his hands with all her strength. "You saved me, you know, put back together my heart after it was broken." She wanted to say more, to hold him, but the look on his face told her he knew he knew all along that it was just a dream.

"We are all slaves in our own ways, some of us to chains, some of us to duty," he said. "Don't worry, I will find your friend... and then, maybe one day, we can be together again."

"One day," said Lucilla, letting go of his hands, racing from the overcrowded room, running from her feelings, running to hide her tears.

———

"They will find him, and bring him to us when they do," said Lucilla a few minutes later, grateful that the dark corner they sat in hid her red-rimmed eyes.

"I feel like a fool. I am not even sure what to say to him, or even why I'm acting this way," said Vesper.

"What do you mean? I have seen the way you look at one another," said Lucilla, sitting beside her on the cushioned bench.

"We are not betrothed, and worse, our parents have not even spoken about a match, although I suppose that will be impossible—"

Lucilla blinked in surprise, a smile coming to her face. "Marriage? I didn't realize that was your intention, or his."

"We have not discussed it, but it must be done. I find it difficult to be around him, and we cannot go on this way," she said with a frown. "Just after the battle, I lost control and kissed him."

"Lost control? Kissed? But surely you have lain with him," said Lucilla, keeping her face steady.

Vesper shook her head, rubbing her palms on the lower half of her tunic. "No, today is the first time. I felt a great shame when my lips touched his, a shame I feel now. Proper Ose women do not do such things."

"By the gods, you have an untouched heart," whispered Lucilla in amazement. "Have you ever been with a man!?"

"No, among my people, it is not proper for an unmarried woman to have relations with a man."

Lucilla threw her head back, covering her mouth to stifle a laugh. "Apologies," she said when Vesper looked away, crossing her arms across her chest while clenching her jaw.

"I am not ignorant to how things are here in Rome," she said, "but we are connected. I feel what he feels... not only that, I have lived in the ludus long enough to know that Narcissus was not like the other men. He was always kind, respectful, and he never lay with the whores provided to the gladiators after a victory."

"Yes, but he is still a man! And he has promised you nothing."

"I know," she growled, "but I cannot help the way I feel... and—"

"Apologies, but I found the man you are looking for." Lucilla looked up to find Thaddeus smiling at them. "If he is in the baths. If you wish to follow me, I can show you the way."

"In the baths—by Olodumare!" said Vesper, her sadness vanishing behind a calm façade. "Lead the way, please." Without another word they followed Thaddeus down one of the hallways that led deeper into the domus.

Lucilla hurried after her as they went from room to room, keeping her eyes firmly ahead of her to avoid seeing the twisting bodies locked together, doing her best to ignore the moaning and grunting, even while the smell of sweat and sex filled her nostrils. They entered a part of the building that was much warmer than the rest, and she knew they were close. Lucilla took Vesper's hand, bracing herself for some sort of emotional breakdown, worrying when she saw that her eyes were bright with unshed tears.

Strolling into the open-air bathing area, the tension faded from her body as she drew in a deep breath, and for a moment she lost herself in the dance of sunlight flashing off the waters. It was clear from the dozen or so men and women that splashed in the waters, that the space was the highlight of the domus, and that the entire home had been built around the large square of bath of blue-green water. Deep as a man was tall, with hints of steam floating just above the surface.

"He's just there," said the attendant, pointing to a shaded corner where a small group was clustered under a wide umbraculum. "Next to the woman with the small crowd gathered around here."

"What woman?" Vesper seethed, squeezing Lucilla's hand so hard she feared it would break.

"I've never seen either of them here before," said Thaddeus with a shrug, "but she was very generous with her coin. Dark of skin with an intricate braid that, in fact, she looked much like you. Is she a relation?"

A shriek escaped her lips as Vesper pulled her along, Lucilla throwing him an apologetic look. "Try and remain calm."

"I can't," said Vesper, reaching the edge of the group, roughly pushing her way through the half-naked bodies.

They had just come to the inner circle when, as a group, they burst out in laughter, and Vesper began to swear. Lucilla almost fell as she came through, her jaw falling open when she realized the person at the center of the group was none other than Lillith, and passed out beside her on a large, cushioned bench that was clearly made for two, was Narcissus, snoring away, a plethora of empty wine-cups around him.

The moment Lillith saw the pair of them, she threw up her arms, a wide grin coming to her face. "Little Empress, Daughter, welcome to the bacchanalia! Have some wine, and then get undressed. We have a party to get started!"

THIRTEEN

RUDE AWAKENINGS

Her mouth was moving, but the words were little more than a jumble of noise that made his throbbing head worse. Groaning in pain, Narcissus buried his face in his hands, struggling to understand what was going on. His mind was blank, and his tired limbs ached from the slightest movement. Nothing around him was familiar, from the baths to the half-naked people, it was all a mystery, with no answers to be found in their mocking stares. Most of all he fought to piece together why Lucilla, the emperor's sister, was screaming at him, while Vesper stood behind her with fat tears rolling down her face.

Lucilla wagged her finger in his face, and something in him broke, and he shot to his feet. "Enough!" he growled, blowing out his cheeks. "I have no idea what you're on about, or what's going on, but given the pain in my head, it would be dangerous for you to continue."

Lucilla squared her shoulders, looking down her nose at him. "Perhaps if you learned to hold your drink better, you wouldn't make such mistakes."

"Mistakes?" he snorted as he looked past Lucilla. "Vesper, what in the name of the gods is this about?"

Vesper met his eyes with a hard look, and he felt like he had been punched in the belly. "Nothing, you have done nothing," she said, crossing her arms. "It is my fault for not knowing the Roman way of things."

"The Roman way?" said Narcissus, clutching at his head. "Make sense if you want me to understand you, woman! I'm in no mood for games."

"Understand this... *Doctore*," said Vesper, her face an unreadable mask. "In three days from now, there will be games in the Colosseum. It will be a contest for the privilege to execute a traitor to the empire. Commodus has ordered that we stand together."

"Stand together... against who—you mean in the primus?" he said, cocking his head.

"Champions chosen by Commodus himself, a battle royal to the death."

Narcissus swallowed hard, catching himself on the post that held up the umbraculum as his head began to spin. "That's madness. Why would you accept such a contest?"

"I told her as much," said Lucilla, looking back and forth between the two of them, "but trust that she did it for the right reasons, for the good of us all."

"Good? What good?"

"I am a slave, remember! I had no choice," said Vesper, looking away, "but I did my best with the hand dealt to me. If we win, we are free."

The word struck him like a heavy blow, and he fell back onto the padded bench, his mouth opening and closing as he tried to make sense of it all. "This still does not explain things, how I am here. Why do you—"

"Lucilla, I'm very tired, and I would be grateful if we could return to the ludus," said Vesper in a hoarse voice, turning her back on him.

"Never mind the ludus," she said, putting an arm around her shoulder and pulling her close. "You will return home with me; you will be safe there." Ignoring his pleading looks, both women put their backs to him, walking away and leaving him with more questions than answers.

They had just gotten to one of the many exits to the baths when she turned and cast a long look at him, and he realized that he felt nothing from their bond. The connection was still there, vague and distant, but nothing came through. He could not feel the tightness of her braided hair, or the heat of the sun on her skin, or not even a hint of emotion. Shaking his head in confusion, he was about to go after her when a strong hand on his shoulder held him in place.

"Going after her will only make matters worse," said Lillith, behind him. "Give her time. Trust me."

He turned while seated to meet her dark, mysterious gaze. "Time... time for what? I don't even know what I've done!"

"Look at where you are," said Lillith, circling the bench while lightly touching his shoulder. "Any woman who found her man in a house of Bacchus would behave the same."

Narcissus looked around the bath, frowning when he saw the intertwining of bodies, the caresses, and the outright lust. "I would never come to such a place. I don't remember coming here."

"Surely you remember. I wanted some wine and a proper bath... you indulged me, and then you indulged yourself, losing yourself in wine and much... much more. You have a worthy constitution, one that would be the envy of even the greatest of lovers."

"I don't remember any of that," he said, glancing down at the scattered cups around the bench, "and I am not one to lose myself to drink."

"I certainly tried to stop you," said Lillith, walking toward the water while pushing the straps of her stola off her shoulders, "but you would not listen, drinking each cup as if it were your last, lost in joys of good wine and beautiful women."

"I don't—I wouldn't," began Narcissus, only for his tongue to catch in his throat when Lillith let her stola fall to the ground, revealing her round hips and shapely bottom.

"Forget my daughter," she said over her shoulder with a coy

smile. "She is still very much a child, and a man like you surely has an appetite for more... experienced pleasures."

Lillith turned to face him fully and the sun was suddenly directly behind her, highlighting her silhouette in all her glory, and he had a powerful urge for her mouth on his, to crush her body against him and take her like they were animals... but then he remembered his dislike for her, his distrust, and with a supreme effort, he rose on shaking legs, letting out a slow breath to calm his racing heart. "I will return to the ludus," he said, averting his eyes. "I have to prepare, if not to win, at least to die well."

"Look at me, boy," commanded Lillith, snapping his attention back to her full breasts and lush hips. "One day you will learn that there is more to life than duty, or playing gladiator. Life's joys are fleeting, and you must seize them when you can. The last thing you want is to be on your deathbed, full of regrets, yearning for one last chance to relive the best moments, to make the right choices instead of the foolish ones."

Narcissus felt the tug once more, and he took a step toward her, his cheeks flushing red as he licked his lips, but then he remembered the look in Vesper's eyes, the sadness and disappointment, the hurt. "I have no such regrets," he snorted, tearing his eyes away, "and I go into battle accepting that I am dead, and only through victory do I live once more. So I live every day to the fullest, and I doubt very much that I will regret not laying with a serpent, no matter how pretty."

Lillith's eyes flashed with anger, and he tensed, expecting her to lash out, but then just as quickly, her smile returned and she shrugged. "I hope you will live long enough to regret your words... but I doubt it," she said, dismissing him with a wave. "I will meet you at the ludus, after I have taken my pleasures here."

Cursing under his breath, Narcissus turned on his heel, clutching at a strange pain in his chest, his mind spinning in confusion. He could not remember anything after their visit to the palace, beyond the fact that he and Lillith had left together; the rest was a blur. He was about to leave when a thought crossed his mind. "Why would you return to the ludus?" he asked over his shoulder, catching a glimpse of her slipping into the water.

Lillith smiled, her eyes bright with amusement. "My dear boy, I have nowhere else to go, but most of all I want to be close to my daughter and, of course... you."

Narcissus was taken aback, a pang of fear boiling in his stomach. Something about Lillith wreaked havoc with his body and soul. "Do as you will. I don't care, but stay away from me. The last thing I want is to have you distracting me or the men under my training. Do you understand?"

"Of course... Doctore," she said, throwing back her head in a laugh. "I am yours to command."

Narcissus stormed from the baths, red faced with anger. He would have to train hard if he had any hope of surviving this nightmare he found himself in. How in the name of the gods would he train with that snake in his ludus? How he was going to fix things with Vesper, and last but not least, survive sure death in the next three days.

FOURTEEN
HIDDEN THREATS

The garden was cold and damp, while the sun above was little more than a muted disk covered by iron-gray clouds. The flowers and plants once vibrant and summer green, were faded to the dull, dying shades of winter.

Vesper blinked in confusion, having no memory of coming here. The last thing she remembered was laying her head on Lucilla's lap, her tears flowing freely while thinking of her faint connection to Narcissus, hardly able to breathe from the hurt in her heart. Drifting in between the waking world and the dream, she had almost fallen into the blissful escape of sleep when something pulled at her, and a short, sharp tug that snapped her to full wakefulness. Now she wandered in this alien place, shivering from the cold.

"Winter is cold here," said a weary voice, drawing Vesper toward it. "Not like at home, but we will adapt."

Pushing her way through thick palms, she found a path that wound its way through overgrown shrubs and flowers. Following the voice, she arrived at a crossroad, the cobblestone giving way to a path of polished obsidian glass on the right, while the path to the left was made of a brilliant marble streaked with gray. Lost and confused,

Vesper opened her mouth to call for help, to shout, but was taken aback when only a faint whisper escaped her throat. Glancing around, she understood what was going on when she looked over her shoulder to find a thin thread of glowing silver vanishing in the distance. The cord would take her back to Lucilla, to her sleeping body, to the pain in her heart. She was about to return when the tug pulled at her once more, and the garden around her shimmered insubstantially for just a moment, like water changing shape.

"It's not just the cold," said another voice, high pitched and child-like. "The people here are mean, even my tutor, he called me a savage."

Vesper took the left fork of the path, stalking toward the voices like a great cat, her heart beating faster with each step.

"It is the Roman way," said the weary voice with a sigh. "They consider themselves far above those they have conquered, regardless of station. As a people, they have been forever cruel in their ways, so much so that they don't even know when they are doing it. Destroying and killing as easily as you and I breathe. All for the glory of their soulless empire."

In the distance, through fluttering leaves and waving branches, Vesper caught a glimpse of a young boy sitting on the lap of a matronly-looking woman with light brown skin and silver-gray hair braided thin, flowing down past her shoulders.

"Then why come here?" asked the boy in his small voice, his cherubic face reddening. "Why make me learn their ways? I don't want to be like them."

As she drew closer, Vesper wrinkled her nose at the smell of rot that filled the air, her stomach heaving in protest to the vile odor.

"Because the hunger for vengeance never dies," said the matron, her voice tense and full of anger, "and you must learn their ways because you pass, and we intend for you to be our instrument to their destruction."

"Pass?"

Vesper came in close enough that she could see them clearly now, sitting on a stone bench. The woman's angular features, high cheek-bones and square jaw, twisted to bitterness as she lectured the boy. "Look at me, and look at you," she snorted. "We may be of the same blood, but with your mother's lineage, you shall pass for a Roman. Our people are already in place, and as you can see, they have already secured everything you need for a life here."

"But... how... I can't... These people, they will not accept a stranger in their midst no matter how much I look like them."

Not understanding, Vesper moved closer and was almost on top of them when she gaped in horror, hurriedly covering her mouth to stifle a scream. At their feet, in a pool of blood was the body of a young boy.

A smile creased the matronly woman's face, and without pause, she dragged her hand along a deep wound in the fallen boy's neck, covering her palm with a deep crimson stain. "We shall use the old ways, long forgotten by our people."

The matron brought a bloody finger to his face, and he recoiled, turning away from her. For a split second he met Vesper's prying eyes, and without warning something passed between them, a pulsing connection that dug deep into her spirit. Before she could draw another breath, Vesper's head snapped back, and the garden became a green blur, and she had the sensation of falling into a deep well of darkness.

"Do not be afraid; through the pain you will be reborn," said the matron, her breath suddenly caressing Vesper's ear.

With a start, Vesper found herself looking deep into the matronly woman's eyes, her entire body tingling while her skin felt tight, like leather stretched out on the rack to dry. "I don't understand."

"You will," she said, placing a single bloody finger on Vesper's forehead. A raw scream that was not her own escaped her throat, and she gritted her teeth as her nostrils were filled with the smell of burnt flesh while the woman traced lines on her face, cauterizing skin, and charring bone. Fighting with all her might, she flailed, her arms and legs kicking in all directions in an attempt to escape the piercing agony, but the old matron was strong, holding her in place with an iron grip, all while humming vile words under her breath that sent waves of terror through her. Sobbing through the pain, Vesper was struck by a distant memory, a memory of her Aunt Magda, drawing the baobab tree on her then flat chest, the symbol that represented the Ose, and the chosen who could wield Ase to force their will upon the world.

"What are you doing to me?" she said through tears, seeing her hands were pale and thin, her voice high pitched... the boy's voice.

"Symbols are important to our people, and even hidden among these Roman fools, we must be true to ourselves. The boldest of us, like me, wear them in plain sight," she said, narrowing her gaze as she worked, "but you, with this new face, do not have such a luxury; our symbols will have to be hidden. The iboju will not only change how the Romans see you, but allow you to still channel our power."

Looking at the matron fully for the first time, Vesper gasped when the meaning of her words hit home. Her motherly face was covered by a whitening makeup, a simple powder that wealthy women often wore to keep them from looking too dark. Her earrings, made of hammered silver, were shaped like animal bones. The most shocking were the bead-like skulls woven into her braids. All of the symbols she knew too well, out in the open for everyone to see.

"Sandawei," she croaked through the pain, hardly believing her eyes.

The old matron smiled at the mention of the name, her eyes shining with pride. "Yes, the first people, this is who we are, now and forever. Made by the great god Olodumare to rule the world. Never forget this, no matter how high you rise among the Romans."

Vesper opened her mouth to ask more when a great weight pressed against her, and before she could blink, there was a rush of motion once more, and she found herself looking up at the gray sky, sucking in deep breaths of cool winter air to calm her racing heart. Patting down her chest, she sighed in relief while holding up her arms in front of her, happy to find the familiar concentric patterns on her arms, bright against her sun-brown skin. A shadow fell over her, drawing her attention to a thin man with a purple embroidered toga folded over one arm, above her. His face was hidden behind a mask made to resemble a human skull, painted a deep shade of crimson with yellowed teeth. "Foolish Ose, is nothing sacred to you! You have no right to be here," he said in the overly formal accent of a Roman patrician, his voice hollow behind the strange mask.

"You are the one Narcissus spoke of," she said, scurrying back on her palms and backside, "in the market yesterday."

"Did that witch lead you here?" he said, ignoring her question. "Traitorous woman! But I thought at least if—"

"You're the one who brought me here!" she snapped back, reflexively opening herself to the weave, shuddering as the Ase from the garden flooded through her.

A hollow laughter echoed from behind mask as he fell back, his entire form dimming like the sun had turned away from him. "You wish to challenge me here, in this place where there are no limits on our power?" he said as dark threads spun into place around his hands, while thin filaments writhed around him in a dark halo. "If you truly wish the final death, I will see to it."

Vesper hesitated, narrowing her eyes at his words. "What... what do you mean?"

For a moment, he stopped, cocking his head. "You really don't know, do you?"

"Know what?"

"Your ignorance is impressive, even for an Ose," he said, shaking his head, "and to think we feared you because you killed Jufari and Saoterus."

Drawing deeper on the power of the weave, Vesper combined it with her own strength, the raw Ase that coursed through her blood. The concentric patterns covering her arms and legs glowing like the noonday sun from the torrent of power running through her. "I'm sure you'll fall just as easily," she bluffed, not daring to take her eyes off him as she stood. Even holding all of this Ase, this potential, she was still unsure of what she could do, but she hoped the display of strength would be enough to make him back down.

"You hope to draw me into a conflict," he said, backing away. "No, I don't think so. Plans are already in motion to deal with you. I have waited too long, sacrificed too much to risk it all for the joy of killing an ignorant Ose. I will take my leave, but... to show that I am a generous host, I will leave you a parting gift." The man in the mask drew out a bone dagger with a leather-wrapped hilt, and for an instant, Vesper tensed, thinking he was about to attack. Instead, he drew the blade along his open palm, and his blood snaked out in a torrent, circling him in a whirling vortex of crimson and black that hid him from view. Then, before she could react, he exploded like a dark star, and she found herself stumbling in an unnatural darkness that burned her skin and stung her eyes.

Thinking quickly, Vesper poured Ase into the patterns decorating her skin, their normally blinding glow pushing back the cloying shadow that covered her. The man in the mask was gone, and in his place was a rippling doorway the color of midnight. Vesper peered into its dark surface, mesmerized by pinpricks of amber starlight that danced along its surface. At first, the lights appeared to be random, flickering in and out of existence, fireflies against the curtain of night, but the longer she stared, the more they bent and twisted, until finally, they took the shape of a woman made of dazzling light. "You look tired, child," said a voice that sent a shiver down her spine.

Vesper shook her head, backing away slowly while she clutched at her belly. "Magda?"

"Yes, child, it's good to know you haven't forgotten me so soon," said the voice in a tone that brought Vesper back to her childhood. To a simpler time when she didn't have a care in the world.

"No," she said, squeezing her eyes shut. "Magda is gone, dead. I can see your image in the tapestry of night when I look to the sky."

"And who showed you such wonders?" it said in a sweet tone. "Come with me and I can show you more. Take my hand, child, and I will teach you all you need to know."

Vesper's eyes shot open when the pinpricks of light shifted and swirled, and for a moment she recognized the kind eyes and warm smile, the gentle hands that would braid her hair ever so patiently. A glowing hand emerged from the pool of darkness, waving her closer, and in her heart, Vesper began to reach out with a trembling hand, wanting nothing except to once more be safe in her arms, to be protected from the harshness of the world. But just before she brushed the glowing tip of the hand, the image of Papa Jufari's spear piercing her chest flashed through her mind, and she remembered Magda's heartfelt goodbye as her spirit faded from existence, giving Vesper a chance at life when she was on the brink of death not so long ago. "No," she said softly, stepping back from the shimmering pool. "I don't know what you are, but you are not her. Magda is dead."

"Then you will die here!" screeched the voice, full of hate. "Trapped forever in the dream!"

The outstretched hand curled into a claw, and Vesper leapt back as the midnight shade emerged fully from the pool of shadow, its body shimmering like the curtain of night, while streaks of light danced along its surface. It shot toward her, its talons digging into her flesh, leaving deep, bloodless gashes in her shoulder. Waves of despair rolled over her from the creature's touch, and she was suddenly overcome with doubt, regret, and guilt, every bad decision, every mistake filling her mind, and she wished for nothing more than the escape of death.

"I see your heart! So much pain for one so young," said the shade, its dark shape pulsing, growing as it lunged toward her for another attack. Vesper raised her arms defensively, but it brushed past them, tearing at her belly, shredding the hardened leather vest she often wore, a vest Narcissus had found for her. At the thought of the big Celt, the memory of him in that horrible place exploded in her thoughts once more, and the monster shuddered in ecstasy. "A feast of disappointment, of failures."

Watching the shade relish in her pain, Vesper grit her teeth, fanning a spark of anger in her belly. "I am more than my pain." She seethed, drinking in more power from the weave, stretching to her full height. The glow from the tattoos on her arms made the creature flinch, "I cannot control the bad things that happen to me, but I can control what I do." A memory from her battle with Saoterus echoed in her mind, and she remembered for an instant how she beat him. Weaving together the threads of Ase coursing through her, she wove a blade of pure light, bathing the garden in a pale glow.

"You are nothing, no one," said the shade, raising a hand protectively from the light. "A failure!"

Vesper took a step forward with the glowing blade in hand, and the creature fell back. "I have known pain, but also joy. Family and friends," she said, slashing and cutting, hacking at its limbs. "I have stood against the Sandawei, against Roman gladiators, and even to the dead. And I have been victorious."

The creature screamed, a pitiful wail that drew a great swell of pity from Vesper's heart, and for a moment she relented, lowering her blade of light. "Luck and lies," it whispered, repeating her own doubts, while its claws stretched toward her. "Like the fat doctore, they never cared for you."

The claws were a hairsbreadth from her face when Vesper roared, slicing off the tips of the vile creature's hands, before ducking under its reach, and plunging the weapon into its heart. "You are not real," she said, fighting against the despair pouring out of the dying shade. "You cannot hurt me. You cannot hurt me."

With the glowing blade deep in its chest, the shade began to fade, vanishing like morning mist against the rising sun. It was almost gone when It clutched at Vesper's arms, its icy claws digging into soft flesh as it leaned in close. "You will forever be alone," it whispered. "Your power will consume you, just like your mother before you... forever alone, forever alone."

"I will not," shouted Vesper with a shuddering breath, tearing her blade from the shade's fading form and plunging it deep once more. "I will not."

The portal, the shade, even the garden began to fade away, and Vesper's heart skipped a beat, terrified that she would be trapped here. Turning away, she raced blindly through the garden at a breakneck pace, hunting for a way out through thick brush that slapped against her skin and tore at her flesh. She had almost given up hope when she found the path once more, only to collapse to her knees when she saw the same bench. The boy's body appeared to be long gone, but a stain of dried crimson remained, a reminder of the horrible things that had happened on this spot. The garden and everything in it was almost gone when Vesper felt a tug at her midsection, and she looked down to see the silver cord stretching off in the distance. Like a drowning woman she grasped for the cord, shuddering in relief when the world around her shifted and streaked, spinning and twisting until everything was still once more.

"Vesper—Vesper, are you all right?" said Lucilla's familiar voice. "You were crying out."

Her entire body shook, and she opened her eyes to find herself once more in Lucilla's bed, wrapped in soft silk sheets, while the patrician woman looked on, worried. She nodded, trying to piece it all together, trying to remember every moment in the garden. The old matron and the boy. Lucilla offered her a cup, and she drank deeply, coughing when she realized it was wine and not water. "Gratitude," she said at last, swallowing the last sip of the dry, tangy vintage.

"The wine should help with your nerves," said Lucilla. "Try and go back to sleep; morning is a long way off."

"We can't. We have to tell someone, anyone who will listen," said Vesper, throwing the soft sheets off.

"Listen, listen to what?"

"The Sandawei," she said, hugging herself. "They are here; they've always been here, and now one of them is a powerful Roman, hiding in plain sight, waiting to land the killing blow."

FIFTEEN
WEAKNESS

"Defeat begins in your mind," boomed Narcissus, slamming his meaty shoulder into the wooden shield of the attacking gladiator, the mighty blow sending his opponent tumbling face-first onto the burning sands. "Long before an enemy's blade kills you, defeat will pierce your heart, rob you of your strength, stealing any hope for victory." Without missing a beat, Narcissus pounced and was almost on top of the fallen man when another pair attacked. Verus and Attilus, men he had known for years, men who he had trained from raw recruits. Verus was a dimachaerus, fighting with a pair of wooden swords, foregoing a shield for the powerful offense of a second blade, which in the right hands, was devastating. Attilus preferred a buckler and spear, better known as a hoplomachus. He fought just behind Verus's right, taking advantage of his blunted spear's long reach while using the other man to conceal parts of his attack.

"Your hunger for victory has left you open to defeat," said Verus, slipping in low with a double-bladed thrust, mocking Narcissus with the very words he often spoke to new recruits when giving them their first lesson in humility.

"And you overreach, my friend," said Narcissus, spinning to his right to avoid the wooden blades, then with a meaty hand, chopping Verus on the back of the neck as he glided past him. The dimachaerus tumbled to the dirt, unmoving, and Narcissus found himself face-to-face with Attilus. The spear wielder flinched, clearly not expecting to be so exposed. Taking advantage of his hesitation, Narcissus charged in before he could recover, and once inside the man's defenses, used his greater height and strength, forcing his arms wide and then slamming his head into the bridge of his nose. Attilus staggered, shaking his head, defenses forgotten. With a smile, Narcissus gripped the smaller man by his leather vest and spun him in a circle, heaving him across the training yard.

The men watching the training sessions broke out into fits of laughter as they often did whenever Narcissus managed to throw anyone a fair distance. Verus was on his feet moments later with his training blades raised high, but Narcissus waved him off, bent in half with his hands on his knees while he struggled to catch his breath, his lungs burning like they were on fire. Narcissus had never felt this tired in his life, and part of him suspected that it was more than just the wine from the day before: the wine, for the life of him, he couldn't remember drinking.

"You look tired, Doctore," said Linus, shuffling over to his side and offering him a waterskin. "You have been at this since dawn. Perhaps it would be best to take a moment to have some water in the shade."

Narcissus snorted at the old gladiator, drinking deep from the offered container. "I will rest when I'm dead, my friend. Which will be all too soon if these fools keep fighting this way."

"They are not you, Doctore," said Linus, his face a mask of pain as he stood straight, twisting his back. "Not all men are as disciplined, or as driven. Most simply fight to survive another day, no more."

"I don't think you understand, old friend," he said, casting side-long glances at the assembled men while they laughed, his blood starting to boil the more they mocked Attilus. "I don't think any of them do."

Linus glanced at the men and then back at the big man, the crow's feet in the corner of his eyes crinkling as he smiled. "Something tells me you intended to teach them."

Narcissus stretched to his full height, uncoiling the well-worn whip on his hip. "You all think this is funny," he shouted, the crack of his whip overhead silencing the laughter. "In three days' time, we will face a challenge that few have ever known... and you jest and pass denarii like it shall be a day like any other. It will not! Now, assemble, line up. I will make you understand what we face."

"Yes, Doctore!" they all shouted in unison, racing to do as told.

"In three days' time, we will face off against the emperor's chosen champions for the privilege of executing a sitting senator," he said, strolling down the line of assembled gladiators, his whip coiled comfortably in his hand. "Every gladiator in Rome will be fighting for the privilege, meaning you may very well be facing the man to your left or right... or even me! If you hope to survive, you must have discipline. Long before an enemy's blade kills you, this lack of discipline you've shown today will rob you of your strength, stealing not only any hope for victory, but your life." He spoke to the men as much as to himself. Angry, that for some reason he had lost his way, his focus that had kept him alive all these years, and somehow he seemed to have lost it. He had spent a fitful night struggling to piece together yesterday's events, only to find nothing. His memory was blank, and he couldn't remember how he ended up in such a vile place, and worse, he couldn't remember having even a sip of wine. When he had finally fallen into a fitful sleep, he was plagued by bizarre dreams. Dreams of insects crawling all over him and being lost in the other place, the voices of the dead wailing in the distance, calling his name. When the light of the morning sun finally found him, it was like he hadn't slept, but he was grateful for it to be away from the horrors of the night.

"Yes, Doctore!" shouted the assembled gladiators in unison, snapping him from his thoughts.

Shaking away the burning fatigue in his eyes, he continued, "In the arena, you will face death and the end of your wretched lives, but worse than death you will face fear. Fear is the harbinger of defeat" he said, drawing in a deep breath of hot air that burnt his nostrils, "Fear is what we will learn about today, how to control it so that it does not control you. In the end I will teach you to embrace it, and ultimately you will learn to empower yourself beyond your limits."

"Yes, Doctore," they shouted once more, many of the men puffing out their chests, pride filling their eyes.

"The emperor has decreed that I fight alone, and I do not expect to live, but I will make a good death of it. But I expect better of you. I intended for every man I have trained to live, so we will all need to train harder, better. And if any of us fall, we will give them a death they will speak of from one corner of the empire to the other!"

Many of the men fell silent, some bowing their heads.

"Now, pair up, begin with advanced forms. I will call on you for testing once more." With a nod from him, the men dispersed. The older, more experienced gladiators matching up with the younger recruits. When Narcissus had come to the ludus as a boy, it was not so. The newer slaves were given the basic drills but then left to face off against one another, while the more experienced men trained against their peers. He had learned with time that it was a poor way of teaching. The experienced men fell into easy routines, never seeing their bad habits until they had a sword in their bellies. It was worse with the newer men; in fighting with those at their skill level, they rarely advanced, and few survived their first matches. He changed that when he became doctore, and it had born fruit. Teaching gave the more experienced men a unique perspective, and some of their wisdom was passed on to the new men: as such, the Ludus Magnus now produced the finest gladiators in the empire.

"Has the emperor gone mad?" said Linus with a grimace on his face as he stretched his back.

"I am fairly certain he was mad before this," he said, eyeing the old gladiator's shuffling gait, worrying over the pained look on his face. "Are you all right? Your back seems more bent than normal."

"It is nothing, Doctore. The weather is turning, and the rains will come soon; I feel it in my bones," he said, again stretching out his back with a groan. "But may I ask a private question?"

Narcissus frowned, already knowing the question. "She is with Lady Lucilla," he said.

"But why?" asked Linus.

"I've never known you to be so nosy, old man," growled Narcissus, scratching at his beard and ignoring the question. The last thing he wanted to talk about was her.

The old gladiator frowned at him. Deepening the lines on his leathery face, "Answer the question, Doctore. Where is the girl, why did she not return with you, and who is the woman who has taken up residence in the main barracks, and why does she look so familiar?"

"By the gods... s-she is in the main cell?" he stammered, knowing how brutal some of the men could be. "Is she well?"

"Yes, but no one has touched her. Even that Lugo, that vile German has stayed clear of her," said Linus, looking up at him expectantly.

Grinding his teeth, Narcissus gripped tightly to his whip, wanting nothing more than to lash out. Instead, he met the old man's gaze and slowly breathed out. "That attack on the market yesterday had unintended consequences," he began in a halting tone, searching for his words, "and as a result, Vesper returned with Lady Lucilla to her villa. As to the woman, she is... her mother, and a dangerous creature at that. Tell the men to stay away from her."

Linus looked at him like he was a fool, shaking his head in disbelief. "Something about her frightens the men, so I doubt it will be a problem... but Vesper's mother? Is she not dead?" asked Linus, blowing out his cheeks. "And while I am an old man, Doctore, I still have my wits about me. Only a fool would believe such a tale. Come up with a better story before I challenge you on the sands and beat the truth out of you."

"I have had enough of this," he snorted, walking away from the old man. "Bring me my armor, and then bring steel for the men I call out."

"Doctore?" said Linus, shuffling behind him with a frown. "What's this all about?"

"You won't stop digging, will you, Linus?"

"No, Doctore," he said, "and if I looked as you do now, would you not press me just as hard?"

"I suppose not," said Narcissus, sighing, resting a heavy hand on the old man's shoulder. "You have been a loyal friend, so it is best you know.

Narcissus told him about the incident in the brothel, about the holes in his memory. To his surprise, Linus only nodded. "Matters of the heart are difficult, but I'm sure she will come around," he said, giving him an odd look, "but if you say she is with Lucilla, that she is safe, well, that's good enough for me."

"Good," he grunted, letting out a deep sigh. "Now, get me my armor. The day is not done yet, not by a long shot."

Linus didn't move, instead staring up at him with an odd look on his wrinkled face, staring as if Narcissus was a prized bull. "Another question, Doctore," he said at last, nodding to himself as if he came to a decision.

"Why are you looking at me that way, old man?" asked Narcissus.

"A plan, Doctore, an old one concocted by drunken gladiators long ago."

"Well, spit it out, man," he said, having little patience left, knowing that if he stopped moving, he might never start again.

"Patience, Doctore, I will return in a moment," said Linus, motioning for him to wait while he gathered together with a few of the older men, murmuring among themselves, nodding and whispering in low tones. After a few tense moments, Linus waved them off with hard looks. Stepping forward, the old gladiator cleared his throat. "I have lived long enough to see such things before, Doctore, and we have waited and watched for an opportunity."

"Opportunity? What in the name of the gods are you talking about, man?"

Linus moved in closer, lowering his voice so that only he could hear. "There will be men from every ludus in the city, many more in the Colosseum than normal," he said, the men around him nodding. "We will take advantage of this; plans were made years ago, and now... now we have a chance to see them through. If we have the courage to risk it all."

"He who risks nothing, wins nothing," he said automatically, looking around to see if any of the guards on the periphery were close enough to be listening. "Perhaps it would be best if we spoke in private, and you can explain what madness you intend."

———

After his conversation with Linus, Narcissus was still at a loss to understand it all and stalked the corridors of the ludus to clear his head. He was seeing the old gladiator in a whole different light after their tense conversation in the barracks, and his head was still spinning. A wise warrior knew the value of patience and when to throw patience aside in relentless pursuit of victory. And after listening to the plan Linus had laid out, he understood why his old friend had not left for a different life after his retirement, that Linus was patient beyond measure, bold beyond madness. Before he had even had a chance to think about it, he had agreed, prepared to risk it all on a single act, a single roll of the dice. "Crazy fool," he muttered under his breath, still in shock.

"Who is the fool?" whispered Lillith, emerging from around a blind corner to fall in beside him.

"Jupiter's beard!" he swore, flinching away from her. "You could frighten a man to death like that."

"I have better ways to kill a man than with fright," said Lillith, throwing back her head in laughter.

"Enough of that," he growled, wanting to shake her, instead

crossing his arms across his massive chest. "I was looking for you. I need—"

"I'm flattered," said Lillith, speaking over him, "but after yesterday I'm surprised you have the energy... but if you insist, I'm sure we can find a dark corner."

"We did not!" He seethed. "Nor would I ever."

Lillith gave him a brilliant smile, reaching out to touch his chest. "No, we didn't, but if you have such an appetite, I would be inclined."

He recoiled at her touch, his belly churning with nausea. "Never touch me; never come close to me," he said, slapping her hand away. "I don't know what you did to me, but it will be the last time."

She backed away, clutching at her hand and feigning hurt. "Oh, so you are as Nabil called you, a Celtic sheep lover," she laughed, "or have you been in Rome so long that you have become a boy lover."

Narcissus showed her his teeth, snarling like a feral dog, "Just because I don't enjoy laying with whores, does not make me a boy lover. I wish for a proper wife, with a proper hearth. Nothing more... not that it's any of your affair."

Lillith's smile vanished, and she stepped in closer to him as if daring him. "Fine... what is it you wanted from me?"

"Linus told me you were sleeping in the general barracks: it's not safe. I will ask the dominus to provide you with your own cell."

The dark-skinned woman's brow shot up, her brilliant smile returning. "No, I don't think so. I will stay with the men; they satisfy my needs."

"But—"

Lillith came in closer, almost touching him but keeping her hands at her sides. "If anyone steps out of line, I will... take care of it, like your friend Lugo back there," she said, pointing with her thumb over her shoulder. "Now, if you will step out of my way, I must go see to my daughter."

Narcissus stepped aside, and she gave him a coy smile as she walked by. She had almost vanished down the tunnel when her words rang in his head, and he raced back to the main barracks where most of the men slept. Slamming open the door, he found nothing out of order in the wide cell. The thin cots were laid out of the floor as normal, and a single guttering oil lamp lit the windowless barracks. Shaking his head, he turned to leave when he caught a glimpse of a crumpled-up form in the corner of the room. "Lugo, is that you?" he said, dashing to pick up the lamp from a corner of the room where the men often diced.

Kneeling beside the still form, he cursed under his breath when he recognized Lugo's blond, braided hair that fell down past his shoulders. The rest of him was a thing of nightmare, his pale skin was blackened and burnt, and in some spots bleached bone poked through. The worst of it was his chest: his leather vest had been torn open, and at the center, just above his heart was a sunken handprint, too small to be a man's.

Narcissus shuddered, remembering how close she had come to him, in that moment a memory hitting him like a bolt of lightning, a memory of Lillith's hand on his chest, right before he woke up with no memory. Throwing down the lamp, he tore open the leather armor he wore, tearing at the straps, his heart beating in panic. There, just as she had done to poor Lugo, was a mark of her hand, burnt into his chest.

SIXTEEN
THE WALLS OF DANUBE

"I thought we had agreed to forget this foolishness," said her husband, placing his hands flat on the cool marble of the table. "It's bad enough you take a gladiator to bed! Next, you will have a troupe of actors living in my house."

"It's nothing like that, Husband," said Lucilla, tossing a quick glance at Vesper, who sat at the edge of the table with her arms wrapped around herself. "This was simply the safest place for her, given the day's events."

"I am going to have the slave who let that idiot Magnus into the house yesterday whipped!" said Tiberius, stepping away from the table, then pointing to a timid girl in the corner, who could not have been more than twelve winters. "You, bring me wine, nothing watered. A strong red, from the clay pots in the cold room."

"The Sandawei are very real, and very dangerous," said Vesper, rubbing sleep from her eyes.

"They attacked in force yesterday. They were organized and if—"

"You don't think I know?" said Tiberius, starting to pace. "I was chief general to Marcus Aurelius, and consul... more than once. I still get reports of the goings-on in the city... and the empire."

"Then you know that we must act!" said Lucilla, meeting his gaze with a pleading expression.

Tiberius bowed his head, pushing out his lower lip. "Act how? Hmm..."

"We must tell the senate; get them to assign you a military command so that you can—"

"With what proof, Lucilla? Do you have a name, or even a face? Did you remember where this garden was, which house? No, you don't!" he said, answering for her. "All we have is some dream... and from a gladiator, no less. I will not risk my name or my legacy over such things. History will not remember me as a fool!"

"Husband—"

Tiberius raised a hand to silence her. Sighing, he returned to the table, sitting across from Vesper. "Young lady, make no mistake. I believe you," he began, bowing his head in thought before continuing, "I was with Marcus during the Parthian War; your mother was with us for much of the campaign. To this day I still remember the destruction of an Armenian city, Artashat, if I remember correctly. Your mother did something to the ballista; I cannot say what, but wherever our stones struck, it burned. By nightfall, the entire city had burned to the ground, leaving nothing but blackened rubble that smoked for days afterward.

"So you understand, about Ase, about Djambe, and the Ose."

Tiberius nodded, looking old and weary. "Yes, I didn't at first, but after that battle, she explained it all over a few cups of wine... And I understood why Marcus kept her at his side." he finished with a shrug.

"If you believe, then why not do something?" said Lucilla, leaning forward on the table.

"Because Romans are practical people," he snorted, rapping his knuckles on the table. "We only believe in things we can see, feel, and touch."

Lucilla sat back, her shoulders slumping. Not so long ago, she would have made the same argument. Most of her life had been spent focusing on position and legacy; this was the way life was in Rome, where station was all that mattered. But with all she had seen in the last year, it was no longer enough. "I understand, Tiberius, I do. But I fear the time to sit aside has past. We must commit to protecting our home, our way of life, or we may lose it."

"You doubt the most powerful fighting force in the world?" said Tiberius. "Rome is—"

"It is not invincible," said Lucilla. "Yesterday proved that. The barbarians were not in some far-off, distant land. They were here. In the western market!"

The timid slave girl squeaked into the room with her husband's wine, running in and out of the room like a frightened mouse. Tiberius looked grateful for the distraction and sipped the wine, tapping a finder on the table, before at last shaking his head. "I cannot help you," he said, looking directly at Vesper. "The men of the senate fear that Commodus will seize their lands if they go against him, and so do I, for that matter. I told you, Lucilla, let someone else take this risk; let someone else lose their head. We will go to the country and wait for this to all be over."

Lucilla stood, pressing her lips together. "You can go and hide. I will remain and fight."

Tiberius glared at her, gripping his cup tightly. "Do not embarrass us, or me," he said at last, downing the rest of his wine in a single gulp. He stood to leave just as the slave girl ran back in, squeaking in his ear. His face grew redder by the moment the longer she spoke.

"What's wrong?" asked Lucilla, putting a hand on her stomach.

"In all my years," he mumbled, running a trembling hand through his shock of white hair and straightening his tunic, "it seems that Vesper has a visitor."

"Visitor?" said Lucilla. "No one knows she's here.

"I do!"

"Lillith," said Lucilla, smiling as the dark-skinned woman glided into the room as if she owned the villa. She looked regal despite only wearing a simple tunic, and without a word, went to her husband, wrapping her arms around him in a warm embrace.

"Tiberius!" Lillith said, holding him at arm's length. "Still handsome, even for a Syrian!"

Lucilla's jaw fell open when her husband, instead of bristling, actually blushed, a boyish grin spreading across his face. "And you're still beautiful for a provincial witch!"

"Mother," said Vesper as Lillith and Tiberius fell over one another laughing, "what... what are you doing here? Did something happen at the ludus?"

"Oh, don't worry about your Celt. I've taken good care of him," she said, plucking the wineglass from Tiberius and motioning for the timid slave girl in the corner to fill it.

"They told us you were dead," he said. "You look like you haven't aged a day!"

"You wouldn't believe me if I told you," said Lillith, "but it's been a long road home, best not spoken of. I see that you finally found a wife worthy of your charms."

"Lucilla is a good woman, brash at times, but she keeps me young."

Lucilla's face reddened at the way they talked to one another. She had only known Tiberius in his later years, long after his campaigning days were behind him, and had always found him somber, even boorish, but when Lillith spoke to him, he lit up in a way she had never seen him, looking at the Ose woman with a passion he had never shown her, his wife."

"Answer Vesper's question: why are you here, Lillith?" she said, crossing her arms.

Lillith squeezed her husband's hands once more, winking at him in an impish way. "Don't worry, Little Empress, I am not here for your handsome Syrian, but for my daughter."

At the mention of her, Vesper's eyes narrowed, and she rubbed her palms against her knees. "Why?"

"Because, dear Daughter, I am not going to let you die in the arena like some common slave. With my help, you will learn what you need to lay these savages to waste. I will show you what true power is, to teach you all that you need to know."

SEVENTEEN
LESSONS

Vesper sat cross-legged, mesmerized by the beautiful lines of her mother's face, an odd sense of déjà vu washing over her. Everything about her mother felt that way, almost as if they had done this all before. She had resisted at first, still not trusting her mother, or herself, but it was Tiberius, of all people, who had convinced her. Explaining that she had nothing to lose as her life was already forfeited, and that she was doomed to the arena in only a few days.

"What do you see, child?" said Lillith, her hands moving with a deft confidence as she drew a cross on the dark earth in front of them. Lillith had asked Tiberius for a quiet space, away from prying eyes, and he had generously offered the villa's garden which, despite the small size for a city home, was private enough that Vesper felt like they were in a world all their own.

"I'm not sure: a memory, maybe something that happened long ago," said Vesper, hesitating as her mother added three straight lines above the drawing, transforming the crude cross into a trident. "It feels like we've done this before."

Lillith smiled her brilliant smile, her white teeth glowing against her smooth, dark skin. "Very good, Daughter. This is the true power of the chosen, of the Djambe. We see the future, the past. We are meant to use this knowledge to guide our people, to keep them safe."

"I don't understand."

"You will. Now quiet yourself while I finish this. It will be your first step to acquiring the tools you need to survive," said Lillith, her eyes narrowing in concentration.

"I don't see what drawing in the dirt will do to help me avoid having a gladius in my belly."

Lillith then drew a circle on each end of the cross, making the trident appear to have a guard and hilt. "Have the dreams started?" she asked in a light tone. "I was about your age when they did."

Vesper leaned back as a chill ran through her, the memory of the red-skulled Sandawei and the shade fresh in her mind. "Yes," she said in a small voice, wondering how her mother would know of such things.

"Good," said Lillith, drawing another line at the base of the trident, underneath its hilt. "Pay attention to them. They often come in times of dire need, of great conflict."

Digesting her mother's words, another memory flashed through her mind, a dream she had just before the Sandawei attacked her village, the night when her aunt fell to Jufari's spear. "You used to do this with Magda, didn't you?" said Vesper. "Sit face-to-face like this."

"Yes," said Lillith, glancing up from the symbol she was drawing as beads of sweat formed on her temples. "We often played mancala, an old game played with stones, squirreled away in some part of the village, or in our parents tent when we traveled as a family."

"And you always cheated," said Vesper.

Her mother's brow shot up in surprise, not bothering to look up. "Your aunt and I were very different. Our parents raised us in the spirit of Omoluwabi, that the chosen were children of Olodumare, and must be people of good character, honest, hardworking, and above all, respecting others."

"And you did not think this way, or accept that lesson," said Vesper, shaking her head, already knowing the answer.

Her mother sighed, holding her palm over the drawing in the dirt. "No, and wipe that look of judgment off your face," she said as a shadow passed over the drawing and it began to darken. "I was raised to be a warrior! Destined to fight and defend our people. As such I never had the luxury of seeing the world as only black and white. Good or evil."

"No, it is simple! There is good and evil, no more."

Lillith threw back her head, her mocking laughter filling the garden. "Oh, my dear, you have much to learn," she snorted, putting a hand on her chest as she tried to catch her breath.

Vesper ground her teeth, uncrossing her legs and moving to leave. "You have, no matter how many times I try, you're always the same," she began. "Selfish to the core, only thinking of yourself."

Her mother's laughter stopped abruptly as Vesper stood, and she motioned for her to sit. "I'm sorry. Please sit, stay," she said hurriedly. "I forget myself sometimes."

"What is all of this supposed to do?" said Vesper, pushing back her anger with a sigh while casting a weary glance at the symbol her mother had drawn.

"You'll see, it won't be long now," said Lillith, holding both hands above the symbol. "Can you answer a question... while we wait?"

Choking back harsh words, Vesper sat once more, adjusting her tunic so it covered her thighs. "You may."

"Is a man who murders, evil?" she asked, raising her chin. "Is a man who steals, a criminal?"

Vesper narrowed her eyes, her lips turning down in a frown. "I am not a fool, Mother. I understand that sometimes you must cross the line for the greater good. That does not justify your behavior. You—"

"Who decides where the line is?" said Lillith, raising finger. "When is murder good? When is it evil?"

"I—" began Vesper, her voice catching in her throat. "I cannot be sure, but murder and thievery must be exceptions, not the rule."

"You are wise, Daughter," she said as the garden around them grew darker, falling deeper into shade. "Rule of law is important in society, or even in a game. But what happens when your opponent does not play by the same rules... What happens when you think you are playing one game, but they another?"

Vesper's breath caught in her throat when the garden faded from view, along with the light, until it was only the pair of them, alone in the darkness. "What did you do, Mother?"

"Answer the question."

Licking her lips, she opened herself to the weave, grasping for Ase, for power as her heart beat out of her chest. "I don't care! Life is not a game," she gasped, shocked when she found nothing, only emptiness, the weave gone.

Lillith stood, her hands balling into fists as she peered out into the darkness as a cold wind kicking up all around them. "What happens if your opponent has no honor, and you face false accusations, and are unjustly enslaved?"

"Mother, please," said Vesper, as the ground's icy coolness numbed her bottom, spreading up her spine until her bones ached. "Stop this!"

"What happens if your opponent steals your land and murders your children?" Lillith was seething, shouting over the icy wind. "Do you keep playing by the same rules? Do you play the game until you're broken and beaten?!"

"I don't know," said Vesper, screaming to be heard over the cacophony filling her ears.

"You cheat! You break the rules!" shouted Lillith, pulling Vesper to her feet. "That's what you do. Because history is written by the victors! Because those who lose a war are always cast as the villain in the tale, no matter how good or fair you were in reality. In defeat, you are damned for all eternity!"

"By Olodumare... where have you brought us?" said Vesper,

shrinking in on herself as she eyed the endless planes of blue gray that stretched across the horizon for as far as the eye could see.

"This is a world of the damned," said her mother, squatting down and scooping up a handful of ashen sand, and then letting the loose dust fall between her fingers. "One of many."

"You mean the place in between? This doesn't look like anything I remember."

Lillith stood, dry-washing her hands. "No, Vesper, look up. This is one of the many places beyond the weave, where the damned and doomed linger for all eternity. Poor, forgotten souls without hope."

Vesper's jaw fell open when she saw the sky was filled with a bright whirlpool of stars, circling a massive sphere of infinite blackness, while jets of light erupted from its surface. "Take me back... please."

"We are not going back," said Lillith. "I have a bargain to fulfil, and a lesson to teach you."

Vesper bared her teeth, instinctively drawing on the well of Ase in her own blood to weave a gladius of pure light, pointing the blade to within a hairsbreadth of her mother's face. "I should have listened to Narcissus. You can never be trusted."

In response, Lillith smiled brilliantly, singing under her breath while swaying to a song only she could hear. A tremor of fear shook Vesper to the core, when all around them humanoid shapes erupted from the ground, their forms composed of the blue-gray sand, the faceless creatures swaying in unison to Lillith's movements. "Perhaps," said Lillith, "but it's too late for that. Now move!"

Vesper adjusted her stance, intending to use the glowing blade to cut her way through and find some way to escape, but Lillith made a vague gesture with her hand, and one of the faceless creatures seized her arms. Their touch sent waves of numbing cold shooting through her body, shattering her concentration while freezing her to the bone. Fighting for breath, she managed to channel some of the limited well of power in her blood to enhance her waning strength, pulling away from creature's grip and spinning like a dervish while her glowing blade slashed through the ashen limbs just as easily as flesh and bone. Her vicious attacks driving the creatures back with deft cuts and brutal strikes. "I must be the most foolish person in history," she said, cleaving a path to her mother.

Lillith's laughter echoed across the barren plain when just as quickly as Vesper severed the reaching limbs, they regrew. "You can't win, Daughter," shouted Lillith, increasing the tempo of her song so more of the creatures appeared. "The dead are beyond counting. Stop your foolishness!"

"And do what? Let you steal my life!" said Vesper, cutting one of the faceless creatures in half, and then using her enhanced strength to leap over the rest surrounding her. She landed in front of Lillith, once again placing the burning tip of her blade to her throat. "I don't think so."

"Impressive," she said, her smile never wavering as the ash beneath Vesper's feet came to life, crawling over them and up her legs, locking her in an iron vice. "But you lack imagination." Gritting her teeth through the pain, Vesper flipped the blade to cut away at the growing bonds, when once again the creatures lunged for her, taking hold of her arms and trapping her in place.

"Why are you doing this?" she shouted, straining until the veins in her forehead felt like they were going to burst.

"This for your own good... mine as well."

"I find that hard to believe," said Vesper, breathing hard while continuing to twist in a vain effort to escape.

"You are going to have to trust that if all goes as planned today, no harm will come to you, and we will both survive to see tomorrow.

"That's our history... isn't it?" she said, shivering uncontrollably. "I trust you—you betray me. Again and again. Because you'll do anything to win... to survive."

"Survival is the most important lesson I can teach you," said Lillith in a solemn tone, "because while you still breathe, anything is possible... even convincing your wayward daughter that you have her best interests at heart."

Vesper rolled her eyes, frowning at her. "You ask for the impossible. Each time I trust you, I pay for it with a little piece of my heart, my soul."

"Well then," said Lillith, her smile vanishing, "you have a choice. You can hope that my words are true, and that I have a plan, or..."

"Or what?" said Vesper.

Her mother shrugged, glancing up at the sky. "There are worse places to spend eternity. At least the view will be spectacular."

Looking around at the endless plane and whirlpool of stars, Vesper searched for another option, a way home, like the cobblestone path in the place in between, but there was nothing. This place was too alien, too bizarre, and without her connection to the weave, she doubted she could survive long. "I don't have a choice... just as you intended," she said, locking eyes with her mother.

"A wise choice, Daughter," she said, rubbing her hands together like she had just won a throw of the dice, "one that you won't regret."

"But you will!" said Vesper, the cold touch of the dead numbing her to the point that a calmness fell over her, and her vision was clearer than it had ever been.

"I regret nothing. I am doing this for—"

"The greater good... I know," said Vesper as the ash binding her fell away, her flesh tingling as feeling returned. "But after today, if I survive, I want you to go."

"Go where?" said Lillith, raising an eyebrow. "You mean you don't want to learn? You don't need me to teach you? No, that would be a fool's bargain. You need—"

"Then I will be a fool," she said, flexing her fingers and rubbing her hands together. "Your way, will not be my way. I will not be you. I will not be the monster you became."

Lillith cocked her head, tapping a finger against her full lips before finally shrugging. "Very well, but you may change your mind once you see what we face. Once you understand."

They resumed their march, and Vesper did her best to ignore her mother's stare, saying nothing while focusing on putting one foot in front of the other through the bizarre landscape, thinking of how far she'd come from her simple days playing in the baobab tree and running errands for her aunt around their village. Part of her wondered what would have happened if things turned out differently, and by some twist of fate, the Sandawei hadn't attacked that fateful night. What kind of life would she have; who would she be if she didn't have to grow up so fast, if she did not have to live with the constant danger and fear of death that was part of her days now. She just managed to lose herself in a fantasy where Jufari had never come to their village and taken her away, when one of the faceless drifted closer, and for a heartbeat its features bent and twisted into the menacing dark eyes and angular nose of the wicked vodun she had been just thinking of, then just as quickly, it shifted again, returning to the blank visage.

"By Olodumare," she cursed over her shoulder, sucking in a deep breath to control her racing heart, "did you see that!"

Lillith hesitated, her eyes darting in all directions. "What did you see?"

"The shade, just for a moment. It was Jufari... the Sandawei vodun who killed Magda."

Her mother nodded, eyeing the faceless forms that guided them. "It's best not to let your mind wander in this place. Your thoughts can have dangerous consequences."

"Was it really him?" she asked, swallowing hard.

"No, just a reflection of your thoughts, your fears."

"Fears?" she said, blinking in disbelief. "Don't you think I've enough horror to deal with, that you need to bring me to such a terrible place and frighten me half to death?" said Vesper.

"Death is your burden, you must learn to live with fear. To embrace it, or it will destroy you."

"What about hope?"

"Hope is for fools and children," said Lillith, silencing her with a raised hand. "We are here."

Vesper's eyes narrowed in confusion when she looked around,

finding only the same endless planes of gray-blue ash. "There's nothing here, just more—" She took another step, and suddenly the lifeless terrain vanished, replaced by a sloping path that descended to a narrow valley that wasn't there moments before. She gawked when she saw that the ground here was different, matching the sky in a river of glowing stars against a dark velvet cloth that stretched onward to a narrow road that ran through the valley. "It's like walking among the stars," she said at last, the cold in her bones vanishing as her blood pumped with excitement.

"It is the second most beautiful thing I have ever seen," said Lillith in agreement, motioning for her to follow as she descended along the path.

Vesper followed, gingerly at first, the terrain beyond smooth, while a warmth spread through her with every step. "What is this place?" she asked in a quiet voice, worried that her words would echo in such a strange place.

Her mother glanced at her over her shoulder, giving her a small shake of the head. "No one knows for sure, but some of the chosen have claimed that this is where Olodumare created the world, and the first loa meant to guide our people."

After only a short decent, they were deep in the valley, its towering walls stretching high above them, while scattered across the valley floor were massive trees with thick trunks and wide canopies of branches, trees that brought a smile to her face. "Baobabs," she said, drinking in their sweet smell. A sense of peace coming over her.

"Yes. The great baobabs spread the first life to our world," said her mother, bowing her head. "They only exist here now; the ones in our world are offshoots, man's attempts to mimic the hand of the great god. Small by comparison."

"The one at the heart of our village was the last," said Vesper, her gaze lost in the sprawling branches above her. "Burned by the Romans, after the Sandawei—"

"I told you we would see each other again soon," shouted a

hollow voice, drawing Vesper's attention away from the ancient trees to a lone figure lingering near the base of one.

Vesper shook her head, her stomach turning over as if she'd been kicked in the belly. "History repeats once again," she said to her mother, shaken to her core yet outwardly staying calm. There, at the base of the tree, was the Roman in the red mask, its garish yellow teeth almost smiling as Lillith took her by the arm, leading her to him like a lamb to the slaughter.

EIGHTEEN

REFLECTIONS

"Why not just kill me?" said Vesper, bowing her head as they walked toward him, too tired, too heartbroken to resist Lillith tugging her along. "Why drag me to this place; why not simply do it in Rome?"

"Power," he said without hesitation, drawing a bone dagger that hung off his hip. "You Ose swim in so much of it, you forget the rest of us are denied the touch of the weave."

"Olodumare cut the Sandawei off from the weave long ago," she mumbled, remembering a lesson from her Aunt Magda, "so you had to find other sources of Ase."

"The planes of the dead and damned offer power enough for some things, but that power has limits," he said, eyeing her with a hungry glare as they drew closer to him. "You are the last of the Ose who can draw Ase from the weave. I intend to take what is yours and make it mine, so that at long last the Sandawei will have the power to restore our rightful place in the world as kings and conquerors." Coming closer, Vesper noticed that the baobab he stood under had jagged markings gouged into its trunk, similar to the ones the Ose used but twisted into odd patterns that made her stomach churn with nausea the longer she looked at them.

"And her," asked Vesper. "Did you somehow bring her back to the world of the living just to draw me in?"

The man in the red mask threw back his head in laughter, his high-pitched voice echoing strangely across the alien landscape. "No, she is an unintended consequence," he said, starting to unwrap the purple-trimmed toga he wore. "When I reached out through the worlds of the dead, to find a way for my people to touch the weave once more, imagine my surprise when I found one the Sandawei's greatest enemies, someone so connected to those who had unraveled so many of our plans."

"My spirit was as you left me, Daughter, lost in time, drifting between the worlds of the living and the dead. He found me somehow, wrapping me in the chains of his will."

"And you chose to betray your own blood... for what? For a chance at life again!" said Vesper, pushing her away, and to her surprise she let go. Stumbling away from her.

"Oh, it was not her choice," he said, pulling his tunic over his head so that he stood before them naked with only a white subligaculum covering his loins. "She had part of the knowledge I required, the location of this realm, but her thoughts were disjointed, and she still had the will to resist me. I solved that by bringing her back to our world... once I found a suitable vessel, of course."

"The Sandawei are masters of death," said Lillith, casting a hateful look at the man in the mask, "and this body is long dead, an empty shell held together by his will."

"The only Ase she has is what I give her. She is powerless, alive only as long as I will it."

Vesper frowned as she glanced around the strange valley, not understanding what was going on, "And this place," she said, wrinkling her nose in disgust at his scrawny body. "And why in the name of Olodumare are you naked?"

In response, he drew the bone dagger across his naked arm, a hollow grunt echoing from behind his mask. "Because here, in this place, what has been made, can be unmade," he said, carving jagged runes in his own flesh that mirrored those on the tree. "What was can be again!"

"Mother, please, don't let this happen," she said.

"Enough talk! Bring her here. I am eager to have what's mine."

"No!" said Lillith.

Vesper's head snapped around, a flutter of hope springing in her heart when her mother's face lit up with a self-satisfied smirk. "Mother?"

A loud snort escaped from behind the mask, and he pointed the dagger at them. "You Ose are truly weak. To come so far, only to falter now—such a waste." Dipping a finger into his already open wound, the red-masked Sandawei deftly traced a series of bizarre symbols in the air. Glowing runes that burned with blue flame appeared in the air in front of him, while in unison, he screeched vile words that made the hair on Vesper's arms stand on end.

Dark strands erupted from the tip of his dagger, at first flowing around him in a writhing aura, and then snaking out, stretching like clawing fingers toward Lillith, wrapping her in a cocoon of dark, pulsing filaments.

Lillith stood stock still, her brilliant smile never fading as the filaments tightened around her, coiling around her hands, arms and chest. "And you Sandawei are ever the fools, blinded by your hunger for power so that you'll believe anything."

"Shut up, witch," he shouted. "Do as I say, or I will take back what I gave you, and you can return to oblivion."

"Try it," said Lillith, ignoring the insult. "Prove how much of an idiot you are to trust. What did he call me—one of the greatest enemies of the Sandawei people."

"What's going on? What did I miss," asked Vesper, backing away from both of them.

"No, I controlled you completely," he shouted, shaking his head. "From the moment I touched your wretched soul, you were mine."

"All true," said Lillith, eyeing the writhing thread holding her in place, "but think for a moment—who brought you here? To this place where what is made can be unmade."

"It doesn't matter. Your defiance will not stop me from taking what I want. After I kill you, your daughter has little chance of resisting me. She cannot touch the weave here, not enough at any rate."

"Unless I draw Ase from somewhere else," said Lillith, raising an eyebrow. "A lifeline to sustain me."

"Impossible!" he said, his reedy voice inching higher.

"Is it?" Lillith began to laugh, a rich powerful laugh that made her entire body shake. Vesper's jaw fell open when the pulsing filaments holding her fell away, revealing motes of glowing amber flickering all around her, almost imperceptible at first, but then growing until it was bright enough to be reflected by the valley floor, shining like the stars above.

"Narcissus," said Vesper, covering her mouth to stifle a joyous shout when she saw the amber cord stretching out from her mother's torso, flowing upward and vanishing into the infinite maelstrom of stars, and then somehow reflecting back again, before finally connecting to her.

"A neat trick, Daughter," she said, smiling at their roundabout connection, "Somehow you managed to save me again, this time without even knowing it!"

"It won't save you," shouted the Sandawei, the writhing aura around him creeping toward them, drinking in all the light as it grew. "I will take what I have been promised, and leave you here to rot for all eternity."

"I don't think so," said Vesper, stepping in front of Lillith, her heart singing as she drew on every ounce of Ase in her blood, banishing the creeping dark with a glow so bright that the masked man flinched, raising a hand to cover his eyes.

Turning away from the light, he drew the bone dagger against the inside of his other forearm, then pressing the wounds together, he raised his bloody arms to the stars. "Eshu, father of the Sandawei, master deceiver. Grant me your boon. Give me your power so that I may destroy my enemies. In return, I offer my blood, my life, and my soul."

Vesper and Lillith shrunk back, locking eyes with each other as they waited for some calamity, some powerful loa to join with the masked Sandawei, but there was nothing, only the distant howling wind. "I guess he doesn't like you," she said as he continued to back away, wide eyed while holding the dagger out in front of him as they inched closer.

"I have heard that Sandawei men often have performance issues," said Lillith, pointing and laughing at his crotch. "And what loa would want to join with a skinny little thing like that?"

"Shut up," he said, looking more surprised than they were, his eyes darting in all directions. "I can still win. I can still—

"So what happens now?" said Vesper, speaking over him. "Did we win?"

Lillith smiled, stepping closer as he shrank back. "I guess so. Do you want to do—" the words had just left her mouth when the entire valley shook, and they staggered in unison, struggling to stay on their feet.

"I think we spoke too soon," said Vesper, weaving a gladius as she fell back. "I'm no expert, but a loa couldn't do this... could it?"

"Who knows," said Lillith, holding out an open palm over the ground. She whispered a word under her breath, and the glassy material beneath them twisted and bent, a portion of it flowing into her hand and forming a gladius made from its reflective. A moment later, a shield formed in the same way. "Olodumare created the first loa here; this is their home."

The floor beneath their feet heaved, once, twice, and then a final time, erupting in a geyser of glass, stone, and ash, hurling them high into the air. Thinking quickly, Vesper, channeled more of her meager stores of Ase into her limbs, enhancing her muscles, making her more flexible, and nimble. Twisting like a cat, she spun her body with the strength and skill of an Olympian. Gracefully landing on her feet, she spread her arms wide to keep her balance as she slid to a halt along the glass surface. Looking back, Vesper expected to see some monstrosity, some nightmare loa; instead, a shirtless compact man with tight-knit hair emerged from the thinning cloud of dust. He wore a mischievous grin on his handsome face, like he had a secret only he knew. His eyes were the same: large, expressive, and all knowing.

"Who in the name of Olodumare is that?" said Lillith, appearing at her side covered in grit and dust, echoing her thoughts.

"I don't know," said Vesper, a shiver running down her spine when he looked directly at her. "Whatever he is, it's not natural." He came at them then, moving with a grace and speed beyond anything human, landing a heavy boot into Lillith's chest, sending her reeling and tumbling away. Vesper blinked, and a blade covered in concentric Ose patterns appeared in his hand as he came in to strike. His weapon moving faster than the wind, hitting harder than stone, forcing her back on her heels as she desperately parried his heavy blows with her gladius. The rune-covered blade left deep notches on her own simple weapon, Vesper's hands numbing each time the weapons connected, with only adrenaline giving her the strength to hang on, if only just.

Desperate to turn the tide, Vesper channeled the Ase in her blood into a bright flash, hoping to blind her relentless attacker, only to curse when he ignored the blinding light, feinting to his left and then following back, tripping her with the back of his heel when she tried to follow. Falling hard on her bottom, she shifted back and forth, her heart beating out of her chest as she battled desperately from her back, barely holding back relentless attacks.

"Oh, come come, you can do better. Get up, show Eshu you be worth his time," he said in the halting, overpronounced accent of the Sandawei while dancing back with a twinkle of laughter in his eye.

"Just take them to the tree," said the masked Sandawei, strolling up beside the loa. "I'm tired of their Ose tricks."

Vesper's jaw fell open in surprise when the mischievous loa

backhanded the masked man, knocking out some of the yellowed teeth and sending him reeling to the ground. "You are not in your realm, human," he said with a sneer. "This be the home of the loa, where Olodumare gave us breath. I answer the call only to be in the presence of these fine beauties."

"What?" said Vesper, taken aback, scrambling away from him.

"You... you can't do that," said the Sandawei, getting to his feet. "I command the bargain.

Eshu glanced over his shoulder at him. "Maybe back in the world of the livin' you have some say, but here, you command nothing. The Ose Djambe do be right, and we have no bargain. I don't want nothin' from your skinny little body. You not even really one of us, just a half breed. Begone with ya! If I feel like it, I will call after I'm done." The loa waved his hand, and the protesting Sandawei vanished, fading like morning mist with the sunrise.

"Don't trust a word he says," said Lillith, taking a defensive stance over her, her breath coming in. "He is the master of lies."

"Oh, come come now! Eshu tells little fibs every now and again," said the loa with a laugh, spinning his sword with a flourish, "but my sweet words be good for a mortal's soul. Don't worry, you gonna have a good time with Eshu, a good time for sure."

In response Lillith raised her sword, resting the tip of her glass blade on the top of her shield. "Come any closer and I'll take your tongue," she said, motioning for Vesper to stand, with a toss of her head.

"Can our weapons even hurt him?" asked Vesper, getting to her feet, speaking low enough that only her mother could hear.

Lilith licked her lips, shaking her head ever so subtly, "I don't know, he's pure spirit here...like I was when you first found me in the other place."

Eshu put a hand over his heart, looking hurt, "You know, Eshu spends most of his time in the mortal world, tied up in human affairs. Doing his best to make you do things right, but I guess it might be fun to teach you ladies a more direct lesson."

Vesper narrowed her eyes, wondering what he meant, until Eshu spread his arms wide, spinning in place. She blinked, and where there was one loa, there were two, and then three, until the entire valley was filled with thousands of him, all wearing his grinning face, "It's been a long time since I could really let loose, but if you insist on a fight, I will be happy to indulge you."

"This can't be real," said Lillith, swallowing hard, her eyes ever moving. "It's a trick, a bend of the light to make it look like there are more of you."

The loa laughed once more, and a trio of him came forward, an army of laughing faces with naked blades in hand behind them. "Come, play... and find out."

"They feel real enough," said Vesper, raising her gladius just in time to block a slash, the clash of steel on steel setting her teeth on edge.

"Then we'll die taking as many of them with us as we can," snarled Lillith. "I'm not going to be a slave for that Roman monster." Her mother counterattacked with a fury Vesper had never seen before, her gladius and shield moving like they were an extension of her will, throwing the copies of Eshu off guard. The ancient loa frowned at her, and then shrugged before responding in kind, waving the hundreds of copies of himself onward into battle.

Vesper managed to lock eyes with the ancient loa just before the horde of bodies washed over them. In his eyes she saw a flash of amusement while, at the same time, catching light of a small frown that creased his handsome face. In a heartbeat Vesper replayed his words in her mind, his actions, and came to a realization: "You said he was pure spirit here, a loa like you once were," she shouted to Lillith, who was battling at her side.

"Yes, but what does it matter? He can still kill us!" she answered through gritted teeth, plunging her gladius into the throat of a copy, who vanished in a cascade of dazzling light when she withdrew the blade.

"Then we have to give him what he wants," said Vesper, drawing her blade along her open palm, wincing when bright red blood gushed from the wound and flowed down her arm. Then using every ounce of her Ase-enhanced strength and agility, she leapt upward, bounding over and on the heads and shoulders of the onrushing horde, moving with grace and speed beyond anything human, so much so that the copies of Eshu were nothing more than an angry blur of reaching hands and clumsy blades. Vesper had almost reached him when she pushed off a copy's shoulder, tucking her feet up under her and vaulting high into the air so that she landed with a flourish and kneeled in front of him. Before he could react, she spun her gladius in hand and offered him the hilt. "Eshu, primordial loa, born of the crucible of creation," she said boldly, never flinching as she met his dark eyes, "tell me what you wish of me, and I will see it granted. I offer my blade, my heart, and my soul in your service. In return, I want my life, and that of my mother's."

Eshu raised an eyebrow, and the entire valley fell silent, a slow smile creeping across his face when every copy of him froze in place, a deafening silence falling across the valley as if he and Vesper were the only two beings in the universe. "You be a bold one for an Ose," he said after what felt like an infinite pause. "I like that. I like that very much," said the loa, reaching for the blade.

"The spirit is always weak to the flesh," she whispered, dropping the blade just before Eshu touched it, instead grasping his outstretched hand with her bloody palm.

NINETEEN
LINUS

"What do you mean, she's gone?" growled Narcissus, pacing back and forth in frustration. "How do two people just disappear?"

"I can't explain to you what I don't understand myself," said Lucilla, her face a reflection of his own. "I only know that she and Lillith were in the garden one moment, and gone the next, leaving only an ashen circle in the dirt. I came to the ludus on the off chance that she had returned here."

When Rainar had interrupted his time training on the sands to tell him Lady Lucilla was waiting for him in the atrium, his heart had surged with hope, and he raced to meet her, expecting to find Vesper at her side. He was desperate to finally have a chance to explain what happened, but when he arrived, only Lucilla was waiting for him, standing beside the reflecting pool where they had first met, her pale features twisted with worry. "I told Vesper not to trust that woman," he said. "She has been nothing but trouble since the moment we laid eyes on her."

"You think her mother spirited her off somewhere? Why would she do such a thing?" said Lucilla, frowning at Rainar, who shouted with glee as he tossed dice with another guard in the corner.

"I don't know, but she did something to me. My memory... since we left the imperial palace together: it's all a fog."

"You blame Lillith for you not being able to control your urges," she scoffed, looking down her nose at him. "You should simply have known better."

"I am not some impulsive Roman," he said, scratching at his beard, "and the last thing I wish to do is lie with whores."

"That's not how it looked to me, nor to Vesper," she said, crossing her arms. "You broke her heart."

Narcissus recoiled like she had struck him, his face flushing a deep shade of red. "I didn't wish it! I would never hurt her. I-I—"

"Doctore," shouted a familiar voice behind him, and he immediately swallowed his words, sighing with relief for the distraction.

"Linus," he said, turning to face the old gladiator, who was strangely accompanied by a legionnaire he didn't recognize. "I thought you were preparing for tomorrow's battle on the sands."

"I was, Doctore, but this one," he said, frowning at the legionnaire at his side, "insisted that I not leave the ludus." Narcissus took one look at the stranger's polished, unscarred leather armor, chiseled features, and ornate gladius, and he knew immediately that he was most likely part of the ceremonial legion who served in the capital: one of those soldiers who gained their position through favors and family, who had never lived in camp or slept away from their comfortable beds.

"All slaves have been ordered to remain at the ludus until the games tomorrow," said the legionnaire.

"Linus is a free man," said Narcissus to the stranger, bristling when the man shook his head before the words finished leaving his mouth. "He can come and go as he pleases."

"Then he can go and never return, but he wishes to remain among the gladiators here; he will be confined to the ludus with the rest of you."

"On whose authority?" said Lucilla, stepping forward.

"Prefect Cleander," said the legionnaire without hesitation, puffing out his chest. "Caesar's new chamberlain."

"Do you know who I am, Legionnaire?"

"O-of course," he said.

"Good! Then I countermand that order," said Lucilla, raising her chin. "Linus is a freeman, justly rewarded after many years of honorable service in the arena, and Narcissus is a trusted slave and doctore, free to come and go as he pleases."

"I-I can't allow that," he stammered. "Not without orders from—"

"From who... Caesar himself!? A fine idea, why don't we go talk to him. I'm sure he'll be very understanding of the interruption," she said.

The legionnaire swallowed hard, his bronzed skin taking on a green hue like he was about to vomit. "No, no, that will not be necessary," he said after a moment's hesitation.

"Good, now get out of my sight. I have little patience today for those who don't know their betters."

"I will speak to my first centurion," he said at last, bowing stiffly at the waist and then hurrying off.

"Gratitude," he said once the legionnaire was gone, turning to face the noble woman with a questioning look.

"Cleander is a horrid man, another sycophant that my brother has given free rein to do as he wishes," she said, shaking her head. "Whatever I can do to impede him is a pleasure."

"I, for one, will not question my good fortune," said Linus. "Now, if it's all right with you, there are preparations to be made for the primus tomorrow, and I must see to men in the other ludi."

"Do it with haste; men like him rarely let things go. He will be back soon, and with new orders and more of his cohorts. I doubt I will be able to stall him a second time."

"I will accompany him, then. Perhaps my presence will help speed things along," said Narcissus.

"Then I will return to my villa in hopes that Vesper has returned," said Lucilla, glancing over her shoulder as she turned to leave. "I pray that you have something exciting planned for tomorrow's games. You know how my brother is."

"It will be a grand contest, one that every Roman will remember for the rest of their days," said Linus, bowing with a flourish, a grimace marking his wrinkled face as he struggled to return upright.

"I will send word if Vesper returns," she said, turning on her heel and departing.

"Have we been discovered?" said Narcissus in low tones once Lucilla was out of earshot.

"With a visit like that from the legionary, we must have been," said Linus, "but I don't see how."

"Someone must have let your plan slip; either that, or someone has betrayed us for denarii."

Linus spat, reaching for a gladius on his hip that wasn't there. "I must find out how far this has gone, or tomorrow will be a disaster, and we will pay with our lives."

"I will face my death tomorrow regardless of what happens, quickly if Vesper does not return before the games begin."

The old gladiator reached up, resting a calloused hand on his shoulder. "If my plan succeeds, you will live a long life as a free man... fat, but free," said Linus, breaking into a grin. "Hopefully with Vesper at your side, along with the many children the pair of you will make, I only pray they will look like her and not you!"

"A fine vision," said Narcissus, ignoring the old man's insult. "One that is in danger of falling apart unless we find out who betrayed us."

"Then we should follow that legionnaire," said Linus, rubbing his chin. "Find out what he knows and who he is reporting to."

"And here it was that I assumed that you lived your life getting by on your looks," said Narcissus.

The old gladiator puffed out his chest before poking Narcissus in the belly. "Insulting a man whose appearance is blessed by the gods is the first bastion of the ugly and the dour. Now, he couldn't have gotten very far, but we may have to run to catch this man; hopefully you will be able to keep up."

"One day you will push me too far, old man," growled Narcissus, waving for the old gladiator to follow as he headed for the street.

Exiting onto the wide avenue, he couldn't help but stare at the massive Colosseum that dominated the skyline, a hint of pride swelling in his chest when he thought of his many victories on its sands, of watching battle after battle of the men he'd trained, and the honor he felt to die well with the people of Rome cheered his name. "There he is," he said, finally catching a glimpse of the legionnaire as he elbowed his way through the midday crowds.

"We should wait until he is in a quieter area before we take him," said Linus, glaring at the wayward legionnaire like a hawk studying its prey.

"You mean to kill him in the street? With the whole of Rome watching?" joked Narcissus, worrying when Linus pushed past him.

"Of course not," said Linus, "but I have prepared too long for this, and I will not lose my chance to change things for the better, not when I am so close."

"Is this why you stayed?" asked Narcissus, staring in wonder at the old gladiator, "Why you didn't take your freedom and find a life far away from all of the arena, from the ludus?"

"How could I enjoy my freedom?" said Linus with a shrug, "knowing that I was leaving others to suffer in my place, knowing that men I considered to be brothers would bleed and die on the sands while I spent my days between the legs of some pretty young thing."

"Do you really think we can do this?" asked Narcissus, hurrying after the old man, who raced ahead of him despite his twisted back.

"Of course," said Linus, breathing easily while he ran. "Look around you; what do you see?"

"Men, women, plebeians, and patricians alike," he said, matching his pace.

"I see slaves, my hairy friend, more slaves than anything else."

"And so, this is Rome. There are always slaves," said Narcissus, ducking just in time to avoid being run over by an ornate litter carried by a pair of bulky slaves that were not paying attention.

Linus slowed as they came closer to the legionnaire, bowing his head in hopes of not being seen. "Do you know, the senate once considered giving all slaves a garb to distinguish us from the common laborer, but eventually they decided against it."

"Why?"

"Because they realized slaves far outnumber all the other classes in Rome, and they feared what we would do if our true numbers were made clear."

"Yes, but slave revolts have happened before; they were always crushed. The wealthy of Rome have the legion, weapons, armor. And you know the penalty for harming a dominus... death to every slave in the household, not just the men or those who did the deed, but the innocent as well. Women and children included."

"And the same goes for harming a soldier of the legion," said Linus.

"Yet here we are," said Narcissus, craning his neck to keep sight of the legionnaire who vanished behind a cart overloaded with cabbage. "About to do the very thing that will get us killed."

Linus halted at the mouth of the alleyway, peeking around the corner. "I doubt that," said the old gladiator, a smile coming to his face. "Tell me, Narcissus, are you afraid of men like Rainar and the other legionnaires stationed at the ludus?"

The big Celt snorted, shaking his head. "Of course not. The man can hardly hold a gladius, much less fight with one."

"Exactly! Most of the legionnaires in the city are like him, pretty men in polished armor. One gladiator is worth ten men like him, more than enough to burn the Colosseum to the ground, while we throw the city into chaos as we make good our escape to freedom."

"When you told me of the plan, I thought it was in jest, an old man's fantasy," he said, shaking his head in wonder.

"I can fantasize about far better things," said Linus, showing him his teeth, cursing when the legionnaire threw a quick glance over his shoulder and then bolted down an alleyway.

"He's seen us," snapped Narcissus, breaking into a run after him, his long legs eating up the distance between him and the legionnaire, leaving Linus far behind. Skidding around the corner into the alleyway, he leapt over piles of rubbish, pushing himself hard as his target left the alleyway for another crowded street. Following as best he could, Narcissus bowled over a group of laborers, pulling a rickety wagon, as he attempted to squeeze his meaty body through the dense crowd, ignoring the curses thrown his way as he staggered, briefly losing sight of the man. Recovering his wits, he snarled at the hapless laborers who blocked his path, frightening them away with a feral look, then with his path clear, giving chase once more.

They had just entered a large square filled with people when the legionnaire stopped suddenly, turning to face him. "What are you going to do, kill me me in the middle of the street... with all of these witnesses?" he said, a knowing smile coming to his face.

The big Celt skidded to a halt, sucking in great lungful's of humid air while eyeing the small crowd that was forming around them. "My death is certain in the arena tomorrow," said Narcissus, thinking quickly. "One day won't make a difference to me, but for you... your death will be here and now."

The legionnaire blinked, his shoulders slumping as his smile faded. "You wouldn't," he began, backing toward a marble fountain.

"He can," said Linus, limping up behind the both of them "You'd be surprised what a man is willing to do when he knows his life is forfeited."

"But you have a chance to live," said Narcissus, stalking toward him, "Tell us what you know, and you have my word; you will live to see the sun rise again."

The trapped legionnaire shook his head in defiance, resting his hand on the gladius at his hip. "It doesn't matter what you do to me...he already knows all that he needs to know about your plans."

Narcissus kept his features still, not taking the bait. "I don't know *what* you're talking about," he said finally with a shrug, "or *whom*."

"That's the thing with you slaves," he said, his smile returning. "You don't realize how high above you we Romans are, or how easily you break ranks. It's your greatest weakness, you know, that to a man, you would sell out your own brother for a few denarii."

"You know nothing Roman," said Linus, surging toward him and grabbing his gladius by the hilt before he could unsheathe the fine weapon. "Now, answer my friend's questions before I cut out your lying tongue with your own blade."

"We can't question him here," said Narcissus in a low voice, keeping the growing crowd at bay with a feral glare. "The cohorts who police the city will be along soon enough, asking questions we cannot answer."

Linus ignored him, leaning in close to the legionnaire. "It doesn't matter what you know," he whispered. "You can't stop us all. Every gladiator in the city will be armed and prepared tomorrow. We will take this city and gain our freedom."

"Linus, we have to go!" said Narcissus, shaking the old man by the shoulder.

"Not if the ludi are burnt to the ground," he countered, coming nose to nose with Linus. "And you and all your friends, along with the emperor's whore sister will die having done nothing but make fools of yourselves."

A hollow pit formed in Narcissus's stomach, and he pushed Linus aside and wrapped a meaty paw around the man's throat. "Lucilla has no part in this. Why would—"

"Cleander does not trust her," he wheezed, struggling for breath. "Which means the emperor doesn't trust her. She will die along with the rest of you, although from what I've heard, he has special plans for her."

Narcissus snapped open his hand, letting the legionnaire fall to the ground when a chill ran through him. "We have to find Lady Lucilla," he said to Linus, "before it's too late."

The old gladiator's face twisted in confusion. "We can't just let him go. We need to find out what he knows, or all will be lost."

"It's too late for that," said Narcissus, shaking his head. "He doesn't matter. We have already lost; the only thing left to do is save as many as we can."

"But—"

"Come, my friend, we have to get back to the ludus before it's too late."

Without waiting to see if Linus was following, the big Celt turned on his heels, racing off toward the ludus, praying that he wasn't too late to stop the slaughter.

TWENTY
BLOOD

The moment her blood connected to the loa, her breath was blasted from her lungs while a great weight pressed against her chest, her mind flooded with images she could hardly understand. One moment she was sitting atop a small green hill with the sharp, pungent smell of thousands of sheep filling her nostrils, whispering into the ear of a lone shepherd whose face was little more than tired wrinkles and sunburned skin. Next, she was at the head of a vast army of legionnaires, arguing with a general whose armor was so polished, it almost blinded her. In the span of a breath, she was a pauper in some unknown gutter begging for denarii, a wife whispering in her husband's ear, even a small child curled up in her father's arms begging for sweets. An infinite number of lives flashing before her eyes, flooding her senses until she didn't know where they ended and she began.

"You cannot do this to me... not here," said Eshu in a strained voice, the muscles in his arms flexing like cords of steel as he fought to pull away from her.

"It doesn't matter where we are," said Vesper, her bones aching from the struggle to dominate the spirit, to control him completely.

"You can't fight against your nature, your desire to be flesh bound." Slowly, ever so slowly, she began drawing Eshu into her body, forcing her will on to his, but the loa fought for every inch, tugging and pulling, vile curses escaping, echoing across the valley as he fought to be free from Vesper's grip. Somehow she managed to hang on, shaking her head to stay focused against the kaleidoscope of images ripping through her mind. Not just of people and places, but wisdom, ancient knowledge, long faded from the memory of humanity.

"You think you can control me, girl: a loa of ancient power! Are you mad?"

"I've done it before," she said through clenched teeth, throwing back her head while needles of white-hot agony burned through her veins as the merge between her and Eshu deepened, "with my mother... and Papa—"

"Common loa, simple beings easily controlled," he began, pulling away with a sudden lurch as beads of sweat rolled down her forehead, slicking her body with sweat as she held on for dear life. Eshu was right, his strength dwarfed that of the loa she had controlled before. She had easily drawn Papa Jufari into her body completely, the same with her mother when she had been a loa. The only contest having been for control of her physical form once they had been joined, but with Eshu, she lacked the power to draw him in completely. Vesper fell to her knees as the loa straightened, almost standing to his full height as the mischievous, knowing grin returned to his handsome face as he continued, "You are brave to have attempted such a thing, but you are but one Ose, alone, the last of your people. You never stood a chance."

Vesper curled in on herself, bowing her head, determined to hold on to him, to life, for as long as she could. She almost let go when she saw it at the edge of her vision, reflected in the smooth glass of the valley floor—the symbol of the Ose. "This place, these trees, are special," she said, looking up at the ancient loa with a knowing grin. "Under their branches, things which are not normally possible, are possible."

"The baobabs," cursed the loa, his gaze darting over his shoulder and then back at her.

"Nature's energy is the fire that drives all creation," she said, repeating the words of her Aunt Magda's first lesson. "It is the spark of life, and the path to our power." With a shout of triumph, Vesper reached out to the closest baobab tree, a shudder running through her as she drew in torrents of clean, pure Ase, flooding her blood and body with a primal strength she had not felt since the first time she had touched nature's energy. Rising to her feet, she easily forced Eshu to his knees, matching his strength and drawing him in.

"A good show, a fine show," said the loa, vanishing in a flash of light, his voice coming from everywhere and nowhere, "but Eshu be too slick to be caught with simple tricks."

Vesper's breath caught in her throat when he reappeared a few feet away, bowing at the waist. "How?"

The handsome loa threw back his head in laughter, his entire body shaking. "You mortals call me trickster, master of deception. "What did you expect! At least you passed my test... and won't spend the rest of eternity wandering this place."

"Test!" said Vesper, realization dawning as she rose to her feet. "You didn't really want to fight, did you?"

The loa nodded to her, and the copies of him vanished, and his tight-lipped smile grew into a wide, toothy grin. "Hey, just because Eshu is a primordial being from the beginning of time, that don't mean he wants to conquer and kill!"

"You like us, don't you?" said Vesper, nodding to herself when he shrugged.

"I like all mortals. You're amusing, and I just wanna join the fun, have a laugh, maybe play a prank or two."

"Then what do you want from me?"

"A kiss!" he said suddenly, raising a finger as his face lit up.

Vesper turned away quickly, covering her face to hide her gaping jaw and wide eyes while suppressing a laugh. "We are not betrothed," she said. "I'm not sure that would be appropriate to kiss a being from the beginning of time."

"What are you doing!" shouted Lillith from somewhere behind her, her voice full of rage. "Get away from him."

"I think she be mad," said Eshu, half frowning, half laughing. "I'm gonna give her some time to cool down while I chat you up." Eshu flicked his wrist, and Vesper turned around just in time to see her mother shoot upward.

"Is she going to be all right?" she said, sucking in a breath as Lillith vanished among the maelstrom of stars.

"Oh, yes, yes. They can fall for a long time, and the look on their faces. Priceless. Eshu can spend hours, just watching mortals fall," he said, giggling to himself.

The amused twinkle in his eye was infectious, and Vesper couldn't help herself. She let go, laughing with her whole body until her belly hurt, and there were tears streaming down her face as she thought of her mother and the red-masked Roman, falling, screaming for hours on end. "Apologies," she said at last, letting out a slow breath to calm herself. "It felt good to just laugh; the last days have been beyond imagining. I can't remember the last time I could just laugh."

A serious look crossed the loa's face, and he put a hand on her shoulder, pressing his lips together while his eyes drilled deep into hers. "No need for apologies. Eshu spend a lot a time watching mortals, and it looks like you've had a rough go. And it's not every day that you meet a charming loa like me in such a beautiful place. So take a moment; you look like you need it." For an instant, Vesper tensed, thinking it was some sort of trick, but then, to her surprise, he crossed his arms and looked up to the stars, a deep sigh escaping his lips.

"Okay, why not?" said Vesper, crossing her arms, nervously following his gaze. "This valley, the stars, they're beautiful."

"Olodumare had a good eye for beauty," he said with a half-smile.

"Even now, after an eternity of life, I can still get lost in the twinkle of an eye, and my heart still skips a beat from the right smile."

"I am no one special, just a proper Ose girl," she said, covering her mouth with a hand to hide her smile, not daring to look at him for fear of what she might do or say.

"Not from where I stand," he said with a laugh. "Now, about that kiss?"

"I— My heart belongs to another" she said as her cheeks started to burn, and she forced herself to look away, part of her not wanting the moment to end. The handsome loa almost made her forget that she would have to deal with the reality of fighting and maybe dying in the arena. "It's so peaceful here," she said finally. "I could spend an eternity just... watching."

"Not a good idea for a mortal," he said, looking down at her. "This place be bad for a living soul. You gonna have to go back soon, unless you want to become a permanent resident."

"No," she said, as much to him as to herself. "To be able to leave the world and its problems behind would be freeing, but then what happens to those I care about, to those I am sworn to protect?"

The loa snorted in defiance, frowning at her. "It's a good thing you have your head on straight," he said. "Olodumare knows we need more like you. Djambe that can do the great god's will of keeping the world spinning. Just don't forget to let loose a little, have a laugh at someone, especially if they behave like an ass."

"You mean like throwing them to the stars and watching them fall?" she said, smiling up at him.

"If you listen close enough, you can hear them scream," said the loa with a mischievous twinkle in his eye, nodding to himself as if he came to some sort of decision. "All right, time to make a deal! You wanna live, wanna go home. You gotta do something for Eshu."

Vesper raised her chin, swallowing hard. "That's what I said, didn't I?"

"That you did; that you did," he said, "Listen, Eshu be a busy man. Not only do I gotta keep mortals on their toes, but the great god has me doing all sorts of things across the world and beyond. I need eyes and ears, people with good heads that can be counted on to do Olodumare's will. Djambe that can do what they gotta do without resorting to murder and violence. You seem to have your head on straight, so that can be you... if we make a deal."

"What about all those things that the masked man called you. My mother too. Master of lies deceiver."

The handsome loa waved a dismissive hand, his face looking like he'd swallowed something bitter. "You know, you humans can't always see the pattern through the weave. You miss the big picture and do dumb things, things that hurt people, sometimes even the ones you love. Eshu's job is to put things right. And since people are stubborn, Eshu has to trick them every now and again, just so they do things right."

"Why not just force them? I mean, look at all you can do."

The loa laughed again, his shoulders shaking. "Where's the fun in that? Besides, Eshu has to have a good time too; otherwise, what's the point!"

"You get bored," said Vesper, looking at it from his perspective. If she had spent an eternity trying to get stubborn people to do the right thing, she would probably take every chance to amuse herself at their expense too.

"I knew you had a head for this," he said. "So you ready?"

Eshu offered her his hand, his eyebrows shooting up in expectation. Vesper reached out to take it but then pulled her hand back "What do I have to do? And what are you going to use me for?"

"You gonna have my mark," he said, touching his heart. "And I will call on you every now and again for favors, to take care of loa business. But it's a two-way street, and you can call on me, too, if you need a hand, or if you change your mind... that kiss."

She broke into a smile, showing him the whites of her teeth before giving him a serious look. "I won't hurt people if I don't have to. I won't become my mother."

"A sad thing that happened to your mother," said Eshu, shaking his head. "She made bad deals, and paid the price—a heavy price."

"What do you mean?" she asked, looking up at the stars to see if she could see her.

"That's for her to tell ya, not Eshu. Now, take my hand, and I'll give you my mark."

Vesper took his outstretched hand, expecting the burning sharp needles of pain she had experienced when her aunt tattooed the baobab tree onto her chest. Instead a wave of warmth spread up her arm, and she gasped when a series of stars appeared along her collarbone, spreading across her upper chest, and appearing almost like a necklace. "What's all this?" she said as her head began to spin, and flashes of insight flooded her mind, complex patterns of light and dark, shapes and geometric patterns that were beyond alien, burning into her thoughts and memories, reshaping her understanding of Ase and the world around her. "What have you done to me!"

"Eshu don't just be pretty pictures on your flesh, he be filling your mind with knowledge, wisdom, and ways to bend light and sound to fool the weak minded."

"Why didn't you warn me?" she said, falling to her knees while gasping for breath, struggling to get a foothold of the images flashing through her mind.

"And what would be the fun with that!"

Vesper laughed, starting to get a feel for his humor and his view of the world. "Do I get to trick you too?" she asked, getting to her feet with his help.

The handsome loa nodded with approval, puffing out his chest. "I made a good choice, a fine choice! If you only knew how many times Eshu tricked the great god. Lucky thing he be quick, or there would be nothing left of him if Olodumare catch him."

"I may just help Olodumare catch you!"

"No, girl! Not nice, not nice at all," he said with an angry look, but his voice was full of laughter.

"So now what?"

Eshu shrugged, letting out a deep sigh. "Well, I guess our chat is over, and I still didn't get that kiss, but that's okay. What I got was better, don't you think?" he said.

"I think I got the better deal," said Vesper, crossing her arms.

"Maybe, only time will tell, but for now, it's time for our friends to come on down." Vesper expected some grand gesture or earth-shaking event. Instead, the loa slapped his palms together, and in the distance she heard the faintest of screams, growing louder with each passing moment. Until, at last, a figure was plummeting from the stars, his hoarse, high-pitched screams setting her teeth on edge and making her cringe from the pain piercing her eardrums. He had almost slammed into the ground when he stopped just inches from the reflective surface, and Vesper found herself smiling at the wide-eyed panic in his eyes, forcing her face to stillness when he glared at her.

"You break thousands of years of tradition, vile loa," he said, rising to his feet, his entire body shaking. "Our pact...You are meant to obey—"

"The only one I am to obey is the great god... and if you have a problem with that, you can take it up with Olodumare," said Eshu, "and like I told you before, the pact is only valid in the world of the living."

"What are you going to do with him?"

"And now you bargain with this Ose witch! You will pay for this. I swear by—"

"She's smarter than you, and made a better deal! So take your silly mask and begone from my presence, before I ruin all of your plans in my anger!" The loa waved his hand, and the red-masked Roman began to fade from view, his thin, naked body growing more translucent with each passing moment.

"You mean you won't tell me who he is? What he's planning to do?"

Eshu shook his head, frowning at the fading vodun. "That would be unfair, and—"

"What would be the fun in that," finished Vesper, pressing her lips together.

"Now, you gettin' it!"

"Yes, I think so—and Lillith?" she asked.

"She comin', and don't worry, Eshu was a little nicer to her than that Sandawei boy. I thought I would go easy on her. It always helps to be kind when bad news is comin'," he said as her mother drifted into view, falling slower, almost like she was flying.

"What bad news?"

"Oh, that's between Eshu and her."

Lillith touched down with a haunted look on her face, her mouth opening and closing while she hunted for her words. "I've never been so terrified and awestruck in my life," she said at last, falling to her knees and then sitting on her haunches, "and I never hope to again."

"I'm sorry, Djambe Lillith," said Eshu in a formal tone, bowing at the waist, "I need a moment to talk to Vesper here. You should be proud by the way, she is a fine djambe, with a good heart."

Lillith clutched at her chest, her gaze dancing back and forth between the both of them. "Many thanks, but that was not my doing. What happened to the man in the mask?"

"Mother—"

"Where?" she growled, her breath coming in short gasps. "We can't—we have to stop him."

Eshu walked forward, helping her to stand. "I think it best if we chat a little, away from prying ears," he said, shooing Vesper away with a toss of his head.

"I don't understand," mumbled Lillith, shaking her head.

"You will. You will."

Vesper bit the inside of her cheek, forcing herself to stillness as they wandered deeper into the valley, talking with their heads close together, with her mother, at one point, stopping and shaking her fist at him. She wandered away from them until she found a comfortable spot, nestling herself among the roots of a nearby baobab tree. She waited for what seemed an eternity, letting her mind wander while she re- played events over and over in her mind, amazed that she was still alive, and relishing in the knowledge seeping into her mind, hoping in some way it would be something that could help her in the coming days. She felt a small nudge and came awake with a start, realizing that she had fallen asleep.

"It's time to go home," said her mother, standing above her.

"What's wrong?" she asked, noting the redness of dry tears in her eyes.

"It's nothing: come. Eshu has opened a way for us."

Not far away, the handsome loa stood in front of what looked like a shimmering pool of water, its dark surface reflecting hints of golden sunlight, and faint brushstrokes of white marbled fountains filled with crystal clear water. As they walked along, Lillith clutched at her, holding tight as if she might fall. Vesper tried to probe, to find out what happened, but her mother kept her eyes forward, silent as a grave.

"She will be fine, given time," said Eshu as they approached the portal. "Just remember our deal."

Vesper nodded, saying nothing more as she stepped through the portal, grateful to be alive, terrified at what was to come in the days ahead.

TWENTY-ONE

THE HYPOGEUM

Lucilla watched the city roll by from the window of her carpentum, lost in her thoughts, her mind a jumble of worry and confusion. The city was abuzz with excitement ahead of tomorrow's games, and the legionnaires, who were normally present with her just for show, were forced to ride ahead of her carriage, clearing a path, even through the upper-class streets of Palatine Hill. News of what had happened in the senate had sped through the city like wildfire, and plebeian and patrician alike were eager to see Vesper and her Celt face off against Rome's champions of the arena. That is, of course, if the Ose woman showed up for the battle. She had seen Vesper do remarkable things, things beyond explanation, just as her father had shown here. But to vanish entirely without a trace, it was still shocking to her. Worst, still, her mother, who Lucilla was told was sure Lillith was long dead, had vanished along with her.

The carriage jarred to a halt, and Lucilla came back to herself with a start. "Ekram, why did we stop?" she asked, sliding open the partition between her and her driver, a young Syrian, with a short, neat beard, that her husband had purchased last winter.

"Apologies, Domina," he said in a small voice, "but... the road has been blocked."

"By whom?" she asked, surprised by the panic in his voice, knowing Ekram was not one easily shaken despite his youth.

"Legionnaires," he whispered.

"Who would dare," she snarled, her nostrils flaring, and she slammed open the door to the carpentum, intending to give whoever was blocking the road a harsh tongue lashing, only to curse under her breath when she found that the street was filled with Praetorian guardsmen, their deep-purple cloaks hanging limply in the windless afternoon heat. She was about to demand for their first centurion when a familiar face rode forward on a magnificent stallion, whose coat gleamed a bright white. "Cleander," she said, keeping her tone neutral, "to what do I owe such a pleasure?"

The swarthy prefect showed her the whites of his teeth, his smile never touching his eyes. "I have come to escort you to the palace," he said, not bothering with common pleasantries.

She raised her thin brows, grinding her teeth at his lack of proto-col. "I do not wish to be escorted anywhere but my home. So if you and your men can clear the road. I will be on my way."

"Perhaps I did not make myself clear," said Cleander, dismounting from his steed and coming close enough to her that Lucilla was forced to take a step back. "By order of Imperator Caesar Lucius Aurelius Commodus, you are to be escorted to the imperial palace."

"And if I don't?" she said.

Cleander glanced back at the men with him, resting his hand on the hilt of his gladius. "Then my men and I will do what is necessary to carry out our orders."

Lucilla followed his gaze, understanding that he had almost three times the number of cohorts than she did, and that if she defied him, he had no problem killing her men and taking her by force. "It has been too long since I have seen my brother. Perhaps it's long past time we had a visit together," she said, changing tactics, speaking as if it were her idea and that he was simply a servant doing her will. "If your men would be kind enough to provide escort, we will follow."

The swarthy prefect was rubbing a finger under his nose while frowning at her. "Of course, come along, the city has not been safe as of late, and it would be a shame if something happened to you." Without waiting for her reply, he vaulted onto his stallion, spinning the beast around, its powerful flanks missing her by a hairsbreadth.

Returning to her carpentum, she grasped Ekram's hands, speaking quickly, "Take the carpentum and return home; inform my husband that I have been taken."

Ekram's eyes shot open, and he squeezed her hands back, leaning forward so that only she could hear. "Wha la' I swear, it will be done. Will you be safe?"

"I don't know," she said, her eyes drilling into his, "but hurry. Please."

The young Syrian touched his forehead, muttering a prayer under his breath. "Allah, give me strength," he said finally, coaxing the horses with a series of low whistles to turn the carriage.

Lucilla turned to face Cleander once more, and she screeched in shock when the prefect drew a javelin from a sheath on his back, and in a single, smooth motion, he hurled razor-sharp weapon with deadly accuracy so that it pierced Ekram's throat just above his collarbone, pinning the slaves to the wall of the carpentum, the horses settling down as the reins slipped from his dead hands.

"What have you done!" she screamed at Cleander, her fine features twisting with rage. "Why would you do such a thing?"

The swarthy prefect shrugged, motioning for one of his men to retrieve the bloody javelin, I will, of course, see to it that you are compensated for the loss of your man."

"Compensated," she said as the men around him broke out in laughter. "Have you lost your mind, my brother—"

"Caesar wishes for your conversation to be private... without interruption. The last thing he wants is to be interrupted by your husband or anyone else."

For a heartbeat, Lucilla thought about turning and running, but one glance at her dead driver made her think twice, and she was sure that Cleander was hoping she would try. "Very well," she said, straightening her back. "Get me a proper horse," she said in her most commanding tone.

Cleander bowed at the neck, a half grin creasing his face as he ordered one of his men to give her his horse. Ignoring the man who tried to help her, she effortlessly climbed onto the beast offered while Cleander's men closed ranks around her. As they departed, she cast one last look at Ekram, wondering if it would have been better off to run. Knowing that the young man had been the lucky one, sure that this visit with her brother would probably be her last among the world of the living.

———

Lucilla had expected Cleander and his men to escort her to the imperial palace, but her belly churned with worry when they turned toward the Colosseum, entering through one of the many archways. The massive structure was alive with activity in preparations for tomorrow's games, with slaves and skilled laborers scurrying around the amphitheater floor, dragging large stone blocks and plants that would serve as scenery for the event.

"Where are you taking me?" she asked, when, instead of taking her to the imperial box, or one of the upper seating areas where she expected to find her brother, Cleander and his men escorted her down a wide ramp, descending into the hypogeum, the underbelly of the great Colosseum.

"Commodus has had special accommodations prepared for you and your friends," said Cleander, shouting to be heard over the clank of machinery and booming voices.

Beads of sweat exploded from her pores the deeper they went, and she gagged when her nostrils were assaulted by a blast of hot, fetid air. "The heat, it's too much," she said, stopping to catch her breath, desperate for a taste of cool air.

"All these years, sitting in the emperor's box while drinking cool wine... have you never been down here?" he said as they entered an open area filled with animal cages and mechanical platforms that were used to lift scenery and animals to the Colosseum floor. "Didn't you ever wonder where all those beasts came from when they appeared suddenly on the sands... or all the fantastic bits and pieces that made up the backgrounds of the battles you watched.

She screeched, shrinking away with a yelp as a caged leopard slammed into the bars, its wickedly sharp claw passing within a hairsbreadth of her hip. "No," she said at last, clutching at her racing heart.

"It looks like she likes you," said her brother, appearing from behind one of the cages, escorted by his usual retinue of Praetorian guards, who hovered just behind him.

"Brother," said Lucilla, her entire body shaking like a leaf as he came closer, "what's this all about? And why in the name of Jupiter are you down here in the bowels of Hades?"

Commodus cupped her chin in a smooth, soft hand, smiling down at her. "Preparing for tomorrow's spectacle," he said, his eyes drilling into hers.

"You look well, Brother," she said, keeping her voice steady as she took her hand in his, pushing it away from her face.

"And you look terrified," he said, waving off Cleander and his men. "Do I frighten you so?"

Lucilla was about to deny it, to play the game they always played, with her pretending the things her brother did were not terrifying, but then she glanced up at him towering over her, his eyes glittering like a madman in the dim light. "Of course you frighten me," she said, laughing nervously. "Your men took me against my will, killed my driver, and brought me here, to the bowels of the Colosseum. Even the bravest hero would be terrified."

Commodus raised an eyebrow, and for a moment he very much

looked like the brother she knew. Arrogant and prideful, but caring and kind, even apologetic in moments when they were alone. "That was the most honest thing you have said to me in years," he said after a moment, adjusting the purple toga trimmed with gold that he had expertly wrapped around himself. "I suppose that's why you tried to kill me, because you were afraid."

Lucilla staggered as if she had been punched in the belly, her breath catching in her throat. "What? I don't... what are you talking about?"

Her brother looked down, unclasping a pin that helped to hold his toga in place. Without a word he began unwrapping the fine silk, letting fall to the filthy floor. "Your friends managed to kill my guards, even land a few glancing blows," he said, lifting his tunic to reveal his taut stomach, marred only be a wide scar on his side that was pale and sickly against his bronzed skin. "But it was you, my own sister who would have landed the killing blow."

Despite the heat of the hypogeum, Lucilla's blood ran cold as she stared at the pale scar. Squeezing her eyes shut, she tried to drive out the memory of charging at him with the gladius, deftly sliding the blade into his belly, but she could still remember the look of pain and horror on his face, the look of betrayal in his eyes. "I'm sorry," she began, pressing her lips together before she raised her chin in defiance, her voice seething with rage as she continued, "I'm sorry we failed! I'm sorry that you lived on to terrorize Rome and her people!"

Her brother met her gaze once more, and Lucilla fell back, catching herself before she was too close to a leopard's reaching claws. The eyes staring back at her had gone from their normal brown that matched her own, to a milky white, similar to what she had seen among the Sandawei dead. "I should thank you," he said, pulling her away from the cage. "I became truly myself that day. A good among men! The son of Jupiter himself."

"What's happened to you?" she asked, not having the strength to pull away from him. "What vile spirit has taken hold of you?"

"I have been deified by the gods themselves," he said proudly. "Hercules reborn, as I have been saying for all my life."

"Then my brother is truly lost," she said, "replaced by a monster."

"I have never been more myself," he said through clenched teeth. "The conflict I have felt for my entire life is gone; the mortal part of me is gone... leaving only the divine!"

"Madness," whispered Lucilla, hugging herself as she fell to the floor, not daring to look at him.

"Not madness," he said, lifting her up, "but glory! Glory so great that all of Rome will bask in my greatness for a thousand years!"

"And what of me? What horrors do you have for me?"

"If I were cruel," began Commodus, squaring his shoulders, "you would be crucified like a common criminal, but... you are my sister and a former empress. Today will be your last day at my side, and after you witness my glory in the arena, I will tell the senate that I have banished you for your crimes, but for your betrayal, I will do much worse. After tomorrow, you will never leave the bowels of the hypogeum again. You will remain here, laboring among the lowest of the low, until you take your last breath, then I will see to it that you are buried without glory or recognition: a failed, forgotten empress, with no legacy, buried in a nameless grave.

"You can't. People will search for me. The slaves here will know my face."

Commodus threw back his head in laughter, his deep voice echoing in the dim light. "These poor wretches have forgotten the feel of sun on their flesh. To them you will be nothing more than another slave, suffering alongside them."

"No, Vesper and Narcissus, they will look for me; they will find me."

"I'm afraid your friends will not see the sun set tomorrow," he said, leaning over her. "They have planned a slave revolt, and I intend to teach all of Rome a lesson. When the day is done, everyone will know my power, and no one will ever defy me again!"

TWENTY-TWO
TO RISK NOTHING

Narcissus had expected to find an entire legion waiting for them when they returned to the ludus, prepared to execute every last man implicated in the rebellious plot. But when he slowly entered through the main gate, cautiously walking the halls to the training grounds, he found everything in order. Even when he descended into the barracks, he and Linus found nothing amiss, with the men going through their normal end-of-day routine. Eating their evening meal, washing away the day's sweat in the small baths of the ludus, with a few of them dicing with Rainar and a few of the other legionnaires in a corner.

"Apologies, Rainar," he said, approaching the legionary guard as he crouched with a few gladiators and other guards. "May I speak with you in private?"

The guard cursed under his breath, a sour look passing over his face as the clattering dice bounced into a bad toss. "I suppose it would be best for my pocket to quit now," he grumbled, standing to his full height, which was still a head shorter than the big Celt. "What do you two want?" he said, looking back and forth between him and Linus.

Narcissus pulled him away from the circle of men dicing, looking around to make sure no one was listening. "Have you had any strange orders, anything out of the ordinary?" he began in a halting tone, not sure how to broach the subject with the guardsman.

Rainar shrugged, casting a hungry look back at the dice game. "Is this why you disturb me!" he said with a sneer, shaking his head before continuing, "No! Nothing beyond the normal day to day. Why?"

The big man scratched at his short beard, searching Rainar's eyes for any sign of deceit. "Nothing, are you sure?" he said, sensing that the man was being honest with him. "I worry for the games tomorrow, that's all," he lied.

The legionnaire frowned at him, pushing out his bottom lip. "You know, I never liked you very much. You never learned your place," he began. But... you are a fine doctore, and you do not deserve the death coming for you tomorrow. I would have preferred that you die in a fair fight, against an equal, or at least at the end of my gladius," he finished with a smile.

Narcissus chuckled, not sure how to take his words. "Well, I think that's the kindest thing you have ever said to me," he said, offering his forearm.

Rainar clasped him back, squeezing hard. "Die well."

"Gratitude."

"Come, Linus," he said, glancing around the barracks, waving off invitations from the men to sit with them: the last thing he wanted was to be around the men right now.

"What could it mean, Doctore?" said the old man, his eyes darting nervously.

"I don't know," he said, "but I will have some of the men stand guard in case they come for us during the hours of night. Beyond that, we can only assume that they will be waiting for us when we arrive at the Colosseum."

"I agree," said Linus, limping behind him. "What are we to do if Vesper does not return?"

The big Celt stopped in his tracks, frowning at the old gladiator. "Death was a given—whether she was at my side or not," he said, "so nothing has changed. I intend to die well, fighting to my last breath."

"And what of the revolt," said Linus, "of freedom for all?"

Narcissus pressed his lips together, not sure what to say. He knew from experience, and from history, that the legion and the empire, in turn, were vicious when it came to rebellious slaves. They killed not only those involved but often executed anyone even remotely involved, just for good measure. The thinking being that it was far easier to replace dead slaves than risk the lives of Roman citizens. Order above else, this was the strength of Rome, and order had to be maintained, no matter the cost. "We cannot risk lives for a failed cause," he said at last, flinching when the old man surged toward him, gripping the front of his leather vest with surprising strength.

"You intend to surrender before a drop has been spilled," he seethed, pushing him against the wall. "I never took you for a coward!"

Sucking in a deep breath, he gently grabbed the old man's wrist, prying his hands from his vest, shaking him hard a single time. "I am no coward, Linus, but I see no need to throw lives away for nothing."

"Not nothing, for freedom. For a life beyond these drab walls, not just for me and you, but for generations not yet born."

Narcissus looked away, unable to meet his intense stare. When Linus had explained his plans, had told him how many of their fellow gladiators were involved, he was stunned. The old man had seemed so simple, kind even, but now he understood it was all an act to make the Romans complacent. "Look around you; everything is far too calm, especially after the visit from that legionnaire today. Think, why would they restrict your moment for no reason? We have been found out; there is no other explanation."

"No," growled Linus, shaking his head. "We have spent too many years preparing. We don't know when—"

"Why throw it away when the risk of failure is so great. Don't be a fool!"

"He who risks nothing... has nothing, is nothing, becomes nothing," said Linus. "Whether you are with us or not, tomorrow every gladiator in Rome will rise up. We will slay anything and anyone in our path, and we will bring freedom to all who want it."

"A good idea in practice," said Narcissus, shaking his head, "but how strong will the resolve of your men be when the legion garrisoned in the city is set upon you? How many will stand and fight at your side?"

"Weak men," spat Linus. "Fat and soft from too many years of drinking and whoring away their denarii on easy city life."

Narcissus stared into the old man's unblinking eyes, finding only desperation, not sense, and he knew what he had to do, regardless of the cost. "I will stand with you, my friend... no matter the consequences."

Linus stepped back, blowing out his cheeks as a smile came to his face. "I knew there was still sense in that fat head of yours."

"I intended to die anyway," he said, looking away, not having the heart to disappoint him. "At least I shall do so for a good cause."

"I swear on my sword that you will see the sun set tomorrow," said Linus. "Now, I must finish my preparations. I will see you at daybreak."

He watched the old gladiator hobble away with more spring in his step than he'd had in a long time, cursing his own weakness at not being able to convince him to abandon this mad plan. Narcissus was not often one for worry, or doom and gloom, but he couldn't see a way out of this mess, and because of that, Linus, and many of the men he had trained, that he liked and respected, would die on the sands tomorrow. Drawing their last breaths in the hope for freedom but ultimately failing when the legion's sword fell on their necks. Shrugging off his melancholy, he headed to his private cell, intending to get some much-needed rest, knowing that he would get none. It had been this way since the days of his first battles on the sands. With him wanting nothing more than to sleep, but finding comfort only in wandering the empty halls of the ludus until the sun rose.

He was almost to his cell when a tug in his midsection drove him to his knees, blasting the air from his lungs as he found his torso glowing a pale amber, casting everything in a warm radiance Then, ever so slowly, his breathing returned to normal, and he felt what he had not felt since that day he had left the palace with Lillith. It was subtle at first, an odd sensation here and there that he knew was not his own, and he found himself turning in a circle, trying to scratch an itch that wasn't there, or catch a glimpse of something he couldn't see. "Vesper... where are you?" he whispered, his pulse quickening.

He blinked, and a shadow was in front of him, like he had stared at the sun for too long. Then, when he could see clearly once more, she was there in front of him, with her mother draped over her shoulder. "Narcissus!" she said, breathing hard from her nostrils, her chest heaving as if she had just finished a sprint. "We made it! We're back!"

He was at her side in an instant, helping her with Lillith. He wanted to ask a thousand questions, but in the end asking only the one that mattered. "Are you all right? Have you—"

"I'm fine," she said, smiling at him in a way that let him know she was. "More than fine!"

Part of him wanted to let her treacherous mother fall to the floor and wrap his arms around Vesper, but something in the way Vesper was holding her up, told him that Lillith had once again wormed her way into her daughter's graces. "Come, we will go to my cell," he said at last, unable to stop himself from smiling at her, getting lost in the curve of her face. A sense of relief washing over him just knowing she was home.

"I feel special," she said. "I've never been to your cell. I always assumed you slept out on the sands."

"As doctore, the men would have gossiped; you know this," he said, shaking his head.

"And now..." she asked, raising an eyebrow.

"Now... the men can all burn in Hades for all I care," said Narcissus. "It only matters that you are safe. Now, what happened to you, to your mother?"

Vesper was silent for a moment as he guided them through a part of the barracks few people were allowed to see. As doctore he was privileged to have private quarters, far better than any of the others who lived under the roof of the ludus. As such, not wanting to make the men jealous of him, he never brought anyone here, fearing it might send the wrong message. "I'm not sure; she couldn't tell me, and she fell unconscious when we arrived back here."

"Where did you go, and what happened to your neck?" he asked, noticing for the first time the stars that began on her collarbone and stretched across her throat.

Vesper hesitated, adjusting her stance to better carry her mother. "It is difficult to explain," she said in a halting tone, "but it was like when we ended up in the world in between... only worse... far worse."

A chill ran through him, and his throat was suddenly dry. "I don't see how anything could be worse than that place."

"The man with the red mask was there," she said. "He is far more dangerous than we imagined."

Narcissus grunted, licking his lips. "Vesper," he began, his words catching in his throat, "that day in the house of Bacchus, I did—"

"It does not matter," she said, looking away from him. "It is my foolishness for assuming things. I have little experience with men... or matters the heart."

He stopped, almost dropping Lillith. "Your feelings were not wrong!" he said, clenching his teeth in frustration. "My feelings are not—"

"Then why do such a thing?" she said with an accusing stare, her eyes unblinking. "If your heart was for me, why lay with other women!"

"He did no such thing," croaked Lillith suddenly, her normally powerful voice thin and raspy.

"What?" asked Vesper.

Lillith pushed away from them, gingerly holding on to the wall to stand on her own. "He didn't simply pass out after I drew on too much of his strength," she said, clutching her head. "After I joined with your connection, he was weak, like he had drunk too much, so I took him to a place where no one would notice."

"Witch! I should kill you for that!" he said, towering over her with flaring nostrils.

"You could try, Celtic dog," said Lillith, "and perhaps I would let you. I deserve no less."

"Narcissus, please," began Vesper, stepping between the two of them. "She had her reasons."

He wanted nothing more than to smash Lillith to a pulp, to make her pay for violating him, for making a fool of him, but worse, for almost ruining his relationship with Vesper. "Know that you only live because of your daughter's mercy," said Narcissus, pounding his fist into the wall beside her head, dust and grit scattering over her face.

"Daughter, know that this man did nothing wrong," said Lillith, her eyes never leaving Narcissus. "He is a good man who holds you, and only you, dear to his heart."

"You corrupt everything you touch," said Narcissus, stepping away from her, his broad chest heaving as his anger faded. "Stay away from us. Do you understand?"

Vesper looked up at him, anger flashing in her eyes. "You cannot decide that."

"No, Vesper, he's right," said Lillith, ducking away from him, backing away slowly down the dimly lit hall. "I have ruined too many lives in my pursuits, but no more. I must find a new path."

"Mother!"

"I will see you later. Go, be together, don't waste a moment. I will be fine."

Lillith faded from view, and Narcissus could swear he heard sobbing. He was about to follow her as a wave of guilt washed over him, but a light touch on his arm held him back. "Let her go," said Vesper. "She has been through enough. We both have."

He stared at the empty hallway for a moment longer, then shook his head. "She's a strange woman," he said. "Infuriating and inspiring all at the same time."

"If you only knew," said Vesper, standing at his side, taking his hand in hers and leaning into him. Narcissus didn't want to move, enjoying her warmth, her smell, the feel of her soft skin against his.

"We should talk about tomorrow," he said at last, drawing in a deep breath. "About the primus, and Commodus."

"I'm sorry I got you into this," she said, looking up at him. "I never thought—"

"You were trying to have freedom for the both of us," he said, pulling her onward toward his private cell. "You could have just done as Commodus wanted, be the murderer he wanted. Instead, you chose your own path."

"I have forfeited our lives," she said, "for my selfish desires."

"There is no shame in the desire for freedom, that you chose to include me in your desire tells me everything I need to know about you."

"By Olodumare, what's all of this?" she asked as they rounded a corner that led to his cell. "It's breathtaking. I could almost swear I was outside, with the mountains in the distance and the sun in the sky.

The wide-eyed look of wonder brought a smile to his face, and offering her his arm, he led her into his personal space, a space where he had never brought anyone. "These are the Celtic Highlands I grew up in as a boy. I've drawn them from memory mostly some of it imagined, some real," he said, pointing at the green and gold murals that decorated his walls, the blue skies he'd drawn making the cell look far bigger than it was.

"And who's this?" she asked, eyeing a gray-furred mastiff sleeping in the corner, who raised its head, growling at her for waking him, only to roll on his side and return to his dreams after a moment.

"Cúchulainn," said Narcissus, fondly eyeing the sleeping dog. "Once the greatest guard dog and gladiator in the empire... now just a tired, old mastiff who sleeps and eats too much."

Vesper raised her brows, giving him a quizzical look. "You mentioned Cúchulainn when we first met. I'd always assumed it was a man, or at least something more terrifying than what you made up to frighten me."

Narcissus scoffed, gently patting the dog's flank before sitting on an extra-long cot that was clearly where he slept. "Back in his day, he was truly terrifying. When I came to Rome, he was my only friend. Kept me safe. But now, aside from a few moments before the sun rises, and a few late into the night, he rarely goes out, and sleeps away most of his days."

"I'm so sorry," she said, sitting beside him on the cot, her hand brushing his knee. She leaned against him once more, and he could feel her trembling, and he pulled away, terrified that she was somehow afraid of him.

"Cúchulainn is in the twilight of his life, but it has been a good life, and I will miss him dearly, but I couldn't ask for a better friend, a better protector."

He was about to say more when Vesper leapt over him and was suddenly in his lap, her lips hungrily finding his, her hands gripping tightly to the back of his head. "You don't have to do this," he said, breathing hard. "We can wait—take things slowly. I know how you wish to be proper."

"I don't want to be proper anymore," she said as her tongue found his. "I have wanted this for a long time, longer than I've cared to admit."

Narcissus took her in his arms, crushing her against him as they fell onto his cot together, his heart pounding out of his chest. He wanted to tell her so many things, to tell her how he felt, how he would never hurt her again, but the longer they kissed he only knew the taste of her tongue, and the smell of her body, while the rest of the world, along with its troubles, vanished, and he only knew her, and that was all that mattered.

TWENTY-THREE
SUNRISE ON THE SANDS

A thin line of gold sunlight was just peaking over the horizon when Vesper stepped onto the sands of the training ground. The rest of the sky was fading from an inky-black night to the pale glow of dawn's twilight. The majority of those who lived in the ludus were still slumbering as she drew in deep breaths of cool air, with only the occasional shout beyond their walls breaking the silence of early morning. Without thinking, she drew on the Ase coursing through her, weaving threads of power into a simple yet balanced gladius, a thrill rushing through her when she grasped the leather-bound hilt. A wide smile spread across her face, and she relished in the moment. After months of struggle, she created the weapon as an afterthought, almost without effort. The few moments her mind had touched with Eshu's primordial spirit, had expanded her skills in ways she was still trying to understand. One thing was certain, her terrifying trip to that terrible place had given her control of Ase far beyond what she had known only the day before.

Raising the blade above her head, she shifted from one form to another, the gladius whistling through the air as she spun it in figure eights. As she flowed through the simple exercise that built endurance and strength, a rush of joy made her blood quicken in her veins. Her night with Narcissus had been magical and uplifting, and while it had begun slowly, even painfully at times, he was kind and gentle, and after a time she encouraged him to go faster, harder. The memory of his touch still sending shivers down her spine. They had hardly slept, and yet she was not tired. In fact, she was invigorated and full of energy, hence why she was out on the sands before the entire ludus had awakened.

The sun was a full disk in the sky when Vesper realized she was no longer alone, and with a start she came back to herself, shocked at how much time had passed. Glancing around the sands, she found her mother sitting cross-legged, facing Linus and quietly laughing with the old gladiator. "You have good form," she said, with a nod, "but you should train with a shield; it will build a better balance of strength and endurance."

Vesper let the gladius fade back to nothingness while she wiped beads of sweat from her brow. "Are you all right? I was worried when you left the way you did."

Her mother unfolded herself and stood, dusting herself off. "You did not worry for long, it seems," she said, showing her brilliant smile. "You have the look of a woman now, no longer a child."

Linus cracked a laugh and winced, clutching at his back as he used the wall to help him stand. "I told you," he said, wagging a finger at her. "You'll be naming your first child before year's end."

Vesper stared at the ground, her face growing hot. "You two should be looking into your own affairs, not mine," she said. "Not that we will see the end of the day. Commodus will see to that... even if we somehow win."

Linus waved her over, a serious look crossing his wrinkled face. "Has Narcissus spoken to you of my plans for today?" he said, his eyes darting around to make sure they weren't being overheard.

"He mentioned it in passing... while we, umm, were resting."

Her mother covered her mouth to hide her laughter, and Linus raised his chin, looking at her with pride. "Good. I am happy for the both of you. I think the entire ludus was getting tired of waiting for the two of you to—"

"Linus! Please, I'm already ashamed of what I've done."

"There is no shame in being with someone you care about, Daughter ."

"More so when you look so happy," said Linus, patting her shoulder with a wrinkled hand. "I'm sure everyone will be happy for you, and I think Atilius chose the right date and will wake up this morning a wealthy man, perhaps with enough to buy his freedom."

"You gambled on Narcissus and I laying together," she said, throwing her hands up in the air and blowing out her cheeks.

"Only for the last month," said Linus, having the decency to look away, "when we realized it was more of a *when* instead of an *if.*"

Vesper buried her face in her hands, reeling from what she was hearing. "Everyone," she whispered.

"Well, except Nabil. Not that it matters. Listen, Vesper, today we have a chance to change the empire for the better, to raise up the low, and bring down those highborn, who have profited from our labors and misery."

"Narcissus thinks it's a fool's errand," she said, shaking her head.

"And you?" asked Lillith, watching her with an unblinking stare.

Vesper bit her lip, hesitating. "I don't know, but with what I've learned from Eshu, combined with your wisdom and strength with Ase, I doubt even the full legion on reserve in the city will be able to stop us."

Lillith's eyes shot open, and she put an arm over Vesper's shoulder. "Give us a moment, Linus. There are things I must discuss with this one."

The old gladiator winked at them. "Just remember, it does not matter how many Romans stand against us, every gladiator in the city will be armed today. Do you understand what that means for our chances?"

"Of course," she said, taking her mother by the arm. "If you begin to draw anything on the ground, or mutter a single word, I'll do what Eshu did, and cast you among the stars."

Lillith's eyes widened, and for the first time since they'd met, Vesper saw worry in her eyes. "No, I wouldn't," she began, swallowing hard. "You couldn't do such a thing... could you??"

Vesper frowned at her mother, not really sure if she could. "I doubt that I could. Eshu somehow poured some on his knowledge into my mind, but I understand only bits and pieces of it. I was hoping that you could help me understand it all, to help train me."

"This is what I wished to speak to you about," said Lillith, her eyes downcast. "This body... it's not mine, and the only reason I was able to touch the weave is because the man in the red mask let me."

"What does that mean?"

"It means that today, the burden of using Ase will be on your shoulders. I can do nothing. I am just... nothing beyond a simple woman who has made more mistakes than I can count."

Vesper raised her brow in surprise, remembering the look on her mother's face when they left the world beyond. "Is this what Eshu told you, before we left?"

"Yes, the master of treachery had one final trick up his sleeve," she said. "He would permit me to keep this body, to live a full life, but I would never be able to channel Ase, to touch the weave ever again. He said it was payment for my past sins."

"It doesn't matter," said Vesper, taking her by the shoulders. "You are still Lillith, hero of the Ose, a person, a cunning warrior, and strangely the one person who seems to know everyone in Rome."

"But without power..."

Vesper bowed her head in thought, thinking of everything she had done since she had come to Rome. "If I have learned anything from watching you, is that it's your drive, your wisdom, and charisma that gives you power over others, not Ase, not the weave."

Lillith cocked her head, an odd look crossing her face. "I thought I was supposed to be teaching *you*?"

"I think we can teach each other," said Vesper, nodding her head.

"Now do you think Linus and his plans are truly a fool's errand? Or can we really do as he wants?"

She was taken aback when her mother suddenly put her arms around her, drawing her close into a tight hug. "Thank you, Daughter."

"What for?" asked Vesper, returning the awkward hug.

"You have a power I never had," she said, stroking her cheek. "The power to look beyond the failings of others, the power to forgive."

"Vesper said nothing, only nodding. "Well then, does that mean you will fight with us today? Is the fight even worth it?"

"Yes. It doesn't matter if Commodus knows. Today we will do what I never could... and free the slaves of Rome!"

TWENTY-FOUR
BROKEN

The heavy iron shackles chafed her wrists, bruising her delicate skin, and she wrinkled her nose in disgust at her own smell. She had only spent a single night in the hypogeum, but already her once fine stola was filthy, and she could swear lice had infested her hair because her scalp itched constantly. Her first night beneath the great Colosseum was a nightmare. Every time she had almost found sleep, an animal roared, or worse, the skittering of rats' claws scraping on the stone kept her awake, or she found roaches crawling on her skin, scurrying under her clothes.

When the Praetorian guard came for her, she had wept, swearing that she would throw herself at her brother's feet and beg for mercy. Anything to not spend another moment in that horrible place. When they had dragged her into the light of morning, she had thought they would take her to her brother's chambers, or even home to her husband. Instead, she was taken to the empty emperor's box, shackled in a corner and left alone to wait.

With nothing to do, she did something she had never done, watched as the plebeians and slaves prepared the Colosseum for the day's events. Lucilla was fascinated by their labors, knowing she lacked the physical strength, or the endurance to clean and scrub away the filth left from the past day's attendees, and she was disgusted by the lack of respect those who came to the games showed for the majestic building.

The sun was high in the sky, and the day's heat was suffocating when her brother's usual retinue of sycophants began to arrive. High-placed officials arriving early in hopes of currying favor with the young emperor: legionary officers whose connections granted them the privilege of serving in the capital instead of on the frontiers, even men and women from noble families who thought they could gain some advantage in being close to Commodus despite his hatred of them. Lucilla stood, ignoring the pain in her wrists and the shame in her heart, shaking out her hair, daring anyone of them to look at her.

"Magistrate Crastor," she croaked, calling out to a pale man with white-blond hair and a round belly that she knew all too well. "A word please."

The magister flinched, his body tensing while he kept his gaze firmly fixed in front of him, not daring to look at her.

"I made you, you old relic" she snarled through clenched teeth. "The senate voted for you on my recommendation. Without me you would still be a nameless questor without an ounce of power, a shame to your family name." While the powerful magister continued to ignore her, Lucilla wanted to scream, to gnash her teeth in rage, but she held it all in, knowing that it would only make matters worse. Only a day ago she was the same as them, obsessed with protocol and appearances. If they spoke with her it would shame them, make them look less than what they were.

"They'll never talk with you," said a full-figured woman who pushed through the growing crowd, her words slurred despite the hour of the day. "They never talk to me, even if your handsome brother does."

"I remember you," she said, vaguely remembering her. "You were with my brother, that day in the baths?"

A sour looked crossed her face, and the curvaceous woman

emptied her wine cup in a single gulp, shaking her head after she did. "Apologies," she said, squeezing her eyes shut. "Yes. Marcia, courtesan to the great Commodus, at your service. Your brother and I... I was there that day."

Lucilla couldn't help but stare. The drunken woman certainly didn't look like her brother's type. She was round of face with dark hair and eyes and her stola clung to her wide hips and full breasts, but she had been her brother's courtesan for longer than most. "If they won't talk to me, why would you?"

Marcia shrugged, swaying in place. "Because they don't talk to me either," she said, sneering at them over her shoulder. "If they only knew how much your brother hates them, or how easy it would be for me to whisper their names in his ear, and he would make them disappear."

"Where is my beloved brother?" she asked, spitting out her words with a look of disgust on her face.

"He prepares for today's games, readying his surprises for the rebels," she said, swaying.

Lucilla perked up, her curiosity getting the best of her. "What rebels?"

The courtesan slid closer, her voice dropping to a whisper, "Haven't you heard?" she said, giggling. "Some old gladiator has planned a revolt, and plans to kill us all."

"That sounds unbelievable," she said, eyeing the drunken woman. "I doubt Commodus would let such a thing happen."

"That's true. We thought the same when we first heard the rumor, had a good laugh at it too. But it seems like it's been in the planning for years... not that it matters."

Lucilla raised an eyebrow, searching for lies in the woman's dark eyes, "I assume he is preparing the legion for an attack."

Marcia leaned in closer, and Lucilla gagged on the smell of sour sweat pouring from her skin. "In the old days, he would have done such a thing," she began, pushing out her lower lip. "We would have stayed in the bath and drank until it was all over, but since the change... well, things are different now."

"What change? Different, how?"

"I don't know when it happened, but he is not the same man. He no longer drinks, and our time in bed... well, it doesn't matter. It's like someone has taken all the joy out of him."

"What does he plan to do?" said Lucilla, clutching at her.

Marcia opened her mouth to speak, only to snap it shut when a hush fell over those in the emperor's box. "I should go," said the drunken courtesan, rising on shaking legs. "He doesn't like to be kept waiting."

"Marcia, please," demanded Lucilla, pawing at her as she pulled away. "What is he going to do?"

"Apologies," she said, her face paling as Commodus called for her, "but you'll see... along with everyone else. I just hope we survive to see the sun set."

Lucilla swallowed hard when she realized Marcia was being serious; she could see the fear in her eyes as she pulled away. Her brother appeared among the crowd and she gaped. He was once more dressed as Hercules, wearing little more than a loin cloth and brandishing a giant club while that ridiculous mane was draped over his shoulders. She understood that whatever her brother planned to do, would be far worse than anything he had already done to her, and that all of Rome would pay with blood and suffering.

TWENTY-FIVE
FOR THE GLORY OF THE EMPIRE

The roar of the crowd thrummed through her when she stepped out onto the sands, sending her heart beating faster with each step, her pulse quickening in the anticipation of battle. They were so loud that she did not hear the auditor announce her name, or Narcissus who followed closely on her heels. While she thought they were loud for her, the moment the giant Celt raised his arms, they leapt to their feet in unison, thousands of Romans cheering his name. "It looks like they haven't forgotten you," she said, shouting to be heard.

"I had forgotten what this felt like," he said, breaking into a wide grin as he tore off the thin tunic he wore, exposing his bare chest. Like a pack of howling wolves, many of the women in the crowd did the same, exposing their breasts and screaming words that made Vesper's cheeks burn hot.

"Should I be worried?" she asked, leaning in close enough so that she could be heard.

The big man shook his head. "Never!" he said, raising his arms once more, "It was, and is, always for show."

"Good, I don't want to battle an entire Colosseum full of women for your affections."

"Let us survive the day first before you start attacking women for looking at me the wrong way," said Narcissus.

Vesper stared hard at the crowd, hunting for signs for the legionary but finding none, with the only legionnaires in sight being those who were always present near entrances to the Colosseum floor and around its perimeter. "Perhaps your worries were misplaced. It seems like a day like any other on the sands."

Narcissus only grunted as the auditor called for their first opponents, and she sucked in a breath of hot air when the gate of life on the other side of the great arena clanked open, and a dozen men surged under the rusted bars, charging at them like a wild pack of dogs. "It looks like we are to face the criminal and the condemned in our first match of the day," he spat, sneering at the oncoming men.

"Not gladiators?" asked Vesper, noticing their crude blades and lack of armor of any kind. "Why?"

"They want us to entertain the crowd for a few challenges," he said, flexing his thick arms. "This gives them a chance to get rid of the riffraff, while making us look good. Are you ready?"

Before they had come out on the sands, she and Narcissus had prepared as best as they could, using every advantage they had. She had weaved together a set of bracers and greaves far stronger than anything forged in Rome for him, and she had done the same for herself. Creating a perfectly balanced shield and gladius. In addition, she was prepared to share her strength, her Ase with him through their bond, just as they had done during the Sandawei attack. "I am," she said at last, her heart singing as the Ase in her blood poured through her limbs and toughened her dark skin.

They waited, letting the disorganized group come to them. The lead man came at Narcissus, filthy and disheveled, his crude gladius raised high overhead. Without pause, his meaty fist connected with the man's jaw in a brutal uppercut, and he bounced away from them like he had run into a wall, falling onto the sands without so much as a whimper.

Three of them then came at Vesper while the rest circled Narcissus. Thinking of her as easy prey, they surrounded her, but she quickly drove that idea from their minds as she spun in place, her perfectly balanced gladius, formed from primal forces, shattering the crude blades they wielded while she used her shield to knock them senseless in rapid succession.

"You have to kill them," shouted Narcissus, stomping on the head of a fallen opponent, bloodying his caliga, the heavy, metal-soled sandal splitting the man's skull.

In response, Vesper slashed at the fallen men, neatly slicing their throats or vital organs, leaving them to bleed out on the sands. Seeing how easily their fellows were dispatched, the remaining criminals turned and fled in wild-eyed fear, only to be cut down by javelins, hurled by legionnaires stationed around the outer edge of the sands. "There will be no escape for anyone today," said Vesper, shaking her head as the auditor called for the next round of challengers, his booming voice just barely cutting through the cacophony of Romans hungry for blood.

"Linus and his men should be taking control of the underbelly of the arena before long. Be prepared to run when the signal is given," said Narcissus.

Vesper cursed as a javelin whistled past her head, and she managed to raise her shield just in time to block another that came in rapid succession. "That didn't take long," she said, eyeing another group of men pouring from the gate of life. This time they were better armed, and wearing the more common armor types associated with the style they fought with. Spear-wielding hoplomachus, along with murmillos with their towering shields and gladius encircled them. Vesper and Narcissus were forced to adjust their stance so they could fight back to back. While their enemies fought with vague coordination, he and Vesper could feel one another through their bond; as such, they moved in unison, ducking, defending, and then striking with ruthless efficiency, killing as if they shared one mind, their strange dance frustrating the men attacking them, forcing them to make mistakes, mistakes that cost them in blood.

It continued on like this for most of the morning, with her and Narcissus facing off against unskilled or barely trained men, surviving against many, with only minor cuts and scrapes, their only moments of respite coming from when they dragged away the broken and battered corpses, leaving a bizarre trail of blood and gore in the sand. Then, during a pause in the fighting, while Vesper sucked in deep breaths of hot air that burned her chest, the auditor stepped forward, calling for silence. "My fellow Romans," he shouted, the perfect shape of the Colosseum amplifying his deep voice, "I present to you the sponsor of these games, Caesar Marcus Aurelius Commodus Antoninus Augustus."

Vesper gasped when the emperor stepped forward, her brows shooting up. "What in the name of Olodumare is he wearing?" From this distance she could just make out the emperor's features under a hideous lion's head that he wore atop his own, and she frowned at the tiny loincloth, which was all he wore.

"Has he gone mad?" asked Narcissus, shaking his head in disgust.

"Citizens of Rome," he shouted, "I present to you, the criminal, Senator Decimus Annius Magnus. Convicted of the high crime of attempted murder."

The gate of life screeched open, and a group of cohorts dragged the thin senator onto the sands. The man looked worse for wear. His once fine white tunic was filthy, stained with streaks of brown and gray, while his face was a map of abuse, purple and black, and his eyes were swollen shut. Following the legionnaires were a few laborers, carrying wide planks of wood and coarse lengths of rope. "What are they doing?" asked Vesper, her voice sounding loud to her ear now that the deafening shouts had been silenced.

Narcissus clenched and unclenched his fist as the laborers nailed the planks of wood together without ceremony, while a few others rapidly dug a hole just in front of the emperor's box. "They are going to crucify him."

"But isn't he meant to be killed by a gladiator, the one who wins this contest?" she asked, frowning in confusion.

"Oh, he will die by the sword once the day is done," said Narcissus with a shrug, "but that's often too quick, especially when they want to make an example of someone." It was clear the men were practiced at this form of execution, as the wooden cross was assembled in mere minutes, and Senator Magnus was laid out on the instrument of his punishment. The crowd cheered when the crude cross was raised in front of the emperor's box, with Commodus raising his arms, inspiring the people to greater applause.

Commodus brought down a muscled arm, and the packed arena went wild as scores of bronzed men in rough brass armor raced from the gates, and they were surrounded by scores of trident and net-wielding retiarii, thick-bodied murmillos with their faces hidden by wide-brimmed helmets, and vicious dimachaeri wielding pairs of wicked blades. "This is it?" she said, licking her lips, her body shaking with nervous adrenaline.

"Stay in form: don't panic," said Narcissus, crouching down with his meaty hands in front of him.

She tensed, every muscle like a rope drawn taut. Then, before the army of gladiators attacked, a single note from a horn sounded, deep and clear, piercing the roar of the masses. Vesper's jaw fell open as one the gladiators turned, some charging at the unprepared legionaries who stood guard on the perimeter of the sands, while a hail of javelins flew toward the emperor's box, some clattering uselessly against the stone, while others found their targets, and ear-piercing screams filled the air.

"Come, let us play our part and send this tyrant to the afterlife," said Narcissus, charging to where Commodus and his ilk watched the games. Vesper followed, her legs pumping hard to keep up with his long-legged strides. They were almost to the emperor's box when she channeled her strength into Narcissus through their bond and was preparing to leap when Commodus appeared, standing on the lip of the opening, brandishing a giant club.

To her eyes, time slowed as Narcissus leapt, his powerful Ase-enhanced legs sending him high to meet the mad emperor of Rome, his meaty paws outstretched toward his neck. Commodus jumped to meet him, the two massive titans clashing midair, the emperor's club smashing the big Celt in the shoulder. The pair of them sending up plumes of dust as they fell in a tangled heap.

Commodus was up first, stomping at Narcissus's prone form, only to stagger as the bear of a Celt caught his foot and then slammed the palm of his hand into the emperor's groin, sending him careening over into the dust. Vesper was at his side in an instant, helping him to his feet, her eyes and hands hunting for injuries. "I'm fine," he said with a grateful nod. "Better than fine."

"What are they doing?" she asked, staring helplessly at the chaos surrounding them. Everywhere she looked, gladiators fought legionnaires, while some of their own men climbed into the seating, slashing and killing patricians and plebeians alike without regard. "This was not the plan."

"Some men cannot help themselves," said Narcissus, shaking his head. "They only see this as a chance for revenge, not freedom."

She was about to say more when Commodus was on top of them suddenly, moving with surprising speed and agility for a man his size. Without thinking, Vesper stepped in front of Narcissus, using her shield to absorb the brunt of the emperor's wide swing, the force of his club numbing her arm and sending her staggering back. Blinking away stars, Vesper looked back to see Commodus and Narcissus trading heavy blows, the big Celt using his bracers and greaves to absorb wild swings from the emperor's club, while he pummeled the other man's flesh with his fists to little effect.

Without missing a beat, Vesper charged back into the fray, fighting like a legionnaire, using her shield to defend, while at the same time stabbing with her gladius, only to curse when her razor-sharp blade scraped off Commodus, leaving his skin untouched.

"It's not like the last time, Ose witch," he shouted, backhanding Narcissus with enough force that he was blasted away, flung a dozen feet and sliding along the bloodstained sand. "You fight me at the height of my strength, with the blood of Hercules coursing through my veins."

Her stomach churned with fear as he stalked toward her, his face twisted with rage. "You are not a god," she said, resting the tip of her gladius on her shield. "Just a man corrupted by the Sandawei, by Saoterus."

At the mention of his former chamberlain, his nostrils flared, and he charged at her with reckless abandon, ignoring the few glancing strikes from her sword. She managed until he was on top of her, pounding on her shield. Vesper gave up on attacking him, using her gladius to defect his heavy blows as she desperately fought to avoid the club.

Vesper missed a beat, moving too slowly, and the wicked weapon clipped her on the side of her head, her world going dark for a moment. She opened her eyes in time to find herself on her back, his club about to fall on her. Not having a second, she channeled the Ase in her blood to shove her away on a jet of air, the blast wind kicking up a plume of dust that blinded Commodus, his massive club falling where she was only seconds ago and burying itself deep in the sand. She cocked her head while she watched the emperor rip the weapon from the ground, the sound of splintering wood filling her ears.

While Commodus scrubbed at his eyes, shaking his head, Vesper bounced on the sand, realizing that some parts of the Colosseum floor were made up of wooden platforms that they used to change out scenery for events.

"I am here," said Narcissus, appearing at her side, his arms covered in ugly scrapes and bruises, while blood flowed freely from his nostrils and ear. With a nod, they stood their ground as Commodus came at them, the pair of them acting in unison, one defending while the other attacked, Vesper deflecting vicious strikes with her gladius while Narcissus attacked the emperor's sensitive areas: eyes, throat and groin, landing blows that would have crippled an ordinary man, only to have Commodus ignore them like he were made of stone.

"It doesn't matter what we do," she said, grabbing his hand and pulling him along as she backed away. "He's too strong! Your fists leave no bruises. My blade can't pierce his skin."

"Then what do we do?" he said as Commodus swung wildly at them, his wicked club hissing as it whistled past them. "We can't just run."

Vesper channeled another gust of wind, sending a torrent of sand at the mad emperor's face, slowing him as he rubbed the grit from his eyes but hardly stopping him. "We trick him," she said, thinking of her time with Eshu, the primal loa. "We use his strength against him."

"Whatever you're going to do, do it quickly; we can't take much more of this," said Narcissus, blocking another swing with both of his bracers, his brow shooting up in awe when the metal bent under the unrelenting attack.

The air was blasted from her lungs when she raised her shield to block another strike, the club splintering the wood and leaving deep cracks in its surface.

"Cover me!" shouted Vesper, wincing as Narcissus did as told, dodging and deflecting blow after blow. Focusing for just a moment, she reached into the filthy weave, her stomach turning as she drew on the few trickles of Ase that she could from its tattered form. Then, combining it with all of the strength she had left, she poured it into the emperor's club, weaving layers of potential atop layers of energy. When she was done, the weapon hummed with power, promising death to anyone who touched it.

"Ready," shouted Narcissus after she gave him a signal through their bond.

"Run!" shouted Vesper, easily switching places with him so that he had room to turn and race away.

Commodus sneered, ignoring Narcissus as he turned and ran. "You should have let the ugly Celt fight for you while you ran. You would have lived longer."

"Not much of a god, are you," mocked Vesper, tucking in her stomach and jumping back to avoid having her ribs pulverized. "You can't even end a pair of slaves!"

With a roar, he redoubled his efforts, his club little more than a blur. Vesper desperately avoided his attacks, sweat rolling down her temples as they circled one another, her breath coming in ragged gasps as she fell back. She had just managed to dodge another series of attacks when she stumbled, twisting her ankle and landing hard on her bottom.

"I have you," said Commodus, raising his club high, his face lighting up with a wicked smile.

"No, I have *you*," she said as the club fell, smiling as her physical form vanished in a cascade of dust and light, appearing a short distance away. The Ase-enhanced club fell with a terrible crash, and the wood beneath the emperor's feet splintered like rotting wood, the normally strong support platform crumbling under the weight of the mighty blow.

The look on Commodus's face shifted from one of triumph to one of wide-eyed terror as he vanished into the dark, without so much as a scream. A smile creased her face, and she was about to get to her feet when the floor beneath her gave way, and she screamed as she slid on the sands. She was almost over the edge when a meaty hand found hers and she came to a halt. "Narcissus," she said, fighting to catch her breath.

"Don't forget *me*," said Linus, appearing beside him. "I can't let him get all the glory."

Vesper shook her head as the men pulled her up and away from the broken platform, and they fell in a heap together. "Gratitude," she said. "To the both of you."

"We must hurry," said Narcissus, pulling her to her feet. "This chaos won't last long, and we have to get out of the city before things returns to normal."

She glanced around to find the great Colosseum almost empty, with only a few stragglers fighting among the plebeians in the high seating near the top. Even the cross holding Senator Magnus had fallen, and the weak-chinned man was nowhere to be seen. "What happened?" she asked as they ran."

Linus slowed, spitting in disgust. "Those fools lacked the discipline to carry out the plan. Too many of the men lost themselves in petty revenge, or simply taking the chance to rape or rob the wealthy in the stands."

"It doesn't matter what they did," said Narcissus. "We cannot control what others do, only what we do, and right now, freedom is at our door. Let's not waste it."

Vesper nodded as the three of them vanished in the streets of Rome, racing to freedom and hopefully a new destiny.

EPILOGUE: REPERCUSSIONS.

"I will find her, and kill her...slowly." he said, pacing back and forth in his garden, wincing from wounds suffered during the revolt.

"It was your fault," she said, gazing at herself in the mirror, "I told you Commodus would not take well to the plan, his will is too strong, despite him spending most of his life as a spoiled emperor's son."

"Do you never tire of that joke?" he said, watching in fascination as she braided her hair, weaving in the tiny skulls of their people as she often did.

"No," she said with a laugh, "twenty years in Rome and these fools have never noticed that death walks amongst them. They only see a kindly matron who bows and scraps to their every need...at least, until it is too late."

"It doesn't matter," he said, returning to his pacing, "Hundreds of our people died in that botched attack on the city, hundreds of people you have placed and replaced over those twenty years. And to make matters worse, that fool loa promised to give us Commodus, but now it seems he has taken him for himself."

"No," she said once more, patting on a soft white powder on her skin, "The loa is loyal to the Sandawei, bound to us...There is more going on here than we can see, some trick played by someone who is moving pieces on the board we cannot see."

"So what do we do now?" he asked, falling into the seat beside her.

She stood to her full height, putting a smile on her face that never touched her eyes, "You will go home. Sit and wait for word from me, nothing more."

His nostrils flared as he pushed his anger down. He would do as he was told, it was never good to argue with her. He had tried once, when he was a boy, he still sometimes woke in the middle of the night drenched in sweat from the memory, "Very well." he said, adjusting his toga and turning to leave.

He was almost to the door when she called out to him, "Senator...don't forget this." she said, and he turned to find her holding the hated red mask. He had hoped he would never have to wear it again, but Vesper and her mother had seen to it that he would have to wear it a little longer, and for that, she would pay with her life.

The End.

DID YOU ENJOY THIS BOOK? YOU CAN MAKE A HUGE DIFFERENCE

Reviews are the most powerful tool in my arsenal when it comes to getting attention for my books. As much as I'd like to, I don't have the muscle of a New York publisher. I can't take out full page ads in the newspaper.

Honest reviews of my books help bring them to the attention of other readers.

If you've enjoyed this book I would be very grateful if you could spend just five minutes leaving a review (It can be as short as you like) on the book's page. You can jump to the page by clicking on the link below.

Gladiatrix: The Last Witch of Rome: Book Two

ABOUT THE AUTHOR

Rhett's love for all things science fiction grew out of a Sunday morning family tradition of watching Star Trek re-runs on the CBC. His love of storytelling is the result of too many hours as a dungeon master trying to murder his players!

He lives in Pincourt Canada with his wife, daughter, and a crazy calico named Maggie.